T0285465

THE
LAST
PROPHET

THE
LAST
PROPHET

A NOVEL

MOSAB HASSAN YOUSEF
AND JAMES BECKET

Forefront
BOOKS

Published by Forefront Books, Nashville, Tennessee.
Distributed by Simon & Schuster.

Library of Congress Control Number: 2024918053

Print ISBN: 978-1-63763-320-5
E-book ISBN: 978-1-63763-321-2

Cover Design by Bruce Gore, Gore Studio, Inc.
Interior Design by PerfecType, Nashville, TN

Printed in the United States of America.

CONTENTS

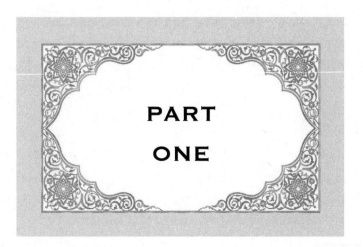

PART

ONE

THE ARABIAN DESERT

611 CE

Dawn. The sun peeks over the eastern hills, sending the first rays of morning light streaking across the desert floor and lighting up a long camel caravan. The white-robed leader, his gray beard a testament to his long experience in this perilous vocation, takes a leather waterskin from his saddle. He shakes it, holds it up over his dry, open mouth, and tries to squeeze something out of it, yet is only able to get out a couple drops of water. As is the practice in this season with temperatures that soar up to 120 degrees Fahrenheit, caravans travel in the coolness of the desert night on their months-long journeys. Bleached animal and human bones protruding from the white sand testify to a lost caravan in the unforgiving desert, mixing with the few plants that grow in the desert, like the sand shrub. The stars and the moon cast faint light on the rough, rock-strewn desert track from Mecca to Damascus. A veteran leader knows the territory of each Bedouin tribe on the trail, who is the sheik, and what deal Mecca had struck with them to allow them to safely pass through their domain.

In Arabia, there are more hungry people than available resources. Raiding other tribes is an accepted part of the culture, a rather brutal redistribution of scarce wealth. It is the end of one of the holy months, where fighting is forbidden. The caravan leader must now decide whether to rest here, setting up the sheepskin tents, which offer some protection from the relentless sun and give the travelers the chance to sleep, or continue into the Devil's furnace of daytime and head for the oasis of Yathrib with its desperately needed cool water and nutritious dates. He searches the sky for a sign of cumulus clouds that would give some relief from the scorching sun. Only blue sky. Raising his left arm, he signals the train, which is moving at the pace of a man walking, to halt. Word goes down the line as the travelers dismount and unpack their tents and cargo to the braying of camels. They then pile the cargo in a defensive perimeter against animal and human jackals.

Not only is the leader, the guide, responsible for the lives of all the men, women, children, and animals on the journey, but also the precious cargo they're carrying back from the Damascus trade fair. They have carried northward ivory from Ethiopia, black African slaves, silk from Asia, jewelry, decorated leather, and, most important in terms of weight versus value, frankincense and myrrh. The caravan is bringing home to their anxious investors in Mecca fair-skinned Circassian women slaves, just-harvested Syrian grain, wine, armor, metal tools, and weapons, including the prized Damascene steel swords. Some travelers heading south have also joined the caravan, which affords more protection for the solitary pilgrim.

Straggling far behind the caravan, a young man, Abdullah, leads an adult camel and a baby camel. His pregnant child-wife, Zaha, bent over in the saddle, cries out in pain. Abdullah lays a blanket on the ground, and their leather waterskin beside it. The camel obediently drops to its knees as Abdullah lifts Zaha from the saddle and lays her down on the blanket. Her bronzed face drips precious sweat as the next labor pain grips her. Abdullah, uncertain what to do, drops down next to her and puts his scarf in her mouth to bite down on when the next labor pain hits. The baby camel lies close to her as though it can feel her pain.

The earth suddenly begins to tremble and shake. A breeze from the south carries the drumbeat of thundering hooves. Abdullah looks up as the sound travels from over the dune in the direction of their caravan. He wonders if it is a herd of oryx, the fleet desert gazelles who can go for long periods without water and run in herds of up to six hundred.

The breeze carries human cries mixing with Zaha's wails.

The travelers, caught at their most vulnerable as they dismount, look to the east. Some twenty Bedouin horsemen charge out of a dried wadi, waving their swords and screaming, the blinding dawn sun at their backs. Roman-trained as light cavalry, their stocky chief with piercing green eyes directs them as they cut down the traders reaching for their weapons and chase others fleeing into the desert. With skilled horsemanship, the warriors corral the women to be sold as slaves, as well as the animals. Well-practiced chaos.

The caravan leader grabs his sword as the chief pulls up in front of him. The two lock eyes.

The caravan leader speaks. "Are you crazy? We're Banu Hashim from Mecca, protected in this holy month by the gods of the Kaaba."

"Mecca has an unpaid blood debt to us. We collect now."

He slides off his stallion and with his sword confronts his adversary. The steel blades clang and ring, blocking thrusts and parries until the caravan leader loses his footing. As he falls backwards, a powerful overhead blow to his right shoulder severs his arm and an artery spurts bright red blood, soaking his dusty white robe. Dropping his sword in a state of shock, he tries to shove the severed arm back into the shattered shoulder socket. He wavers, still on his feet trying to stay conscious, as the chief winds up to deal the *coup de grace*. In the middle of the desert, this is an act of mercy. Having survived too many close calls to count, this is the end of the trail for him.

On the other side of the dune, Abdullah reaches for his knife. He looks down at his blood-covered wife and his new baby, who is crying to open its lungs to draw its first breaths. Abdullah slices the umbilical cord, freeing the newborn. Always alert as a son of the desert, he spots a lone dark figure on horseback at the top of the dune. The figure waves behind him to another horseman. The two riders set off down the slope, the horses plowing deep through the sand.

They rein up, towering above the bloodied couple. It's the Bedouin chief with the startling green eyes and, next to him, a boy whose eyes are the same shade of green. Abdullah picks up his newborn child and stands, facing the intruders. Zaha quietly sobs, gasping for breath.

Screams drift over from the other side of the dune. The chief grabs his reins to turn back.

"Kill them!"

Seeing the hesitancy on the youngster's face, he gives him a hard look. "They showed no mercy to your mother. Be a man, son! Honor our tribe—our gods."

The boy nods and thrusts his sword, which glistens with fresh red blood, into the air.

The father's powerful steed fights its way back up the dune.

The boy looks down at Abdullah holding the baby, who has stopped crying.

"No . . . no . . . no . . ." Zaha softly pleads.

The boy glances back toward the dune and sees no one watching. He grasps his sword, so heavy in his hand, and looks over at the mother and then at the baby. His determined expression softens. A flicker of empathy or nausea?

The young warrior urges his mount forward, and, as the horse rears up as though to trample the couple, the rider leans way over in the saddle, grabbing the couple's waterskin off the ground. Pivoting around, he sets off at a gallop, attacking the steep slope of the dune. Let the desert take them. A worse way to die.

Abdullah falls to his knees. He will live to see another day in this most uncertain of worlds. Holding the baby in the cup of one hand, he wipes some of the blood away with his other hand. A baby girl.

He lays the newborn down in a slight depression in the sand. Zaha turns her head to see, and her moaning—"No . . . no . . . no . . ."—takes on a renewed urgency.

With his two hands, Abdullah scoops sand over this makeshift grave, stifling his daughter's cries. One more sputter, then silence. Only a tiny grasping hand is visible. Abdullah thrusts it back into the sand.

As Abdullah stands to walk back to his wife, a sand squall kicks up, covering both the grave and his footprints.

---- TWO ----

MECCA

Mecca—the most powerful city-state in Arabia. It is the pilgrimage season, and for three months the holy city is crowded with pilgrims and merchants. Outside the city walls, thousands of Bedouin tents dot the desert floor. Mecca is a sacred zone where fighting among warring tribes is forbidden and no weapons are allowed. Palm leaf mud huts and stone mansions surround the bustling center of the city, where two landmarks stand out—landmarks that make this human settlement in the desert possible.

The first is the Kaaba, a cube-shaped building with a stone base, its four walls draped in strips of purple and red cloth. The story goes that the first sanctuary built by Adam, the first man, was destroyed in the Great Flood. It was rebuilt by Noah, then forgotten under the sand until Abraham found it when he went to visit his older son, Ismail, who had been banished by Abraham's wife, Sarah. It is here that Abraham nearly killed his favored son, Isaac, to prove to God his undying faith. As a result of this fealty, God promised that both sons would found powerful nations. For Ismail, his nation would be founded from this very spot in the unforgiving desert wilderness.

Meccans believe they are the descendants of Abraham. Inside the Kaaba and alongside it are more than 360 idols, totems of the countless tribes of Arabia. It is said that whoever controls the keys to the Kaaba controls Mecca. In the last three generations, the Quraysh tribe has taken control of the Kaaba, making them the most powerful and prestigious of Meccan tribes.

The other landmark is the Zamzam spring, which produces abundant water, making human life and commerce sustainable. A long queue waits their turn to go down into the spring to fill their empty containers. The spring's known existence for many years has no doubt resulted in tribes fighting for control of it. When the water source surrendered to the desert, covered with sand, its location was forgotten until a Quraysh named Abu-el Muttalieb rediscovered it. As the holder of the keys to the Kaaba and the one who had control of the Zamzam spring, he became the most powerful man in the city.

The brilliant exploitation of these two landmarks in this barren desert made Mecca the richest of Arabian city-states, despite being unable to grow any food in the desolate valley. They depended on fertile neighboring towns for vegetables and fruits, and on nomadic Bedouin herders for meat and milk. The Meccans mastered long distance trade and with their caravans, the slave trade, commercial fairs, and pilgrimages, the ruling elites gathered great wealth and even owned mansions in Damascus, Jerusalem, and Egypt. During the seemingly eternal conflict between East and West, in a period of intense warfare between the Christian Roman Empire and the Zoroastrian Persian Empire, the pagan Meccans, dependent on far-flung trade, became excellent diplomats, whether negotiating with the Bedouin tribes along the trade routes for safe passage or maintaining a neutral posture between the two clashing empires.

Outside the heart of the city, beyond its walls, is a livestock area with stables full of camels and horses and pens holding sacrificial sheep and goats. Noisy with braying and neighing, it's teeming with arriving pilgrims and slaves tending to the animals. One majestic black Arabian stallion stands out, attracting the admiration, if not envy, of those who pass by. The horse stamps a hoof, prompting a man, his white skin tanned by the sun, to come around the animal's flank to face the stallion. He caresses the steed's muzzle, making calming sounds. The man has a large head, broad shoulders, a well-proportioned body, coal-black hair tied in plaits, and a black beard, which, now that he has turned forty, is slightly flecked with white. He has the aquiline nose prized by society, though it is his compelling brown eyes that those who meet him never forget. He lifts the horse's leg, examines the hoof. He pulls out a large thorn, and, smiling, shows it to the sufferer.

"Muhammad!"

The man turns to see Sufyan, a friend of patrician bearing and the same age. They resemble each other in features; everyone in Mecca is related in some form to everyone else, all cousins at least. Sufyan is with his elegantly attired wife, Hind, who wears the haughty expression of privilege. An entourage of attendants and slaves accompany them. A tall slave from Abyssinia, Washi, stands out with his muscular African body. On the sartorial front, Muhammad, with his patched homespun and worn-out sandals, hard at work with the livestock, could be taken for a slave like Washi.

"Sufyan. Hind. Good morning," Muhammad greets them with a smile in his resonant voice.

"Twenty camels I offer you for this old animal that has seen its best years." No pleasantries from Sufyan, only business.

Muhammad makes eye contact with the stallion as though asking for an opinion. The horse throws its head back.

"They will make your next caravan more profitable."

"Not for sale," Muhammad responds.

"Everything's—and everyone's—for sale at the right price." Sufyan reacts to Muhammad's slightly bemused expression, then tries again. "All right, fifty camels."

Muhammad's answering smile says no.

"Females. Fifty females," Sufyan recklessly offers. Females produce more camels and thus have much greater value.

Muhammad strokes the coal-black coat of his animal as he and Washi lock eyes.

Sufyan shrugs. Then one more attempt. "Your best horse for my best slave."

Hind, glancing at Washi, opens her mouth to protest, but her husband cuts her off, awaiting Muhammad's response.

Once again, a negative.

With a last look at the object of his desire, Sufyan decides to move on. "We'll see you at the Kaaba. Big day for Mecca."

As they walk away, Muhammad jerks slightly as though he's been hit from behind. He turns to see two baby camels nudging his back and four laughing figures approaching. Muhammad joins in the laughter with his wife, Khadija; his uncle Talib, looking younger than his sixty years; Talib's fifteen-year-old son, Ali; and fourteen-year-old son, Zayd. Muhammad kisses his wife on her forehead.

"Muhammad, beloved, can you help unload some goods for the shop? They arrived from the Yemeni caravan." Khadija points to two loaded, hobbled camels.

Khadija, Ali, Zayd, Talib, and Muhammad unload the camels and carry the goods into Khadija's shop, which offers a wide variety of goods from practical items like cookware and spices to luxuries such as prized silk fabrics from Asia. An impatient Talib, helping Muhammad carry in the last items, speaks to him above the din from the busy street as customers enter the shop. "Nephew, we must hurry to the center to offer Meccan hospitality to the pilgrims who have traveled so far."

Muhammad looks reluctant, but an excited Ali responds, "I'll join you!"

"Of course. Come, Muhammad, walk with us as Meccans at this festive time, this time of peace; it is our duty."

Khadija puts dates and a leather waterskin into a cloth shoulder bag for her husband. Muhammad grabs his shepherd's stick, takes the bag from his wife, kisses her on the forehead, and heads out of the shop with his uncle and Ali, while Zayd stays behind to help in the shop. Khadija's expression is one mixed of love and concern as the three disappear into the passing crowd.

The center of Mecca, with its Kaaba and its mansions bordering the large square, is packed with pilgrims, Meccans, merchants, Bedouins, beggars, prostitutes, money changers, guards, slaves, and food sellers. Like any ordered urban society, there are classes distinguished by dress and activity. Most notable is the marked difference between the blasé city dwellers and the nomadic tribal Bedouin, who are marveling at the sights of the city. Towering above the scene is a giant statue of the stern Hubal, Mecca's main god.

Talib and Muhammad are greeted with respect, clearly recognized as significant figures in the city. Despite the carnival atmosphere, Muhammad is not comfortable as the three thread their way through the jostling celebrants. The noise of hawkers shouting and the aromas wafting about in the smoky heat, both pleasant and unpleasant, assault his senses.

They move past the thriving slave market, a pillar of the Meccan economy, primarily full of dark Africans. One vendor specializes in beautiful women, booty from intertribal warfare. Potential buyers examine the merchandise. Some come to great fairs like the one at Mecca with the hope that they might find a kidnapped relative who has been sold into slavery. One fat, bearded man walks around a strikingly beautiful Ethiopian woman, carefully studying her.

Addressing the vendor in an unfamiliar language, the fat man announces, "I like. What tribe?"

"Aksum."

"No. No. Pact." A pact meant they had a peace agreement with a rival tribe, which called for the return of any enslaved tribal members they might come across. The fat man moves on, pointing to another woman.

The trio pass a tent where a money changer stands up respectfully for Talib.

Two drunks stagger by and trip over a blind beggar who is sitting on the ground, his eyes staring straight into the sun. One of the stumbling inebriated men knocks over a tattooed man who is headed to the Kaaba to deposit a heavy totem festooned with feathers and seashells, causing a traffic tie-up.

Muhammad reaches down to help the blind man up and guides him back over to his prime begging position next to the money changer. The blind man recognizes his benefactor by his familiar voice and calls out, "Muhammad!" Muhammad takes some dates from his bag and puts them in the blind man's hands.

They walk on, coming to a raucous crowd cheering a wrestling match. Talib's brother, Abbas, greets them. Though he is Muhammad's uncle, they are about the same age.

"A glorious day, brother. Muhammad, good to see you here for once."

"Indeed, brother, you must be betting on Omar."

They all look at the struggling, sweaty combatants, the local giant Omar pitted against a large, tall African. Omar so towers over everyone, it is as though he is on horseback. A few feints and Omar lands a powerful fist to his adversary's jaw, knocking him out as the man sags to the ground. The crowd cheers or groans, depending on how they placed their bets.

A happy Abbas opens his purse and goes to collect his winnings as Omar muscles his way past the queue to collect his. Muhammad turns away to face a large, disappointed-looking Bedouin with piercing green eyes and a young man with similar green eyes. As they make eye contact, Muhammad smiles, but the Bedouin doesn't respond.

Walking on, they see two guards pull a crying ten-year-old boy from the arms of his father and drag him toward a table.

"Please! Please! My last caravan was robbed, and I lost everything," the father pleads. "I can pay my debt next year—please!"

"If I believed all those promises about next year, I'd have nothing to loan those honest men who do pay their debts," the corpulent money changer at the table responds. The guards deposit the frightened boy at his feet. Seeing the three passersby staring at him, he tells them, "The value of this boy doesn't even cover what his bad father owes me." No doubt this scene is due in part to the exorbitant mounting interest that is part of the Meccan financial system, resulting in the rich getting richer and the poor getting poorer.

"It's not the fault of the money lender," Talib says to a deeply troubled Muhammad. "It's the fault of the borrower who did not keep his promise to pay."

"I'm not sure whose fault it is, but I'm certain it was not the boy's."

The father collapses to the ground.

"Come, Muhammad, it is what it is." There is no societal view of helping the poor beyond family.

"Does it have to be that way?"

The trio walks on past hawkers selling food, medicines, and lucky amulets, and gamblers sitting on the ground playing a game with colored stones. An archery contest has attracted a crowd. Khalid, a handsome young warrior, draws back his bowstring and lets the arrow fly, narrowly missing the bull's-eye. Hamza, another of Muhammad's uncles, an imposing, dark-bearded forty-year-old in flamboyant, colorful dress, steps up, clearly the crowd favorite by the noisy response he elicits. He places the arrow, lifts the bow, and shoots. With the twang of the bowstring, he turns his back to the target, not watching to see where it hits. The *oohs* and *aahs* and cheers report Hamza's arrow striking the target dead center. Khalid embraces his better.

Moving on, Talib and Ali come across Bin Mas'ud, a young shepherd boy who is in tears and holding a lamb in front of an angry man, Jahl, who grabs a stick from a slave and strikes the boy hard. The boy drops the bleating lamb. Jahl sees Talib and Ali watching. Now hesitating to hit the boy again, Jahl feels the need to explain. "The fool lost a lamb."

Muhammad moves on to the next attraction, where he joins an appreciative crowd of men and women laughing. A poetry duel is underway between two veteran poets, Bakr, Muhammad's best friend, and an older man, Othman.

Bakr declaims, "That girl emerged from her lover's soul. Not from any rib or bone. And from her heart comes honey. Amazing! How could honey come from a stone?"

Othman takes up the challenge. "Beautiful women, as experienced men know, are but darkness wrapped in a dazzling light all aglow." This evokes a strong reaction from the crowd.

Bakr spots Muhammad and calls out, "Muhammad, join us, take on the wily Othman here."

The crowd responds by encouraging him. From an early age on the caravans, Muhammad showed his talent as a poetic storyteller, relieving some of the boredom from the monotonous travel across the desert wasteland until they would come to an oasis settlement. This seventh-century desert world is one without books, and while some ten epic poems are known to all, the quality of the recitation makes certain poets, like Muhammad, in demand. A skilled poet produces surprise and drama, both as entertainment and education. And in a culture of warring tribes, poetry celebrating the warrior strengthens the identity of the tribe.

Muhammad declines with a smile. His life thus far has favored the Word, particularly as a mediator, but like every Meccan, he grew up learning the skills of sword combat. Warrior poet?

Muhammad continues with his uncle and cousin to the wide steps that lead up to the inner sanctum of the Kaaba. A queue of pilgrims lines up to enter. They carry totems, some bejeweled, others adorned with gold and silver. Uniformed guards provide security for the sacred Kaaba, which is both a treasure house and the repository of objects of worship. Standing at the top step is the imposing figure of the white-bearded Lahab dressed in black. The enormous key to the Kaaba hangs around his neck, the symbol of his status as keeper of the Kaaba, the high priest of the religion that governs Mecca.

Semi-naked pilgrims ritually circle the Kaaba at a jogging pace seven times in a tradition whose origin is lost in time. They chant and pause to kiss all four stone corners, especially the mystical Black Stone anchoring the eastern corner. They clap and whistle with hundreds engaged, creating a powerful collective energy.

A voice calls out to Talib amidst the din, and they turn to see Sufyan with other burghers dressed in white silk, drinking and laughing on the terrace of one of the mansions facing the Kaaba on the main square. Beautiful women slaves serve them food and drink. "Talib! Muhammad! Come join us to celebrate!"

Muhammad, regarding the scene with disdain, tells Talib, "No, I'm on my way." He looks up at the towering Mount Nur in the distance.

Talib and Ali climb the steps to the terrace, past the giant statue of Hubal, to join Sufyan. From the terrace, the entire animated scene is in view. The two Meccan leaders look down on it with pride.

Talib notes, "This is the only place where during the sacred months, all enemies lay down their swords."

Sufyan agrees. "There's no miracle like Mecca. We spare nothing for our guests."

Ranged against the thick city wall are giant iron pots large enough to hold half a camel. Slaves carry wood to an already large pile while the cooks start the fires under the enormous pots. Smoke rises from various charcoal pits grilling meat as the hungry line up.

Sufyan and Talib, surrounded by their overfed peers, venture to a table laden with delicacies of fruits, meats, and sweets. Sufyan looks out at the pilgrims jogging around the Kaaba as he fills his tray. "Our fathers knew that if you control the sacred, you'll never starve," he observes.

The fat cats all share a hearty laugh.

An urgent voice calls out to Sufyan. The stocky Meccan chief of security, Malik, and two guards stand below the terrace with Abdullah, the rattled survivor of the caravan raid. Sufyan invites Malik and Abdullah onto the terrace and asks Abudullah to tell his story.

From the vantage point above the crowd, Abdullah spots the Bedouin chief with the green eyes standing outside the money changer's tent. They make eye contact, and mutual recognition hits. Abdullah shouts and points at the chief who, recognizing the man who should be dead, slaps his son, knocking him to the ground. Sufyan orders the guards to go after them. Malik jumps down to the ground and, with the two guards following, the chase is on. Their quarry melts into the dense flow of humanity.

Three blasts on a ram's horn blown from the top step of the Kaaba stops all activity and talk. In a few moments, everyone present drops to their knees and leans forward onto their forearms, ritually bowing to Hubal. Muhammad still stands, a striking image of one man above all those paying obeisance. With all prostrated, it would seem no one would notice, but on the terrace Lahab and Jahl scan the crowd, always on the lookout for any offense to the gods. They exchange glances at this flagrant violation, which is worsened when Muhammad turns his back on Hubal to head off toward the main gateway to the holy city. The ram's horn blasts again, and all rise and continue.

Muhammad walks out of the city's main gateway, past four respectful guards, as excited pilgrims pour in. He continues toward a just visible trail that switchbacks up the steep slope of Mount Hira. Leaning into the mountain, he climbs quickly. Stopping for a moment to catch his breath, he leans on his staff. The sound of hammering draws his attention to where dozens of slaves, men and women, labor in a quarry that provides stones for the mansions and walls of Mecca.

A tall young Abyssinian slave, Bilaal, makes eye contact with Muhammad. Bilaal smiles and Muhammad smiles back. In a deep, resonant voice, Bilaal says, "Master." The supervisor, carrying a whip, acknowledges Muhammad, and a threatening lash puts Bilaal back to hammering.

As the sun dips behind Mount Nur, a rising half-moon takes up the job of providing light for Muhammad to make out the path.

❁

Back in Mecca, the joyful party and feast are in full swing. Hundreds of locals and pilgrims sit on rugs and pillows spread out around the Kaaba area, which is lit with oil lamps that give it an eerie quality. Inside the Kaaba, Lahab and his wife, Arwa, move systematically from idol to idol, totem to totem, removing the jewels and gold and placing them in a large box.

Inside Sufyan's mansion, gathered together in an intense meeting focused on Abdullah, are the leading notables: Talib, Sufyan, Jahl, Hamza, Omar, Hind, Bakr, Othman, and Malik.

Jahl rises to his feet. "I say kill them now!"

"Sit down," Talib says. "Not during the sacred month."

"They violated the sacred month."

"They did. We don't. And the month is soon over."

A distraught Jahl looks about for some support, but no one weighs in on his side.

Sufyan speaks. "We're not sure what tribe it was yet. What tribe would be so crazy as to attack a Meccan caravan and its leader and feel safe enough to show up here?"

"I can only think they made a mistake, but the deed is done, and an example has to be made." Talib states what all agree on.

Hamza, in his multicolored outfit, adds in a deep voice, "When the sacred month is over, we will, blessed by Hubal, wipe them off the face of the earth." He looks around the room to general approval, though his gaze lingers for a moment too long on Hind, Sufyan's wife, where there's a connection. She looks down.

As the meeting starts to break up, Jahl calls out, "Wait!" Attention assured, he continues, "How many of you saw Muhammad stand when all bowed to Hubal?"

"I saw this outrage to Hubal," Lahab, who has joined them, states. "This is hardly the first time. I've lost count of the offenses to the gods that he and his friends have committed." He looks at Bakr and Othman. "We must bring him before the council and hold him to account."

Talib looks concerned but doesn't answer.

"Yes," Jahl agrees. "It's important we teach the Bedouin a hard lesson, but we must be honest—they are an outside enemy, and with Muhammad, we're talking about an enemy among us whose disrespect for the gods can spread like a plague in the city."

Lahab says, "We must bring him before us now."

"He's gone off on retreat," Bakr counters.

"Where?" Lahab asks.

"No one knows," Bakr admits, "which makes the retreat a real retreat, severing all connections."

Othman, half joking, says, "Perhaps he will not come back, like many hanifs who live alone never return to the city, thus solving your problem."

"He'll be back; his money is here," Jahl opines. "And his family. I swear by Hubal, whom he has insulted—we will deal with him when he returns."

THREE

THE HIRA CAVE—
REVELATION

If anyone began life with an inauspicious start, it was Abu al-Qāsim Muḥammad ibn 'Abd Allāh ibn 'Abd al-Muṭṭalib ibn Hāshim. His father, Abdullah, died of fever before his son was born. Muhammad was sent to the desert to a Bedouin wet nurse, Halima. This was what the leading families did. Muhammad did his part working as a shepherd, and those first five years of his life growing up in the desert in a Bedouin family meant that he absorbed many of their austere values along with their love of the oral tradition of epic Arabic poetry. He was sent back to his mother, Amina, who died soon after they visited relatives in the northern town of Yathrib. Thus, he was an orphan, though in this tribal society, he had the good fortune to be born into Mecca's most powerful tribe, the Quraysh, and one of its clans, the prestigious Hashim. His powerful grandfather, 'Abd al-Muttalib ibn Hashim, took him in. Two years later, Abd al-Muttalib died.

Fortunately, Muhammad's paternal uncle Talib, a wealthy merchant, popular poet, and now the head chief of the Hashim clan, took him in and put him to work on the lowest rung of the ladder as a camel boy. His Bedouin time stood him in good stead, for this "camel whisperer" showed a gift for handling the temperamental beasts. It would be a couple of years before he was enlisted to go on the caravans, doing the menial chores like the other youngsters. This opened the growing Muhammad to the larger civilized world to the north dominated by the warring empires of Byzantium and Persia. The young man's diverse encounters on the road fed and stimulated his already restless and inquiring mind. It would turn out he had a gift for languages, which made him both effective as a merchant and entertaining as a poet on the long caravan journeys. Still, without a father and with the stigma of being an orphan, Muhammad was not off to a favored start. Yet despite his modest status in society, now at age forty, by any measure his life is a success. He has what any of his peers would want—a reputation of trustworthiness, respect as a businessman, a loving, remarkable wife, children, and no material wants. And yet. And yet Muhammad is a deeply troubled man. He believes there is more than the material. There has to be.

Many of the values Meccan culture is based upon conflict with his belief system, which has been formed from his life experience and an innate sense of social justice. On his travels along the different trade routes north to Damascus and south to Yemen and beyond, Muhammad met with many holy men and spiritual practitioners, some from as far afield as India, others from Persia, but especially Christian monks, who had found peace from this spiritual yearning exploring the inner life. It was in their monasteries where Muhammad would often lodge on his journeys.

Lately, Muhammad has been beset by visions, and this retreat will allow him to decipher their meaning. Meccans have the practice of withdrawing from the world into the wild, and the grottos on Mount Nur are ideal for spiritual retreats. There they engage in prayer, rituals, and self-examination. On their return to society, many give to the poor, honoring the traditional religious practice. No one is a sincerer and more disciplined seeker than Muhammad.

Up on the mountain, Muhammad climbs to the final cliff face that is filled with caves. He disappears into the darkness of an opening in the mountainside known as the Hira Cave.

Blending into one, many days and nights pass with Muhammad in his cave, going ever deeper into meditation and contemplation. With his long fast, Muhammad's senses have become more acute.

Down in the valley, Mecca returns to its normal life, all the Bedouin tents gone.

On the thirtieth night, praying, his eyes closed, without warning Muhammad goes into a free fall, hurtling down a primal bottomless hole. A pure black void. Dissolving into nothingness. Terror seizes him, and his consciousness recognizes nothing to rely on for survival in a realm beyond space and time.

Then a distant, thin light cuts into the blackness. Focusing on the light arrests the uncontrolled falling. Only one form Muhammad recognizes—a steady flame.

The flame gradually transforms into a perfect human form, blindingly radiant, vibrant, stunningly beautiful, the most awesome sight of Muhammad's life.

This perfect form then projects other forms—some are beings Muhammad can recognize, others he's never seen before. Beauty within beauty. A purple color diffuses this phase, transforming into recognizable beings.

Another plane opens to Muhammad, an explosion of color, infinite shades of colors, now shapes, forms, endless dimensions, all woven together in a magnificent thread, with powerful life force in its majestic dance. The diversity of existence is overwhelming. Planets, stars, humans, animals, and plants.

Now, Muhammad for the first time is aware of sound, vibrations at different levels. The vibrations echo, which he can perceive as words manifesting themselves in his consciousness,

I was a hidden treasure . . . I desired to be recognized, so I created the universe. You are in me, and I am in you.

With that, Muhammad opens his eyes and for a moment does not know where he is. The cave. He is back in time. He touches his body to assure himself that he exists. His vision is super acute; all he sees is illuminated as though he is seeing for the first time. He touches his face, feeling sweat and tears, tasting it as salty. He has a sense he is not alone. He tries to get up . . .

A sudden and overwhelming light illuminates the cave. Protecting his sight, Muhammad immediately surrenders his face to the ground as a superior voice commands him:

Muhammad! The son of Abdullah!

Muhammad's limbs shake involuntarily. He feels as if he is at the edge of a seizure.

Terrified, he can only fearfully utter, "Who are you? I can't see."

No man can see me and be still alive.

A deafening roll of thunder crashes on top of the mountain. This is not the pleasant, enlightening encounter with the divine he had anticipated.

I AM YOUR LORD!

THE ONE AND ABSOLUTE!

When I create, I command, "BE—then it IS." I have no partners, companions, nor associates—I am independent, yet everything depends on me. Form originator, yet formless, without beginning and without end.

Not begotten nor begotted/born. No one or anything can be compared to me. Not a son, certainly not a beloved.

Planets, the sun, the stars, move by my power—everything originated from me, and to me everything shall return.

My command, "Thou shalt not make unto thee any graven images," long has been forgotten! I AM the most compassionate, yet my wrath is greater, and killing infants angers me.

Go down to your "village" and warn this wicked generation of an imminent destruction.

When they ask you, "On what authority do you speak?" declare fearlessly, "I speak on the authority of the creator of all that exists, seen and unseen, evident and speculative. The legislator and the ruler of the universe."

Preach to them gently at the beginning, and if they don't listen, fight them! Fear not! For I will send with you the armies of Earth and heavens.

For those who oppose and reject my supreme design will certainly perish.

For many minutes, Muhammad sits immobile with his eyes closed, as though daring not to open them. Finally, he opens his eyes in the darkness of the cave. Behind him the remaining embers of the fire cast a shadow on the wall. The shadow has a human form. When he moves his arm, the shadow mimics his movement.

He rises shakily to his feet. Breathes deeply. Stepping out of the cave, he sees the magnificence of Creation laid out before him. He feels both weightless and exhausted. He realizes he has been a witness to the truth. The truth of Creation. The existence of the Creator. Oneness. One God. This knowledge, this privilege he was granted, thrusts upon him his mission: to bring that truth to the world, to expose the lies of the corrupt. In that moment he feels the weight of the responsibility and the risks to his person, but he accepts that he has been chosen. There is no going back; his life and the lives of those close to him will be forever changed.

He heads down the mountainside still locked inside his mind, his body picking up momentum, careening pell-mell down the trail, loosing stones, tripping, falling, snagged by brambles tearing his clothes.

As usual, Khadija is up with the light of dawn. Though she's accustomed to her husband's long absences when he goes alone on one of his retreats, there's always that worry present when he is gone. Hearing an unfamiliar sound, she opens the front door. A figure collapses on the doorstep, lifting himself up on his hands and knees and wearing a torn and bloodied garment. Overcoming her shock, Khadija reaches down to help up her husband who, with an enormous act of will, manages to get to his feet. With his arm around her, they make their way to a divan in the living room where, once they sit down, Khadija cradles Muhammad's head in her lap. She holds him tight as he convulses, soothing him with caresses until his body stops shaking.

"Cover me!" his shaky voice whispers.

"Tell me, my love." She caresses his brow.

"Cover me."

She reaches for a shawl and covers him.

"What happened?"

No answer. She lifts the cover, sees his eyes are closed. She thinks she hears the word *one*, but she can't be sure. She goes to find a cloth and water so she can clean his cuts. When she returns, Muhammad's breath has taken on the rhythm of sleep. Ali appears, looking distressed when he sees Muhammad bloodied.

"Let him sleep. Don't worry, he'll be all right." Khadija examines Muhammad's wounds and delicately daubs them with the wet cloth, then cleans them more vigorously when he doesn't react.

Muhammad and Khadija are one of the most unlikely of history's love stories, given the mores of the money-driven Meccan culture. Khadija was the town's wealthiest merchant and most eligible young widow. Suitors were stepping over each other to get at her money, offering large gifts to her father, who was required to give his approval. For a woman to reach such a pinnacle of business success was unprecedented in this patriarchal culture that saw women as little more than chattel. It meant she had an independent mind, a brilliant one at that, and kept her own counsel. Her wealth came from the caravan trade, which required considerable capital. A business of great potential profit, it carried the very real risk of losing all to the multiple perils of the desert. Much of the success of a trading mission depended on an experienced leader, and a time came when Khadija had to find a new leader for her upcoming caravan north to Damascus.

Muhammad's uncle Talib had given him a roof over his head and the opportunity to gain extensive experience working in the caravan trade. Sharply observant, Muhammad quickly learned the caravan routes north and south at a time when there were no maps. Early on he would show a precocious talent for politics and diplomacy, which in a world of warring tribes and shifting alliances could mean success or failure for a caravan. He was the son of the desert, embracing its solitude, its deprivation, and its beauty. His life experience, as the least prestigious member of a powerful clan and major tribe, caused him to come across as rather shy, other than when he was traveling in the desert or reciting poetry. There was a nascent charisma in this young, well-traveled man who took in all the marvels of the external world and whose restless, searching mind fed the richness of his internal world.

At just twenty-five years old, relatively poor and with an unpromising future, a good measure of Muhammad's status at the time was his marriage proposal to his uncle Talib's daughter, with whom he was very close. Talib humiliatingly turned him down on his daughter's behalf, which caused a rift between the two men.

To his surprise, Muhammad was called to Khadija's mansion for a job interview. Despite their uneasy relationship, Talib, her fellow caravan entrepreneur, gave his nephew the highest of recommendations, touting not only his experience on the caravan treks but his honesty, reliability, and renowned bargaining ability.

Muhammad appeared outside Khadija's stone residence in Mecca's center, only to find that he was joining other candidates for the job. He was the youngest, and he was familiar with all the other men. Realizing he had little chance against such competition, he let go of what would have been a very natural nervousness. Finally, his turn came, and he was escorted into the luxurious living room where Khadija held court with her male advisers. He stood in front of her. Their eyes met. There was an immediate connection—a soulmate connection. Afterward, neither would be able to articulate that; as their social and economic divide was so great, it was unthinkable that such a union could exist. Muhammad answered a few questions—most from the skeptical advisers—and then left, shrugging to the few candidates still waiting outside.

Surprisingly, he was called back the next day. What was that about? Offered tea and now invited to sit down without the advisers, Khadija spoke right away about the enormous responsibility of leading her next caravan—a caravan twice as large as any other from Mecca, even Talib's. It took a while for Muhammad to realize she was giving him this prized job!

Muhammad didn't need to be told what a heavy responsibility this was, what dangers lurked on these monthslong journeys, nor what a once-in-a-lifetime opportunity this was for a man without means. This extraordinary woman was taking two gambles: the first was the caravan itself, and the second was entrusting her wealth to this young Hashim. She introduced him to her trusted manservant, Maysara, who would serve him, help him with trip preparations, and be at his side during the trip. No doubt this was also a way of keeping an eye on him. Now Muhammad felt the nervousness in the pit of his stomach, for this was becoming very real.

Word traveled quickly around town. Many questioned the widow's judgment; some wondered how the handsome young man had managed to turn her head. But this young man riding the lead camel envisioned the expedition with no other outcome than success.

And that was how it turned out, with the Muhammad-led convoy returning from the north. He went directly to report to Khadija, the dust of the desert still on his simple white gown, describing the trip as she listened intently to his vivid descriptions in animated, compelling language. He had her laughing and marveling at his adventures and misadventures. Khadija would sell the goods he brought back for more than 100 percent profit, though that, while welcome, was not what moved her; it was his character, his being. Indeed, now she felt she had found her soulmate. Did he feel that too?

Life would never be the same for the orphan boy after he was approached by Khadija's friend Nufaysah. "Why aren't you married?"

"I don't have the means," Muhammad replied.

"What if you were given the means, and made a union with beauty, nobility, and property?"

Muhammad quite skeptically asked, "Who, pray, might that be?"

"Khadija bint Kuwaylid."

"You're joking."

"Not at all."

"If this is serious, for my part, with my whole heart I welcome it."

Khadija was determined to make her own choice. Her father, who no doubt would have turned Muhammad down as "a person of no importance," had died. She invited Muhammad to come to her, where she expressed her love for him and told him how much she admired his beauty of character and truth in speech. She proposed marriage to him, which, needless to say, he accepted, hardly believing this turn of events. Keeping with custom, Khadija's uncle Amr represented her, and Muhammad was represented by Hamza, his friend and distant uncle, the warrior of the colorful dress. The young men went to Amr to ask for Khadija's hand, and the dowry Muhammad was to give was set at twenty she camels. It made for good gossip in town, as it was as much a surprise for the Meccans as it was for the bridegroom.

So it came to pass in this particular love story that Khadija and Muhammad were married and would have four daughters together: Zaynab, Ruqayyah, Umm Kulthum, and Fatima. They never considered killing a girl baby at birth. They did have one son, Al-Qasim, who sadly died before he was two. This was an emotional blow, as a father's standing and wealth were based on his number of sons. Yet Muhammad was very affectionate with his daughters. He loved children and joined in their laughter and games. And as it turned out, two boys would later join his household.

One was Ali, Talib's youngest son. A severe drought struck that part of Arabia and hit Talib's enterprises so hard that he could no longer feed his many children. Muhammad proposed to a friend that they take in a child until Talib was once again able to. So, five-year-old Ali joined the Muhammad household, where he would be treated as a son. And he would marry one of their daughters.

The other was Zayd, whose story is more out of the ordinary. Zayd was an undernourished, traumatized child who Khadija and Muhammad saw cowering in the slave market one day. They paid the asking price—with no bargaining—to the surprise of the slave master. Zayd was from the powerful northern tribe of Kalb and had been captured in a caravan attack. In the first year of his slavery in Mecca, each time he went to the Kaaba area, he prayed he'd see a familiar face from the proud Kalb tribe. After two years of living freely as a member of the Muhammad household, he saw some fellow tribals at the Kaaba. They happily recognized him. As was the custom of the time, Zayd composed a poem for them to take back to his parents. He wrote in part, "Weary not the camels scouring the earth for me, for I, praise be to God, am in the best of noble families, great in all its lines." In other words, *I'm fine here.* Not what would have been expected. Of course, his father and uncle soon appeared to recover him, not trusting the message. The four met, and the father offered whatever ransom it would take.

Muhammad replied, speaking to Zayd, "You know me. It is your choice. No matter what you decide, there will be no ransom to pay."

"I would not choose any man in preference to you; thou are my father and mother."

The father and uncle couldn't believe what they'd heard from this young man, now a decisive adolescent. Had they come all this way to be so humiliated?

"So, you choose slavery over freedom, and strangers over your own father and mother and true family. Out of our hearts then, you are not worthy."

"That is how it is. I have seen from this man such things that I could never choose another above him."

Muhammad cut off any further discussion and invited them to the Kaaba. There he spoke out in his loud voice, gathering the attention of all present. "To all of you here, may you be witnesses to my solemn words, that Zayd is my son. I am his heir and he is mine. He will be known in Mecca henceforth as Zayd bin Muhammad."

Zayd embraced his father and uncle, who had to face the lonely trip north empty-handed but impressed by Muhammad's action. They at least were assured Zayd was in good hands as a free person and came to look at it as maybe a good thing. Having a powerful connection in Mecca could help their family.

Muhammad gave most of his money away; thus this happy family had a frugal lifestyle. Talib rejecting Muhammad's marriage request would turn out to be good fortune—perhaps, even, we could say good fortune for the world—as without Khadija, Muhammad's life story would not be worth telling.

Later that afternoon Muhammad stirs, waking. His sleep has been agitated by dreams. When he opens his eyes, he sees his family looking hopefully at him. He smiles and they all smile back. Ali helps him to sit up so he can drink the proffered water. It's evident he's trying to orient himself, to absorb all that happened to him up in the cave. He spots a splotch of blood on his sleeve, triggering the memory of that out-of-control flight down the treacherous mountain slope.

They look to him for an explanation. How was the retreat? How did he get so scratched up?

He manages a faint smile, slightly shaking his head, as though it is not possible to explain.

FOUR

MECCA REESTABLISHES ORDER

The sun rises over the desert as a Bedouin camp wakes to a new day. From out of the black woolen tents emerge women who start cooking fires and draw water from a well. Youngsters head to the animal area to milk the camels, goats, and sheep. Close by the animals, a group of women and children, captives from a recent raid, sleep on the ground. They are roused to search for firewood and serve their captors. From out of the largest black woolen tent—its blackness providing dense shade in the day and warmth at night—steps the warrior chief, the tribal sheikh, followed by his son. He stretches and looks into the sun, scanning the nearby hill.

From behind the hill four men, lying down, observe the waking camp: Hamza, Sufyan, Khalid, and Abdullah. Just then, the loud bellow of a camel sounds from behind them. The warrior chief looks back at the tribe's animals as a few neighs come from the horses, then glances back at the hill, as the sound seems to have come from there. He scans the area for any sign of movement.

The four men, bending low, slip away from their vantage point. Behind the hill, in a slight depression, await an impressive array of some one hundred and fifty mounted Meccan warriors, battle ready. The quartet join the leaders, Talib and Jahl, at the head of this imposing force. They exchange a few words.

At the camp the son hands the father a cup of fresh milk. Reading his son's alarmed expression, he follows his gaze to see fifteen Meccan warriors led by Hamza striding down the hill and bearing down on the camp. The warrior chief drops the milk and shouts to mobilize his warriors. He slips into the tent for his weapons.

Hamza's strong voice echoes off the hillside: "Come out, cowards!"

The Bedouin warriors rush about, gathering their weapons as the Meccans form a small battle line and patiently wait. While there are not rules of engagement, nor can it be said a sense of fair play, the warrior class has some standards for combat. The poets will celebrate their heroes for those values.

Finally, the Bedouin warriors assemble around one who carries the tribe's totem of feathers and beads. Most have armor and shields. The warrior chief, seeing thirty behind him and only fifteen facing him, regains confidence. This does not last long, as Hamza moves forward with Omar and Khalid at his side.

"Hamza!" the warrior chief mutters under his breath.

Two young warriors, eager to do battle, join their chief, three against three. The chief looks back at his warriors and the frightened women behind them. No choice but to step forward.

Hamza beckons Omar and Khalid to stay put and moves alone toward the approaching tribal trio. Momentarily confused at the approach of this lone combatant, they ready themselves with dramatic sweeps of their swords.

Talib and Jahl observe the unfolding battle from the hilltop, knowing they have an overwhelming force behind them. Let Hamza and the others have their moment.

Hamza takes quick steps forward and, in a swirl and blur of superhuman action, his sword sweeps, spurting blood, severed limbs, and one head before three of the tribe lie dead or dying on the ground. There's a moment of awed silence at what has just happened—so quick and so devastating, the collective mind can't accept it as real. Then the silence is broken by the screams of the women and war cries from the men. The Bedouin men are no longer so keen on battle, but behind them is a wall of wailing women.

The three Meccans plunge into the midst of the leaderless Bedouins, hacking, stabbing, slashing their way. Khalid and Hamza fight back to back, an invincible team. The towering Omar is the Grim Reaper with his scythe-like weapon. The totem bearer tries to use the totem as a spear, but his life ends in a flurry of feathers.

Those who can flee into the desert. Shields, swords, and fifteen bodies litter the scene as suddenly widowed women rush to their fallen.

Talib, Sufyan, and Jahl, positioned on the hillock, watch the carnage below. Sufyan, with a wave of his arm, orders the cavalry forward. With thunderous hoofbeats, they sweep down the hill, pursuing those escaping. Some tribals are cut down from galloping horses; others are corralled and led back as prisoners.

The brief battle is over. The freed women and children cry tears of joy for their rescue. Meccan soldiers mingle with them, recognizing some of the people. The Bedouin women and children huddle together, crying tears of sorrow for their lost men and their future slavery. Abdullah escorts the chief's son, who saved his life, to the liberated women and children. Sufyan, Jahl, and Talib stand over the captured men, some wounded, who are sitting in a line. All understand the law of the desert. Most now adapt the classic posture of submission before a superior force, their foreheads to the ground, arms outstretched on the dirt, rears up in the air, hoping for mercy and grace from their conquerors. Talib nods to Hamza, who turns away, wanting no part of what is to come. Talib then looks to the giant Omar holding his sword wet with blood. The women plead and cry. Omar raises his sword above the first in line. There will be no mercy or grace on this day. Many turn away rather than watch the grisly spectacle.

So ends another Bedouin tribe. If the battle is to be memorialized, it will be by a Meccan bard. Those now entering into slavery will have the only memories of their now extinct tribe to be buried with them. Victors write the history.

FIVE

INSULTING THE GODS

Talib appears at Muhammad's door and is warmly greeted by Khadija. "Good morning, Khadija. I need to speak to my nephew."

"He's doing his morning prayers. Shall I tell him you passed by?"

"I need to speak to him now—it's important."

"Please come in, then. I will get him."

Muhammad appears, greets his uncle.

"Nephew, Lahab has called a council meeting to bring charges against you."

"For what?"

"Insulting the gods."

"Have the gods complained?"

"This is serious—I warned you many times not to speak against the gods. You are under my protection, so don't embarrass me. It's this evening they want you to appear before the council. An apology should straighten things out."

That evening, a crowded meeting is underway at the Nadwa House. Muhammad sits, along with Hamza, Waraqa, Bakr, Othman, and other Companions, against one wall facing the rest of the council, all who share family and Hashemite identities. Few in the crowd know about the charge.

Stoked by righteous anger, Lahab rises, the powerful gatekeeper and now the self-appointed prosecutor.

"What a shameful low moment that I have to stand before this honorable council to bring a charge against none other than my own nephew. When the charge is serious, threatening our Meccan way of life, there can be no family favoritism; that would be a corruption undermining our true values. Yes, as painful as it is to say, the charge is insulting the gods!"

An audible gasp rises from the assembly, knowing that this is a capital offense.

Lahab dramatically clutches the Kaaba keys as he continues his rant. "All of you know that his disrespect for our gods has been constant, even at the Kaaba. We the Hashemites have devoted our lives to the temple and its gods, the true gods of Mecca—known to me, to your fathers, to your forefathers. To them we owe our lives, prosperity, and superiority! They are the true protectors of Mecca! Disobeying, mocking, and insulting them is the unforgivable sin, punishable in this life, and their offspring shall carry their disgrace forever! There is no place in this holy city for those who don't bow in humility and gratitude to the gods."

The crowd reacts to his arguments with spontaneous comments. Lahab has the support of many of the conservative Notables. Others find the harsh attack too provocative; they've always known Muhammad as an upright citizen who contributes to Mecca's wealth and prestige. They're suspicious of Lahab's motives. Why does he want to make an example of Muhammad?

All look to Muhammad, expecting him to reply with some conciliatory words to defuse the situation. He remains calm, showing little reaction.

"Nephew," Talib says, "how do you respond to such accusations? Before anyone leaves tonight, this unfortunate misunderstanding must be resolved."

Muhammad rises, surveys the crowd. Many he's known his whole life. He speaks in a calm, even tone in total contrast to Lahab's angry vitriol, as though he is simply stating obvious truths. He directs his words to Lahab and the other hostile council members.

"My people, my tribe, sons of Hashim, young and elders. How can I bow to the part and forget the whole? To a man-made idol? These false gods you've created that you praise in the morning and condemn in the evening, that you worship this year and the next year you forget. When you speak to them, they do not hear; when you ask them for help, they do not answer. Your gods are nothing but the manifestation of your own greed, lust, and hatred. You've made them in your own image to create a Mecca where you are the masters and the people are the enslaved. God is not made of matter—he is the maker! Omniscient, omnipresent, all-knowing, infinite without beginning and without end, the absolute most powerful, the uncaused cause of all that exists, the almighty creator of the universe, the light of this world and other worlds."

Muhammad pauses both to catch his breath and to make sure his description of the true God in his infinite magnificence has registered. "But you turned his house of worship into a marketplace where idols are bought and sold based on your own interests. You've created these gods to maintain your monopoly over wealth and power."

Jahl interrupts, "They are not only stones! They are not only made of wood! There is a force behind each one of them that an illiterate shepherd cannot see! The stone you see is only the symbol of that power. Of their greatness and majesty! *HUBAL!* The god of divination. *MANAT!* The goddess of fate, destiny, and death. *AL-UZZA!* The goddess of might, protection, and love! *AL-LAT!* The goddess of fertility and war! In them we trust—we are ready to sacrifice ourselves at their feet, ready to die fighting for their glory!"

This rousing declaration of faith sets the majority on fire, cheering and clapping. When the room settles down, the participants look back at Muhammad. For the multi-godly, nothing that Muhammad could say would contradict the spirited truth spoken by Jahl.

Muhammad continues in the same calm voice. "God to you is just another object, another subject you own, a thing you praise now and later you blame. You honor the gods for prosperity, and when drought comes you curse them. To those gods, I don't bow! The false shall perish and the eternal, one, immutable, true God shall remain!"

This produces a flurry of talk among the audience.

Muhammad continues, "Noah had warned his people, but only a few listened; the others mocked him, laughed at him for building the ark far away from the sea. They did not believe his warnings, rejecting any change to their wicked ways, arrogant in their traditions, blinded by their desires and hatred until the destructive flood came and wiped them out. Your sins and deceit are greater than the sins of any past generation!"

This produces many reactions, from uncomfortable laughter to total shock at Muhammad's throwing back the accusation against him a hundredfold stronger against the Meccan leaders.

"I tell you, the time has come to renounce and reject slavery, for the true God created all men equal. The time has come to reject murdering female babies, the most innocent of all God's creation; to conduct honest, fair trade and abolish the evil of interest; to forbid usury from destroying so many lives, only making the rich richer and the poor poorer. To turn the Kaaba back to God." Muhammad's resonant voice fills the room, and those present are surprised to hear such eloquence from their kinsman.

Lahab responds, "How can an illiterate, ignorant shepherd dare to speak like the Prophets Moses and Abraham?" He looks around for support, for others to agree that this is clearly an absurdity. While he does get nodding support from many, the room is divided.

Waraqa, Khadija's respected hanif cousin, speaks out. "Moses and Abraham were shepherds!"

That receives murmured approval from many, and even some laughter, as a good retort. Hamza's voice stands out with loud approval.

Lahab furiously grasps his cane, its golden handle adorned with the head of Hubal, holding it in a threatening way, as if he might strike Muhammad. The crowd stiffens. They look to Talib, the Hashemite leader, the peacemaker, to speak. He remains silent.

Sufyan leaps up from beside his wife, Hind. "Those gods this orphan slanders are the gods of our fathers, the protectors of Mecca. What are you saying? We end pilgrimage? Make my slaves equal to me? Share my wealth with those who didn't earn it? Sabotage the status of Mecca among the Arabs and non-Arabs and make it vulnerable to attacks from all the

uncivilized out there who envy and hate Mecca? You are asking us to go totally against man's nature! Every empire has its
kings and its slaves, the natural laws of superior and inferior;
they can't be equal. You say we invented our gods. Is your
invisible god not your own invention? Yes, we respect Al-lah,
but your Al-lah is not the one we know. Without our gods
there is no pilgrimage, no trade, no Mecca! What does your
god bring us, the way you describe it? Only destruction!"

That does connect with the audience as they look around
to see the reaction of their peers. Hind's eyes meets those of
Hamza, expressing a kind of triumph.

The conciliatory Talib stands and addresses Muhammad.
"Nephew, worship the god you wish; just leave the other
gods alone."

That meets with a kind of relieved sigh, as if to say, *May
Muhammad accept that.*

But no. Muhammad replies, "A man carrying his traditions and beliefs like a donkey carrying Holy Scripture without understanding it, to what advantage is this? Especially to
a man mad after money and pleasure."

"Talib," Sufyan interjects, "still your nephew's tongue. For
we all know, the penalty for insulting the gods is death."

"You are not my nephew, and I am not your uncle!"
With that verbal punch, Lahab, the realist, storms out of the
room, joined by his wife, Arwa, and many of like mind, leaving Muhammad, the idealist, facing those who are remaining. They are impressed as much by his calm and confident
demeanor as they are by his condemning words.

All exhale. The Rubicon has been crossed. Mecca will
never be the same.

After the tumultuous meeting, a small group lingers outside, talking with concern about Muhammad. Some attribute this grandiose behavior to a jinn having captured Muhammad's mind. Maybe Lahab was right, after all. Hopefully, with time Muhammad will come to his senses. Until then, let him lay his carpet outside the Kaaba and join the other seers and oracles, these hanifs that no one takes seriously. For Mecca's elite, Muhammad was a rising star of his generation, viewed as one who could play a leadership role one day. But this incident certainly has led them to have second thoughts.

However, the young who were there, while they did not raise their hands to help, are impressed. Muhammad has not publicly preached these revolutionary ideas, but more and more of his extended family, many of them cousins, have been joining the growing circle of believers who gather at Muhammad's for prayers and to listen to the wisdom coming from this man they are beginning to see as a master. Muhammad's four uncles show no interest in following their nephew. Hamza doesn't really understand what Muhammad was going on about, and Abbas is simply noncommittal, but both assure Muhammad of the strong personal affection they have for him. No such sentiment is forthcoming from Lahab, who, immediately upon hearing those first lines that couldn't have been clearer, sees Muhammad as an existential threat to his domain of the Kaaba and thus Mecca itself.

SIX

FIRST BELIEVERS

Night settles over the sleeping city. The stars and a few lights from dwellings provide just enough light to see the outlines of the buildings.

At Jahl's mansion, the tall Ethiopian, Bilaal, moves silently out of the slave quarter, effortlessly scales the compound's wall, and is gone. Washi, the slave acting as night watchman in this wealthy area, spots him, hesitates, but then follows him at a safe distance.

In the poor section of town, a middle-aged man named Yassir comes out of a shack, scans the street in both directions, listens intently, and then, satisfied, beckons his wife, Somaya, and their twenty-year-old son, Ammar, to join him. They move quickly through the dark streets, hugging the walls.

In a wealthy section of Mecca, a young man named Mosaab moves softly out of a luxurious house, slipping past a sleeping guard.

At Bakr's home, Bakr gets up and says good-bye to his dozing wife.

Bilaal moves quickly in long strides up a hill, passing the stone quarry where he labors. Washi still follows, while other figures, glimpsed in the starlight, appear to be headed in the same direction.

When he reaches his destination, Bilaal ducks into a cave, where the dim light of flickering oil lamps illuminates a group of some forty Companions, both men and women. He sits near Khadija and the children and behind Hamza.

Outside, Washi gets as close as he can to the entrance of the cave to eavesdrop.

"Be drunk with love!" a voice from inside the cave declaims. That produces laughter inside the cave and a puzzled look from the spy outside.

Bakr and Othman stand next to a seated, amused Muhammad.

Othman says, "Be drunk with love. For love is all that exists." The assembly makes approving sounds.

The Messenger gestures to Bakr, signaling his turn.

Bakr declaims, "The beloved is alive. The lover is dead." That produces a negative reaction and all look to Muhammad expectantly.

He does not disappoint. "A soul that is not clothed with the inner garment of love should be ashamed of its existence. Love is the way of the heart, the way of the pure. The value of an action is dependent on the intention. If your pilgrimage is to God, then you will reach God. But if your journey is to the world, you will get only to the world, the lower material realm."

Outside, Washi, now intrigued, leans in to hear better, then slips and falls. Hard. Picking himself up, he flees down the hillside path, causing an avalanche of cascading rocks. The noise draws the attention of those in the cave. They look back at Muhammad for guidance on what to do. As tranquil as ever, Muhammad continues describing his experience in that very same cave.

SEVEN

MUHAMMAD ATTACKED

O n a hot summer day at the Kaaba, devotees perform rituals before their idols amidst the swirling smoke of incense. No ritual is stranger than that of Lahab's wife. Arwa cuts a chicken's head off and drains the blood into a bowl. Next, she deftly maneuvers the head of a snake out of a cloth bag and, holding its head over the bowl, extracts a few poisonous drops from the fangs.

There is a lone tree in a removed section of the Kaaba precinct where the poets, magicians, soothsayers, and preachers hold forth, attracting a crowd. Muhammad sits under the welcome shade of the tree. Gathering around him are some of the Believers and the curious. In the middle of telling a story, Muhammad stands up with a broad smile as three pilgrims dressed in white approach.

"Sa'ad!"

"Master," the lithe thirty-five-year-old replies.

"Please, sit, you've had a long journey." Muhammad, both surprised and pleased to see them, indicates the three to sit in front of him in the shade.

Sa'ad looks uncertain, not wanting to interrupt the master's discourse, but with a gesture, Muhammad insists, and they find their place.

Jahl and Lahab hover in the back of the crowd, listening. Who are these new arrivals Muhammad has greeted so warmly? More trouble?

Back in the days when Muhammad was a trader, before Al-lah called him to warn mankind, he often broke up the long journeys by spending time in Yathrib, the oasis town of water and dates. The two leading tribes, the Awes and the Khazraj, were constantly fighting. Muhammad made them realize the power of unity and the benefits of peace. His mediation in helping them reconcile their differences made them the strongest tribe in Yathrib. Since then, they have looked to him with great respect, and Sa'ad, their leader, recognizes him as a master and spiritual teacher.

Muhammad continues his story to a rapt audience. "So this man, one fine morning, made a god for his tribe out of dates, which, after all, had given them their prosperity. Then in the evening he was hungry, so he prayed to his god to give him food. But his god didn't answer." He pauses before continuing: "Then he just ate the god he'd made that morning!"

This gets the desired laugh.

"God is not made of wood or stone; he's not an object nor a subject." Muhammad indicates a man struggling to carry a wooden idol. He scans his audience, and his eyes meet those of a hostile Jahl.

"God is the absolute. Never born, never dies. Eternal." Muhammad closes his eyes as though collecting his thoughts. "The Uncaused Cause of all that exists. There is nothing that can be compared to him."

This puzzles most, as it is much more abstract than the wooden idol that just passed by, yet they're fascinated and want more. A young pilgrim asks the obvious question: "Who are you?"

"Some call me a Messenger."

"What is your message?"

Muhammad points to the heavens, intertwines his two hands together.

"Oneness."

Before Muhammad can continue, there's a scuffle at the edge of the crowd as Jahl, Lahab, Malik, and their guards plow their way through, knocking over some of the listeners.

An enraged Jahl kicks Muhammad in the ribs, slams his face to the ground.

This is, to say the least, a shock to all who were listening to a gentle and wise discourse.

"Get this liar out of here!" Jahl shouts.

The Yathrib pilgrims rush to help Muhammad, who sits back up, not confronting Jahl, a captive of rage.

Lahab pulls Jahl back, realizing he's made a mistake, especially in the presence of pilgrims. It was Muhammad's popularity with them, more than the blasphemy, that sparked his jealous action.

A shocked Sa'ad addresses Jahl: "Why did you do this?"

"You heard him; he's insulting the gods in this sacred place. Corrupting the minds of our youth, dividing our city—father against son, husband against wife."

"We've known him for a long time and have heard him speak only beautiful ideas. A poet."

"A poet of poison."

Muhammad's group and the Yathrib group, fearing more violence, surround Muhammad to escort him past the guards and out of the Kaaba area.

Suddenly, Arwa knifes through his volunteer guardians and throws the chicken blood, bowl and all, at Muhammad.

His white garment is sprayed with bright red blood, just missing Sa'ad's.

Muhammad calmly walks away. Sa'ad walks alongside
him, handing him some Yathrib dates.

Arwa, proud of herself, receives some support—and some
comments of shame. Jahl does his best to convey the impres-
sion that he's won by expelling this fraud from the holy area.

❁

Later that afternoon, a man dressed in black astride a jet-black
Arabian stallion canters through the main city gate as many
are leaving the Kaaba area. It's the hunter Hamza with a bow
and a sack. An older woman also dressed in black approaches
him. Hamza takes a headless snake from his sack and gives it
to her.

"May Hubal bless you, O Hamza, the knight of Arabia.
I've just witnessed a shameful moment where Jahl attacked
your nephew Muhammad in the worst way." The woman
points to the terrace overlooking the Kaaba, where a group of
Notables enjoy an early dinner. Jahl stands out among them.

Hamza hears a few more words about the incident as he
dismounts, and he grows ever angrier. He marches toward the
terrace, passing the statue of Hubal. The Notables stop eating when they see Hamza, a vengeful expression on his face,
bounding up the steps. The Notables freeze as Hamza confronts Jahl, who is guiltily munching on a camel bone. Hamza
grabs the bone and stuffs it hard into Jahl's full mouth, making Jahl gag. "Will you still insult my nephew when I tell you
I support him?" Hamza cries.

No one is more startled than Hind at this surprise double blow—one physical, the other political. Jahl, afraid of the

fierce Hamza, spits out his food as hatred scours his features. Hamza turns his rage toward the startled Notables, who are quickly losing any appetite they had, and angrily turns their food-laden table over, splattering them with their dinner.

Then Hamza leaves the disaster behind and rides off. Some of the Notables go to assist the humiliated Jahl, while others stare at a worried Talib. Hamza is a Hashemite, and Talib as the Hashemite leader bears the responsibility for Hamza's actions.

***

Hamza comes through the front door of his home and hangs his bow and sword on a wall covered with weapons and hunting trophies. Then he heads for his bedroom. There, sitting on his bed, is an angry and seductive Hind, Sufyan's wife.

"Have you gone mad, Hamza?"

"No."

"I can see you defending your lunatic nephew, but not his evil path."

Hamza ignores her, washing his hands in a bowl of water.

"This story's all over Mecca. Everyone must understand it was said in a moment of anger."

"It was. But I meant what I said. My nephew speaks the truth. There has to be a Creator greater than the idols at the Kaaba."

Hind is unsure. Is he playing with her? She goes into her seductive mode.

Hamza is tempted but turns away. "No, Hind."

With that she leaps up, storms past him.

When she arrives home, she finds her husband, Sufyan, hosting a meeting with the key Notables, familiar faces like Jahl, Lahab, Khalid, and the giant Omar. Conspicuous in his absence is Talib.

Jaamil, who acts as a judge in Mecca's rather primitive "eye for an eye" criminal judicial system, opines, "There aren't that many following Muhammad—only slaves because he promises them freedom, and beggars because he promises them gold in the sky."

"What about Hamza and Bakr?" Omar asks. "They're not slaves nor beggars."

Jahl joins in. "Exactly—that's a serious threat, and it shows how this could get out of hand."

"Teaching a lesson to the arrogant Hamza will set an important example," Hind interrupts as all look around to see her there. "You, Khalid, can do that, as there is no one stronger with the sword than you, though the insufferable Hamza thinks he's the strongest."

Jahl does not disagree with the sentiment, but the interruption from this woman, even though it is her house, annoys him. "It's Muhammad who is the threat. We must teach a lesson to those who follow him or are even tempted. Put the fear of mighty Hubal in every Meccan."

"It's useless to step on the tail of the snake. You need to cut off the head. One stroke." Leave it to Lahab to get straight to the point.

"You know that's not possible," the realist Sufyan, a defender of the system, states.

Khalid muses, "Only as long as he's under Talib's protection, and I don't see why we need to—"

Sufyan interrupts. "There'd be a blood feud. A civil war. It would tear Mecca apart. Do you want that?"

"Then the solution is obvious," Jahl says. "Confront Talib and demand he disown his nephew. Remove his protection."

That morning, a delegation consisting of Jahl, Sufyan, and Lahab appear at Talib's house. They meet in the living room where they all sit down. Ali is there too.

After the niceties, Jahl speaks. "We wish to meet with you alone, Talib."

He looks over at Ali, who looks to his father as to what to do. A first test of strength? This is Talib's house and Ali is his son, but these are important elders. He reflects for a moment, then nods to Ali to leave them, which he does.

Jahl takes a deep breath and begins the speech he's been mentally rehearsing. "Talib, you have a high and honorable position among us. We've asked you before and are asking you now to renounce your brother's son, which you haven't done, even though he continues to insult our fathers, scorn our traditions, and revile our gods. We know you don't believe his crazy ideas, and you don't follow him. You know he is destroying our beloved Mecca."

Jahl, looking for an agreement about what is indeed true, gets no response from the Hashim leader. After a long silence, Jahl drops the hammer. "You either make him stop, or we will fight both of you."

Talib, a man of conciliation, replies, "Kinsmen, I'll speak with him."

There's another moment of silence as the threat and promise to deal with Muhammad hangs in the air. Then Jahl stands up, and perhaps the shortest meeting ever ends.

❈

That evening, Muhammad sits with Talib, as his presence had been requested, though Muhammad was well briefed by Ali as to what to expect.

"Son of my brother," Talib says, "spare me and spare your-self. Don't put on me a burden greater than I can bear."

Muhammad well understands that this man he is so close to is caught between a rock and a hard place. Talib believes in the traditional values espoused in Mecca that have kept prosperity for the few and have brought peace, but part of that belief system is to protect members of the clan or tribe. Because the decision to maintain or remove that protection is held solely by the clan chief, all the other clans have an invested interest in maintaining this principle. In part, it's where their power resides. Muhammad would very much like to solve this dilemma for him. A word or even a sign from him would relieve Talib from his ethical agony. How-ever, Muhammad's belief system will not allow it. He does not know how long Talib will be able to hold out maintaining Muhammad's protection.

Muhammad doesn't reply immediately, so Talib ups the stakes. "They're talking about the death penalty, nephew."

"None of us know when we're going to die," Muhammad replies.

Seeing the disappointed look on Talib's face, Muhammad realizes his uncle did not deserve in such a crucial moment such a cavalier, if not stupid, reply that helped no one.

Muhammad takes a calming breath. "I swear by God, if they put the sun in my right hand and the moon in my left, on the condition that I abandon this course of action before he's made it victorious, or that I perish in this struggle, I will not abandon it."

There could not be a clearer statement made. Talib is not surprised, but he hoped for some kind of middle ground where Muhammad expressed that he would remain faithful to Al-lah while not criticizing other gods and those who worshipped them.

Muhammad departs with mixed feelings, leaving Talib with a heavier unresolved burden.

Out on the street Muhammad is aware that people are looking at him differently. The word is out and the rumor mill churns away. At the same time, more and more people are joining Muhammad as First Believers as the schism in Mecca grows.

EIGHT

OMAR'S FATEFUL NIGHT

Omar, Khalid, Otbah, and other fighters are enjoying a drunken night out at a popular lower-class dive frequented by camel drivers, prostitutes, freed slaves, shopkeepers, and workers. The two brothers who own the establishment have a good relationship with a Taif vineyard that produces a wine renowned for its high alcohol content, and they serve the best barbecued meat in Mecca, which will even attract Notables who are willing to go slumming. This night, as the warrior buddies grow more and more drunk, the Notable Lahab, wearing the Kaaba key around his neck, has made a rare appearance. His presence is rather intimidating for the usual patrons on the poor side of the sharp class divide. The brothers make a special effort around him, offering different meats supplied by their hunters. At the moment he's greedily chewing away on a gazelle bone.

The inebriated warriors are discussing their favorite topic, railing against Muhammad.

"Nothing's being done to shut him up," Omar says.

"Why don't you do something?" Otbah asks.

Khalid refills Omar's wine bowl.

Omar, spotting Lahab in a corner, stands up unsteadily and points. "Look at Lahab!"

The room goes silent as all eyes turn toward the Notable.

"Like a hen, he knows how to sit on the Kaaba's golden eggs. But watch over and control his own nephew Muhammad, the destroyer of Mecca? Nothing. Pathetic."

There's uncomfortable laughter as all hope that this is a joke.

Then Lahab speaks. "And you, Omar, so strong—you can't even control your own sister."

"So all you can do is insult my sister," Omar retorts.

"Your sister and her husband are following Muhammad," Lahab says. "What—are you blind?"

Alcohol does not slow the giant down, and in few steps amidst the gasping crowd, Omar rips the Kaaba chain off Lahab and puts two powerful hands around his neck, choking him. Khalid and three others leap up and grab Omar, all four managing to yank him off Lahab. Stunned, Lahab collapses to the floor sputtering and coughing, sucking in air.

"I swear by Hubal she's following him," Lahab says.

"I don't believe you," Omar says.

"Go ask her."

"You son of a whore! If you're lying, your head will be on my spear on the roof of the Kaaba." Omar looks at Khalid. Khalid looks away. The other companions avoid Omar's angry, penetrating gaze.

Omar grabs his sword and empties his wine bowl, throwing it to the floor. Then he heads for the street.

"Where are you going, brother Omar? Sit down," Khalid urges him.

"To my sister's house."

"She's not there."

"Where is she then?"

"At Muhammad's house."

"How do you know that?"

"Everyone knows, Omar, but no one dares tell you."

Drunk and dangerous, Omar staggers down the street. With each step, his anger and humiliation grow, the alcohol erasing any rational restraint. As he approaches Muhammad's home, he hears laughter coming from inside, which in his drunken state he takes personally as mocking him. He slams his heavy bulk against the wooden entrance door, loosening it. With a solid kick, the door falls half open and the angry giant forces his way in.

The laughter dies as the sword-wielding giant finds himself standing in the middle of the large room in a circle of participants sitting on the floor. He looks around the surprised room but doesn't see his sister. Making eye contact with Muhammad and Hamza, who is seated next to him, he sees there are even more people in an adjoining room. When he spots his sister, he rushes toward her, only to be blocked by Saeed. Omar whacks him with a forearm blow, knocking him out as he drops to the floor. He moves toward Fatima, Omar's sister, who tries to crawl away, but he grabs her by the hair and drags her toward a wall.

Fatima pleads, "Brother . . . brother . . . please!"

But Omar lifts her up like a rag doll and bangs her against the wall so unexpectedly and so violently, it's too fast for anyone to react.

Then Omar looks down at his unconscious beloved sister, her head bloodied. A sober moment hits him. Many of the men stand to contain Omar, who is now in shock. An agonized cry escapes the giant's sobering lips. "*What have I done?*" he wails.

Khadija and Muhammad's daughters rush to help Fatima.
Hamza, who has known the volatile giant since his childhood,
steps toward him. Omar makes eye contact with his best friend
and breaks into tears, sobbing. He drops to the floor in shame.

Khadija tapping on Fatima's cheeks brings her back to
life. No one is more relieved than Omar, who gets back on
his feet to see Muhammad standing next to him. Everyone
present is intent on what the Prophet will say. Muhammad
indicates they both sit back down on the floor across from
each other.

"Anger makes slaves out of kings; tolerance and patience
make kings out of slaves," Muhammad begins. "You were
still a little boy when your father almost buried your baby
sister alive, fearful of people's judgment. Your anger springs
from your fear. Today you beat her because of what other men
would think of you. When fear of man's opinion is greater
than love for one's daughter or sister, a man must take a hard,
honest look at himself. You try so hard to maintain your status among men, a giant physically but a midget spiritually.
You don't know this, but your sister is here because it was
Khadija who convinced your father not to kill her. She showed
him how his fears of being judged were false. And you, Omar,
had those wonderful years growing up with your sister. What
is courage, really? Fatima has more courage in her weak body
than an army of angry men fighting for honor and pride.
Those who have the fear of God in their hearts don't fear men;
they are gentle and humble when it comes to the defenseless.
Have you forgotten that this strong body came out of a woman's womb? Are you on the side of truth? Who is your master,
Omar? Who is your idol?"

Omar wipes tears from his cheeks as Muhammad's words
strike deeply into his soul.

"Men arrive at the feet of Truth at some point on their short life journey, but most of them turn their back on Truth when they realize what it takes to be truthful," Muhammad continues. "You go on fighting for status, an idol you create, then you enslave yourself to it. Most men are too weak to live truthfully. Because it means the death of their idols, the truth reveals them as false. The annihilation of the lower self is fit only for this lower realm of existence. No one can enter the higher realm of existence as long as they are still enslaved to the idols they create. God created Adam in his image, not the opposite. I reject bowing to idols, seen or unseen, made of stone, or of words, or of flesh, or even of poetry. The lower self has to die in order for the higher self to be born. This realm is nothing but a mirage, a false existence. Your pleasure in vanity can only die."

"What made Jesus, Moses, Jacob, and Abraham great was their power over their idols, but small men worship their idols, and this is why they remain in slavery. Go on . . . continue wrestling against the external enemies. Punch those who oppose you. Do you think they will stop appearing? But this is your quest to conquer infinity, until it conquers you. I, Muhammad, the son of Abdullah, promise you this: if you conquer your inner enemy, then you have conquered all your enemies. The fine line between Truth and Falsehood is the same fine line between your lower self and your higher self. Now you see. It is your choice to be true or to be false."

With that, both men rise. Fatima steps toward her brother and enfolds him in a forgiving embrace.

Hamza takes his shaken and profoundly moved friend by the arm and escorts him home.

After this, Omar will never drink another drop of alcohol, and Muhammad's words will resonate with him as he takes a hard and honest look at himself.

NINE

THE SPLIT BECOMES A CRISIS

Every day, the Notables grow more aware that Muhammad is making inroads among the youth—even the privileged young. This particularly worries the Notables, especially if the youth are from their own extended families, and they're being pressured by their peers to do something. A mother-son conflict well dramatizes the family schisms that are playing out across the holy city.

In a mansion near the Kaaba, three African slaves attend the denizens, stone-faced as a bitter confrontation between Mosaab and his mother, Zainab, unfolds. Mosaab's handsome brother, Assad, revels in it. The beautiful Circassian woman on his lap tries to distract him.

"My privileged and spoiled son has gone blind," Zainab says.

Mosaab, facing his mother, stares at the ground.

Zainab gestures around her at the ornate inlaid furniture, Persian carpets, gold objects, totems to Meccan gods encrusted with jewels and silver. A small leashed African leopard reclines on a divan, eyeing the caged parrots above him. "But you see this, don't you? You're happy to take advantage of this." She crowds him, lifts his chin so their eyes meet, and feels his silk shirt. "You feel this on your pampered skin. You've been given the life of a prince. Why can't you enjoy this like your brother? Why do you insist on humiliating me, our family, by following a lunatic?"

That energizes Mosaab. "Muhammad is not a lunatic. The lunatics are those who worship idols, who enslave our fellow humans, who kill newborn baby girls—those are the lunatics."

That hits Zainab, who gestures the slaves to leave the room. They drop what they're doing to hurriedly depart.

"Those creatures of God were born equal. Money doesn't give anyone the right to own them," Mosaab says.

"Is this what your Muhammad has been teaching you?"

Mosaab does not reply, thus admitting it is.

"To insult your mother in front of her slaves. I, who gave you status and beauty." She looks admiringly around the golden room. "He gives you lies and ugliness."

"Muhammad gives me true life. You cannot buy that with gold, Mother."

"Get out! Leave my house. And don't come back until you become again the son I bore."

Zainab rejects Mosaab's attempted farewell embrace. His brother watches with mixed feelings his favored brother's fall from grace.

The rejected son heads briskly for the door, strides down the hallway. He makes eye contact with the three slaves who have left the room. Two look away, but one gives him a faint approving smile.

As Mosaab opens the front door to the lonely night, someone grasps his arm. Assad. "Best go back, brother. Apologize to our mother."

"Apologize for what? For telling the truth?"

"What truth is worth hurting our mother?"

Mosaab shrugs, then heads out into the dark uncertain night.

Assad shivers in the cold. "You'll be back."

＊

The number of followers of Muhammad grows steadily, which has the Notables especially worried as the pilgrimage fair is coming up soon. They decide to make a final attempt to confront Muhammad directly, offering him something no reasonable man could turn down.

Again, it falls to Sufyan to make the proposal. "If you want money, we will gather for you all of our property that will make you the richest among us—the richest man in the richest city. If you want honor and power, we will make you our chief so that nothing can be decided without your approval. And if a jinn possesses you and you cannot rid yourself of him, we will exhaust all our means to help you, to restore your health."

Muhammad listens, suppressing the desire to laugh at their transparency and desperation. It's obvious they neither could nor would deliver on this "deal." Their stratagem is to get him to accept, then accuse him of hypocrisy. It only reveals their misunderstanding of what motivates Muhammad. What motivates them is money and power, so they assume it is the same for Muhammad. It is this very lust for wealth and power that Muhammad is preaching against.

Of course he turns them down.

❖

Tensions mount in the City of Peace as taunts to the followers become blows. Muhammad commands the people to practice patience in the face of persecution and not respond with violence. However, when a young follower, an orphan, is killed praying peacefully in a wadi outside Mecca, brawls erupt around the Kaaba between followers of Muhammad and those loyal to Hubal and the Notables. The guards, favoring Muhammad's opponents, have difficulty controlling the mayhem.

Sufyan calls an emergency meeting at his mansion—without Talib—to search for a solution now that both intimidation and temptation have ignominiously failed. Lahab's proposal from the beginning to simply kill Muhammad, still under Talib's protection despite their threats, would produce not just a blood debt but risk a civil war with the Hashemite clan. Lahab, with his hatred of Muhammad and a perverse imagination for punishment, proposes that they go after Muhammad's followers, the majority of whom are not Hashemite. Pain rather than persuasion is the remedy, he insists. This will create a terror in anyone even considering listening to Muhammad. If Muhammad really cares about his followers and believes in his preached message of love, this will finally force him to silence.

As the meeting breaks up and the Notables disperse, Talib passes by Lahab, laughing with Abu Jahal. Upon seeing Lahab, Talib's face darkens with alarm. He sets off at a brisk pace in the opposite direction.

He knocks vigorously on the door of a familiar house. Khadija opens the door to see Talib standing outside. Her smile of welcome drops when she sees his worried expression. He strides past her without a greeting and goes to the prayer room, where he finds his nephew seated on a carpet.

"Get up, nephew!"

Startled, Muhammad stands to his feet.

"Is your one God pleased now? Division. Hatred. War!"

Muhammad is completely taken aback by this version of Talib he has never seen. Is he actually expected to answer him?

But Talib wants an answer, the answer he's always wanted. "What happened up there on Hira? On your last retreat? You came down a different person; the gentle Muhammad I've known my entire life was lost. Tell me. What happened?"

Khadija intervenes. "Uncle, please sit down."

Talib hesitates, calms down, and sits. Khadija offers him milk and dates.

Muhammad sits respectfully across from his uncle, keeping a steadfast gaze on his troubled mentor. He owes this beloved elder his life and understands the increasing pressure on his uncle's shoulders. He owes him an answer, but he doesn't know where to begin.

"I had fasted for thirty days when . . . the cave was lit with a blinding light and a sudden and overwhelming heat . . . The light blinded me and the powerful presence dropped me to my knees . . . A thunderous voice called me by my name and my father's name. I've never heard a voice as deep as that, and the voice was so far yet so near, as though it came from every direction: *I AM YOUR GOD!*"

Muhammad pauses, catching his breath as he delves deep into the memory of the overwhelming encounter. Talib and Khadija listen intently.

"He warned mankind of imminent destruction if killing babies and worshipping idols continued. Then he commanded me to go back to my village and deliver this message . . . and I did."

Talib realizes from the power of his nephew's speech that he truly believes his experience alone there in the cave was real.

"Son, anyone who goes without food and water for thirty days hallucinates, sees unreal things, hears voices. When I got lost in the desert for just twenty days, I thought I saw God too. I heard voices saying words—but they were just words."

Khadija tries to support her husband's veracity. "You should have seen his state when he came down. It was hard to recognize him."

"Uncle, it wasn't the words only; it was the authority, the rhythm, the vibration behind them—they penetrated my bones. I wasn't hallucinating. On earlier retreats I've fasted more than thirty days, and I know both hallucination and awareness."

Talib becomes even more frustrated. *How do you convince someone who is in the grip of delusion?* he wonders. "Delusions and confusion. What can this aged man do to persuade you and persuade your adversaries? Apparently, neither of you have any respect for the wisdom of an aged man."

Muhammad does not know how to reply.

"Listen, son! Many have tried to change Mecca, but they have failed. Mecca changes people while Mecca stays the same. You may be able to change the names of the gods, make it *Al-lah* instead of *Allat*, but this does not change the nature of man. Mecca will never change. Our ancestors circled the Kaaba long before we were born, and our heirs will circle it long after we are gone."

"Truth is beyond the mirage of Mecca, beyond man's delusion."

"You speak repeatedly of 'truth and falsehood.' There is no such thing, son. Meccan gods are made of clay and stone for a reason—they were meant to be fake. They should never become real, because when they do become real, they bring chaos and destruction. We want them to stay at the level of a stone, no more."

"No wonder your gods can't provide protection to a new-born buried in the sand—they can't bring justice to the weak, nor care for the orphaned, nor end a drought."

Talib emits an audible sigh. "When I was young like you, I rebelled. I also thought I knew everything. I thought life had two sides—vice and virtue. I was wrong. In life, there is reason and result; if there is any law beyond man, that is it. Everyone reaps what they sow."

"Uncle, killing infants is pure evil. I will not rest until it ends. Slavery, stealing, honor killing, and aggression are all crimes committed by the lawmakers, who should be doomed to hell."

Khadija offers both men wet towels to refresh themselves in the deadly heat of midday Mecca and soften this unexpected confrontation.

Talib takes a deep breath. He is more than aware of the maladies in Meccan society Muhammad is pointing out. "Son, if you believe you can stop such an evil without creating a greater evil, you are totally mistaken! This has not been the Hashemite approach. It was not the approach of your great-great-grandfather who built the city. I don't doubt your intention to end corruption and bring justice to the defenseless and powerless, but I disagree with your approach, for it will lead to endless bloodshed. Your great-great-grandfather managed the opposing powers of Mecca and rarely confronted them. But you have started a war, and neither of us knows how it will end. The only currency of exchange is blood. All have their gods, all the different colors in a society—the pilgrims, the money lenders, the prostitutes, even the gamblers. Three hundred and sixty-five gods. Don't you see the genius of this, every tribe with their own god and a respect for the other three hundred and sixty-four?"

Muhammad looks skeptical, as tribes often go into battle holding their totems aloft, but he doesn't say anything. What more can be said? The Younger and the Elder. The Idealist and the Realist.

TEN

THE CRISIS BECOMES
VIOLENT

Chaos reigns in the market and the Kaaba area as the Notables' new effort to silence Muhammad goes into brutal effect. Guards on horseback help corral citizens, beggars, and slaves trying to flee. Once guards grab someone, they frogmarch them toward a queue lining up before the imposing statue of Hubal. Notables watch this punitive roundup from the terrace. Finally, some definitive action is being taken.

Malik, the security chief, gestures the next citizen to kneel before the statue of Hubal. The citizen remains standing.

"Kneel before Hubal, the god you owe your life to," Malik tells him.

The young man doesn't move, then abruptly pivots, turning his back on the statue, which produces a gasp from those in the queue. Two guards roughly grab him, twisting his arms painfully before dragging him off to a group of refuseniks sitting on the ground. Many of them are familiar figures from Muhammad's meetings.

The Yassir family waits anxiously in the queue. A momentous decision awaits. The old man in line ahead of them is pushed forward to face Hubal.

"Kneel!" Malik commands.

The old man looks confused, hesitates. Malik indicates with a physical movement to kneel. The man drops to his knees, putting his forehead to the earth. Submission to a greater power. Hubal or Malik? A guard gently lifts him up, directing him to go free.

The Yassirs—father, mother, and son—step together in front of Hubal. Malik looks uncertain for a moment.

"Three together?" Malik questions. "All right. All of you kneel to mighty Hubal, who protects us all."

Ammar looks to his mother, Somaya, and then to his father, Yassir, signaling them to kneel.

"Kneel! No one is above the gods," Malik says.

This family drama has caught everyone's attention, especially those watching from the terrace.

Three guards come up behind the family and try to force them to their knees. Yassir falls down, but Somaya and Ammar resist. All three are brutally dragged off, their feet trailing in the dirt. They're thrown to the ground with the other refuseniks.

In the queue, Bin Mas'ud, the shepherd boy, gets closer to being called when he suddenly bolts. He's quick and evades the guards' attempts to tackle him, darting through the crowd and disappearing into the warren of narrow back streets.

❁

Some thirty of those who refused to bow are marched off to the quarry on Mount Hira, where they are given a final chance under torture to recant. Charged with "insult to the gods," a capital offense, if they do not recant they will not leave the quarry alive.

It is a scene from Hell, with these first-generation Companions of Muhammad being tortured by slaves, supervised by Meccan guards. Overseers Jahl and Malik stand over the slave Bilaal, who is tied by stakes to the ground, his chest a lattice of bloodied stripes from countless lashes. Bilaal refused to whip his fellow companions, meriting a slow death sentence.

Malik puts his face close to Bilaal's. "Hubal!"

There's no response from Bilaal. Whether he is unconscious or resisting is unclear.

Jahl orders Washi and other slaves to roll a boulder onto Bilaal's chest. It's hard to tell if he's still breathing.

His two torturers lean over him to see if he's still alive.

Bilaal draws words from somewhere deep: "One God."

Surely, that was his last breath. His eyes have gone vacant as they unblinkingly stare into the sun. All the frustrated torturers can do now is kick at his lifeless form.

They are distracted by a loud scream from a young man being dragged by two slaves toward the edge of the cliff. He tries to dig in his feet, but the slaves are too strong and they throw the young man off the cliff. His scream fades, then is abruptly cut short. The cries and screams of the victims at the whipping posts continue.

From the crest of a hill above, the shepherd boy Bin Mas'ud watches the horrific scene. A woman's scream echoes off the hillside. The shepherd gets up and scrambles down the back side of the hill to rejoin his sheep.

The Yassir family is being dealt with near the quarry cliff.

Ammar is tied to a whipping post, joining others being flogged by slaves under the burning heat of the midday sun.

Malik puts his face close to Ammar's. "Hubal!"

Ammar emits a cry with each lash to his back.

"Say 'Hubal,' and you'll have water," Malik demands.

"Water," Ammar responds.

Malik grabs the whip from the slave and whips Ammar with all his strength. Tiring, he goes over to Somaya, who is splayed out half-nude over a rock, her back bending in a painful position.

Malik draws his knife and, bending over Somaya, jams the knife to her throat.

"Hubal! Hubal!" Ammar suddenly responds.

Malik indicates a Nubian slave to release her and pull the stakes from the ground. Somaya struggles to sit up, her exposed skin red and blistered from the sun.

Malik leans into Somaya's face. "Say 'Hubal' like your son did, and you'll have water."

Somaya appears barely conscious. Malik presses the knife harder against her throat.

Ammar screams, straining at his bonds.

"Say it!" Malik insists.

But Somaya only says, "You're not worthy of the Prophet's sandals."

Malik slaps her. With a burst of final energy, she spits bloodied spittle into Malik's face. In a fury, he yanks the tiny woman up by her arm and drags her toward the edge of the cliff. Grabbing her by the hair, he forces her to look over the cliff. Some fifty meters below on the jagged rocks are at least ten bodies, many with their wrists still bound, splayed out like rag dolls. Somaya passes out. Malik gives her limp body a push and, looking over the cliff below, he sees that the execution ground has added another body to the group. Another martyr. Yassir, on his knees before Washi's raised sword, witnesses his wife's fate. Managing to roll over and avoid the blow to his neck with his hands tied, he staggers to his feet and leaps off the cliff on his own, cheating his executioner.

❁

Back in Mecca at Muhammad's home, the family sits on the floor before a low table, sharing a meal together. Muhammad, Khadija, Ali, Jaffar, Zayd, Talib, and Fatima, along with a one-eyed man and a disfigured woman—two of the poor and beaten down of Mecca.

A worried Muhammad has his mind elsewhere.

Khadija pats his arm. "Everyone's out looking for them. They'll find them."

Muhammad nods, ladles out some food from a plate. The one-eyed guest, seeing there is not much food on the table, holds up a hand to say no.

"Please, if there is enough for two—" Zayd says.

"There's enough for four—" chimes in Ali.

Fatima adds, "If there's enough for four, there's enough for eight—"

"And if there's enough for eight—" Zayd starts laughing. They've heard this so many times from their father.

There's a rapid knock on the door. The restless Muhammad is the first up, and he opens the door to Bin Mas'ud, the shepherd.

An hour later, Muhammad follows Bin Mas'ud up the familiar mountain path. Behind him, Hamza, Talib, Bakr, and ten other Companions hike rapidly, many loaded down with water. They reach the killing ground with its bodies and feasting vultures. Muhammad, in a rare display of disgust and anger, moves around the bodies, directing his fellow rescuers in a kind of instinctive triage. Chasing off the vultures, giving water to the victims, helping those who can stand up, the rescuers move quickly and efficiently. The horror of it all registers on Muhammad's face.

Bakr looks down at Bilaal's ravaged body, shakes his head, and moves on. Then he hears a moan. He stops, goes back, and kneels next to Bilaal. Could that sound have come from this lifeless form? He feels for a pulse, then pours water on the slave's face and, lifting his head, puts the waterskin to his lips. Bilaal opens his eyes, and the faintest sign of recognition creases his dark face. Bakr tries to lift the rock off Bilaal, but it's too heavy. He motions to Hamza, who comes over and, with the help of others, rolls it off. Bakr helps Bilaal sit up and gives him more water.

Hamza stares down at the body of his friend that bears the marks of a severe beating, and the rage in his gorge wells up. He reaches back to grasp the handle of his sword as though to reassure himself it's still there.

Muhammad sits in front of Ammar, who rocks back and forth grieving his dead parents. Opening his eyes to see Muhammad, he prostrates himself at his feet. "O my lord, I am not worthy. I have betrayed you. Leave me to die with my parents."

Muhammad leans over and pulls Ammar up to a sitting position. He embraces him to comfort him and gives him water. What words can serve here after all?

"This is the evil I have been warning about," Talib says. "And this is just the beginning. Damn you, Lahab, and your witch wife."

The killing ground, where just a short time ago the only movement came from the vultures, is now in motion as Muhammad organizes caring for the survivors, many of whom are gravely injured.

The thunderous sound of hoofbeats grabs everyone's attention, and they look toward a swirling cloud of dust coming toward them. It's Khalid. He slides off his horse, looking Hamza up and down. Only a short time ago, they fought a common enemy back-to-back.

Hamza stares straight ahead, containing his rage. He tries to make eye contact with Muhammad, only to have Khalid provocatively stand between them, blocking any contact. Khalid studies Hamza with evident contempt and casts a provocative glance back at Muhammad. The tension mounts.

Talib finally speaks. "Go back to the city, Khalid. Enough blood has been shamefully shed."

Khalid crowds Hamza's space and gives him a push on his chest.

"His words might be sharp," Khalid tilts his head toward Muhammad, "but we both know the sword will always be sharper." He meets Hamza's stare. "You've forgotten who you are." He reaches out and feels Hamza's bicep. "You've become soft like a woman." Khalid glances derisively at Muhammad.

Almost too quick to see, Hamza strikes a punch to Khalid's face.

Khalid staggers backwards, hand to his face. He observes the blood, smiles broadly. Then he looks triumphantly over at Muhammad.

The two top fighters of Mecca draw their swords.

Everyone quickly falls back from where Khalid and Hamza circle each other, looking for an opening. Their first attempts only fan a breeze until suddenly Khalid strikes closer, forcing Hamza to block the blow in a fierce flurry of clanging swords. Khalid taunts the older man. A veteran warrior, Hamza watches his opponent's breathing. All strike on the outbreath, maximizing the force, while the inbreath offers a moment of vulnerability. Evenly matched, the two fighters are soon winded.

Hamza strikes a mighty blow that Khalid blocks, only to have his sword break. Hamza kicks him in the chest, knocking him to the ground, then jams his foot onto Khalid's chest, pinning him down. An angry Hamza raises his sword to deliver the death blow.

Muhammad's strong hand forcefully grasps Hamza's raised sword arm, preventing him from striking. "Enough!"

Hamza's eyes meet Muhammad's, his arm relaxes, and he reluctantly takes his foot off Khalid's chest.

Khalid scrambles to get up, locks eyes with Hamza, and smiles broadly. Having made his point about Hamza's true nature, he mounts up and rides off as quickly as he rode in.

A furious and humiliated Hamza faces Muhammad. "We must fight them."

"First fight your pride and your anger," Muhammad replies. "You may have mastered the sword, but not the self."

Hamza walks away.

Bakr gets Muhammad's attention. "It's not safe for us to remain in Mecca. It will only get worse. They will not hesitate to kill you."

Muhammad nods to Bakr as he looks out at the carnage. If it were not for him, this scene would not have taken place; these people would still be alive. And yet his hours of prayer encourage him to stay the course.

Bakr leaves to negotiate to buy Bilaal from his owner so he might then free him.

Muhammad walks over to join Talib, whose face reveals deep concern and the realization that things can only get worse. Muhammad gently puts his arm around the elder, leads him toward a horse, and helps Talib mount.

ELEVEN

THE BAN

The repressive efforts of the Notables have some impact, particularly with news of the carnage in the quarry. There will always be defections when the stakes are life and death. However, for some, this only strengthens their bond as a persecuted minority with right on their side.

Meccan society depends on all its participants working harmoniously to survive. Their common principles, values, traditions, and unity are what allows survival in the deadly and merciless desert. It protects them from outside enemies who are tempted to invade to harvest the fruits of Meccan hard work and accomplishments. Every individual is a significant brick in this structure, every tribe a pillar of the foundation. Meccan success depends on each individual in the society, whether traders, poets, warriors, or slaves. Now their differences have become irreconcilable. Attempts to control the Hashim, ranging from humiliation to torture and death, have failed. As the division grows ever deeper, the capital of Arabian culture and power faces the greatest internal threat since its founding.

Jahl calls a emergency night meeting in the Kaaba. Some forty Quraysh Notables crowd into part of the Kaaba around various idols, a reminder of the basis of Mecca's economy. All eyes are on Jahl as a scribe hands him a parchment.

"So, we have decided a total interdiction will be placed on the clan of the Hashim," Jahl begins.

Muttalieb, forewarned of this, immediately interjects, "This has never been done to ban a whole clan. You're declaring war on the Hashemites. You'll start a war!"

"It already has started!" Lahab shouts.

"What is Mecca without the Banu Hashim, the sons of Hashim?" asks Muttalieb. "Without Talib, Abbas, and Hamza? The greatest men Meccan mothers ever bore! Have you forgotten? You are going too far!"

"Do you have a better suggestion that could silence your bewitched cousin?" Jahl waits for a reply. "See, you don't!"

"What makes you sure that forcing an entire tribe into poverty and starvation will solve your problem?" Muttalieb challenges.

"The council's firm position is, and has been, no individual or clan is above the law," says Lahab. "Rebellion against the established law and against the gods will lead us all to starve, thus we have no other option."

"The sons of Hashim have to choose between Muhammad and Mecca," Jahl says.

"None of us doubt the blessings our gods give us," Muttalieb says, "nor the order our laws bring us, but we object to and completely reject your unlawful collective punishment, as it will only bring chaos, not order."

Jahl pays no attention and continues to read, despite the hubbub of reaction to Muttalieb. "No one will marry a woman of Hashim or give his daughter in marriage to a man of Hashim. And no one is to sell anything to them or buy anything from them. Not even basic food. They are barred from the caravans, banned from the markets, excluded from all business deals and partnerships."

All those present rapidly calculate how this might affect them. How can they profit? What about their extended family members who are intermarried with some Hashim? Some see the complexities in enforcing such a ban. Opinions are being formed, pro and con.

It is a collective punishment unprecedented in Mecca. It might force Talib to hand over Muhammad. It could squeeze the Hashim so hard they'll oust Talib and choose a more pliant leader to do as the power elite want. But for a boycott to be effective, it has to be widely observed. The Hashim following Muhammad are still only a minority. Jahl and Sufyan represent the two largest clans, but not all of Mecca. And the motivations of the two leaders are different. For Jahl, it's the lust for power, while Sufyan is sincere in his conviction that Muhammad is destroying his beloved city of Mecca, a just reason for radical measures as a matter of survival.

The leaders come up to the table to stamp their seal on the document. The first one in line is Lahab.

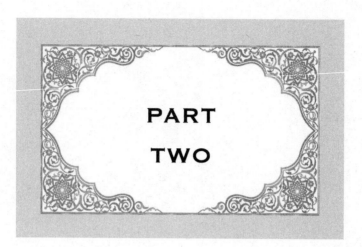

PART
TWO

TWELVE

LIVING UNDER THE BAN

The next morning, with some ceremony, Jahl nails the proclamation, inscribed on sheepskin vellum, to the Kaaba door. A crowd quickly forms and Jahl relishes the opportunity to read it out loud, given that few in the stunned crowd can read. The news spreads to every corner of Mecca, for every individual will be affected one way or another.

Talib's first reaction to the boycott is one of fury. He has led the Meccan council with wisdom through the moving sands of the desert for generations. Many conflicts were solved under his leadership, and many wars were declared as well. Now the Notables, driven by a younger generation, have met without him, violating the long-standing rules. Their dangerous decision means breaking bonds with the Hashemites and stripping them of all their privileges, their economic advantages, and the security and prosperity they enjoy as respected members of Meccan society.

Talib knows lives depend on his response. He faces two ugly options, one worse than the other: reject his own nephew, who will be promptly murdered, or set off a bloodbath in

---

the holy city of peace. His long life has taught him that once revenge cycles begin, they seldom end. Confronted by hate, he has to find a solution that honors his love for his nephew and his love for Mecca.

A determined Talib strides past a group of gossiping, sword-carrying warriors and mounts the steps to Nadwa House, where Notables are meeting with warriors from the non-Hashemite clans to discuss how to deal with the mounting unrest. It is the first time in his life he has attended such a meeting uninvited. As his sister-in-law, Arwa, exits the building, Talib avoids her. Surprised, she indicates to Malik to stop the old man, but Malik hesitates to challenge the authority of this veteran leader of the city and reacts too late to stop him. A scowling Arwa continues downstairs as more warriors gather outside.

All look up to see who has entered, but when they see Talib, all turn their faces away, ignoring the elder. The room falls into dead silence.

Talib walks between the rows of people, many of whom he knew as children, who now do their best to humiliate him.

"So you have made an oath not to talk to this aging man," Talib says. "But what about your oath to keep the sacred place holy? Which oath is greater?"

Silence.

"Answer me by the name of the sacred shrine!"

There is some shifting about, but still no answer.

"By refusing dialogue, you are dragging everyone into the alternative: the darkness of revenge and retaliation. How long do you think this can last before more Meccan blood is shed?"

Talib comes to the end of the first row, approaching his usual council seat as head of the Hashim. Seated there is his brother Lahab, the only other Hashemite present, who looks to the floor to hide his shame.

Talib can only shake his head with sadness and disappointment. "What is your heart made of? Stone? Do you think when you allow Muhammad's blood to be shed, the Hashemites will crown you? And this council will truly respect you? Take the seat, but remember you are nothing without the Hashemites."

Talib leaves his brother to stand in front of Sufyan, who looks straight ahead, avoiding eye contact. "Your father and I ruled the desert from this house! He wasn't quick to anger when poets misjudged him, turning his victories into defeats. True leaders are not afraid of poets. You punish poets by not paying them. You don't behead them for their eloquence. This is the unwritten law of your father! But your father was a giant, and today you prove to be a midget. Muhammad is not the first mystic of our city, and we never before punished mystics or poets. This is what made us the strongest. By killing Muhammad, you would remove the cornerstone of this structure, turning friends into foes, brothers against each other, cousins into enemies."

Talib scans those present, all of whom are avoiding eye contact. "I, the Son of Hashim, Son of Mecca, reject this council's verdict. Let the gods be my witness . . . and let this day be remembered. One Hashemite's blood equals all Hashemites' blood. One Meccan's blood equals all Meccans' blood. Our city has always maintained its status above the sword, ruled by the power of wisdom, logic, and tolerance, not the hatred and vengeance which has so blinded you. That is what has made us superior. Broken is the arm that points a sword against its sons. This is the vow to the forefathers, to Manat and Hubal, to keep Mecca sacred and holy."

No one speaks. They don't know how to respond to his truth.

As the silence and the shame lengthen, Talib moves toward the door with some parting words. "You all have forgotten our common vow. I will not give up my son's head as an offering to satisfy your lust for power, and I will not let you lead Mecca toward destruction. I wish I had died before witnessing such a shameful day."

Talib walks out the door of the dark meeting room. In the bright sunlight, he charges down the steps of Nadwa House and into the crowd of warriors and guards gathered outside. Some, out of respect, avoid making eye contact with the elder. Others whisper; a few laugh. Disheartened, he moves through the gauntlet as the tribesmen open a passage for him.

When Talib reaches an open area, stones suddenly rain down on him, some striking his back. He turns, shocked to see children chasing him with rocks. He picks up the pace but soon stumbles and falls. A few warriors, not liking what they see, scare off the children and help the old man up.

Talib hurries down the street as the citizens he encounters spit on the ground and turn their backs to him.

Once the old man is gone, the children circle back and find Lahab's wife, Arwa, who discreetly gives them the coins and dates she promised them for their actions.

Muhammad is hosting a gathering of his own numerous companions to discuss the ban when there is a knock on the door. He opens it to find a bloodied Talib standing on the doorstep, completely out of breath. The injured man looks like he might fall over.

"O Al-lah!" Muhammad reaches out and supports him as Khadija and others rush to help.

Hamza is furious. "What son of a doomed witch dared do this?"

Helping hands ease Talib into a chair as he winces with the pain, unable to speak for the moment.

Hamza, not getting an answer, heads to the door to track the perpetrator down.

"Hamza," Talib manages weakly. "Hamza. Wait."

Muhammad leads Hamza back to sit down and listen.

"Please, everyone . . . they were just—" Talib gasps.

A vigorous knock interrupts him. Hamza leaps up and opens the door to Omar, who stands there with two other companions. "Is Talib alright? The word on the street was he was nearly killed!" Omar is immediately relieved to see a live, though injured, Talib. "What happened?"

"I was leaving Nadwa House when some children chased me with stones and I fell," Talib explains. "Really, just a minor incident—don't turn it into a fight. The tribesmen waiting outside were not involved, and some even helped me up. They were just children."

"Children? Someone had to encourage them!" Khadija exclaims.

"O daughter!" Talib replies. "The majority is rejecting us, and we have to live with their rejection."

"It is not only rejection," Bakr adds. "They are out for blood!"

"The ban is a declaration of war," says Talib. "This is not the Mecca I know. My nephew is stubborn, his disciples are provocative, our cousins are highly charged. Any incident could spark a war, annihilating our tribe and destroying Mecca."

Those present hear him, but it's not just the other side leading Mecca to war. Strong emotions grip all those in the room.

Talib cries out in despair. "I don't know what to do!" He finally breaks down in gasps. Tears stream down his cheeks.

No one present has ever seen their strong leader like this. They feel helpless. Khadija joins Talib in his despairing cry. The chief of the Hashemites is broken, her husband is sentenced to death, the city is dangerous and divided.

Muhammad kneels at his uncle's feet and, with a bowed, contrite head, reaches out and clasps his uncle's hands. He speaks in a strong voice, "Uncle, I am responsible for all this. I brought you shame and dishonor."

There is no sound in the room other than crying and anxious breathing.

"Give them my head, which is what they want!"

Talib pulls himself together. "No. Nephew, you are not to blame; you did not commit a crime. This is mankind's cruelty. What is seen by some as shameful can be seen by others as noble. A man can be honored by one group at sunrise, just to be dishonored by the same group at sunset. It is mankind's denial, seeing the real as unreal and the false as true. After all, what did this old man do to be dishonored?"

That rhetorical question produces a noisy reaction in the room as all are locked into every word the elder speaks from his battered soul.

"The vast majority of our brethren pretend to be something they are not, siding with the agreeable in order to conform to the current demands of their leaders. Imposture, living in deceit to get something for themselves. You, on the other hand, have sacrificed everything in your quest for truth, not a quest for wealth or power.

"It is not the first dark time our tribe has endured. I will not hand you over to them, even if I perish. We are together in this, in life or death, united."

A collective breath of relief fills the room.

❧

The next day, Lahab, always the opportunist, gathers a hundred Hashemites who have something to lose—property, a relationship, a relative—and who feel most affected by the ban.

Lahab addresses his carefully selected audience. "As you know, Mecca is determined to end Muhammad and his fellowship. If you choose him, you choose to be against a united Mecca. Is it not unjust to make all us Hashemites pay for Muhammad's crimes?"

Abbas speaks up. "These words should have been directed to the council you were sitting on earlier today."

"The council is aware of the consequences, and they assured me to make exceptions for those who don't agree with Muhammad."

"I don't believe in Muhammad's God," Abbas replies, "but he will always be my nephew."

Another Hashemite interjects, "Well, Muhammad didn't regard any of us, totally blinded by his delusions, not considering the pain and suffering our tribe is going through because of his stubbornness."

Many in the room agree with this point.

"We are the Hashemites," Lahab says. "We have set the foundations of Mecca, no one can deny that. Renounce Muhammad and his God and your interest will be protected, but your status will not change. I promise you that."

As the weeks and months pass, a new reality is established in Mecca, the city that once prided itself as the City of Peace. The Hashemites are a shunned minority, and the social and economic impact of the ban is devastating. Greetings in the street are replaced either with insults or the turned backs of old friends and relatives. No more weddings. No more funerals of old friends. No more dinners with the neighbors.

Mecca is a class-divided society, with privileged upper and abused lower classes living in different parts of town, but Hashemites are spread out all over the city. There is no separate Hashemite ghetto, nor do the lords consider rounding them up and moving them into one. Rather, the relentless drumbeat of propaganda emanating from the council builds up a growing hatred toward the newly declared "minority" of rebels out to destroy Mecca. They are public enemies. Efforts to grow small gardens are vandalized; those carrying water from the Zamzam spring are stopped and the water spilled out onto the ground.

Even the Hashemites who renounced Muhammad under the assurance their lives could go on as before find themselves threatened under this collective punishment. Some of them, when they meet alone with a fellow Hashemite who stuck with Muhammad, apologize with understandable excuses. In their hearts, they believe in Muhammad. Muhammad encourages those who are vulnerable and defenseless to migrate to Abyssinia, led by one of his daughters, so they can practice their faith and avoid the hardships of the ban.

With each cycle of the moon, the Hashemite situation for those who remain in Mecca grows increasingly dire. Traders they have traditionally dealt with for their foodstuffs, like Taif, almost universally refuse to buy from or sell to the banned Hashemites. They don't want to violate the ban and affect their more lucrative Meccan trade.

Inevitably, a black market emerges, with food being sold at inflated prices to the Hashemites and buyers taking advantage of their desperation to buy property, animals, and valuables at prices way below market value. Talib harbors some hope that the absurdity and the cruelty of the ban in Mecca will eventually end it—or at least soften it.

Lahab's effort to take the leadership from Talib has failed. Instead of defecting to Lahab, many Hashemites endure the unjust punishment and become even more united, their love for Muhammad—who they have begun to refer to as the Prophet—growing even stronger.

THIRTEEN

ASSASSINATION?

Muhammad fasts to extreme extents, going without food for ten days at time, then breaking his fast with a meal only to repeat the cycle again. Yet as he walks about town, he still appears his vibrant, energetic self.

Both he and Talib spend their wealth exploring distant sources of food untroubled by the ban. When the Meccans tighten their border control, confiscating any goods destined for the Hashemites, the two men come up with a plan. Talib owns a piece of land not far from Mecca called the Shi'ab, which has a spring where goods can be delivered. From there, they can be effectively smuggled into the city.

There is one city-state in Arabia willing to openly defy the ban: Yathrib, the oasis town of water and dates. Ever since Muhammad, during his trading days, helped the warring Awes and Khazraj make peace and unite, he has enjoyed their respect and gratitude.

The united tribes visit the holy city during pilgrimages to spend time with their mentor, and when they learn of Muhammad's and his followers' hardship, they make the long journey to lend their support. An impressive seventy sword-carrying warriors on white female camels, followed by a hundred-camel caravan carrying the famous dates of Yathrib, grains, dried fruits, clothing, and tools, makes it through the northern gate. They head toward the stables, the usual destination for caravans to replenish their water and supplies before moving on or doing business in Mecca.

Sufyan is quickly informed of their unexpected arrival. He sends Kahlid to gather a force of guards and warriors, then leads them to confront the Yathrib tribes at the stables.

Outnumbered, the Yathrib warriors are forced to dismount.

The Yathrib leader Sa'ad shouts, "Our intention is peaceful, our swords are sheathed. What is this all about?"

"Sa'ad, don't play the fool!" Sufyan responds. "We know why you're here! Do you really think you can humiliate us in our own city and not be questioned?"

"Your ban against the Hashemites doesn't apply to us, and we are not here to challenge your authority. We are here to extend a hand to an honored friend."

"You are not going to see your 'honored friend.' You are going to turn around and leave Mecca and never come back."

"And if we don't?"

Khalid intervenes. "We will make you."

Hands grasp swords.

Sufyan hesitates to give the order. Yathrib is an indispensable way station for water and food for Mecca's northern caravans, particularly those heading to prosperous routes like Damascus. He has already made an enemy of this new rising power of Yathrib; he cannot risk war with them, but neither can he afford to have the ban so flagrantly violated.

Sa'ad is reluctant as well. He expected the Meccan lords to object—not to go to war over this ban. He's outnumbered and in the middle of the now enemy camp.

"Understood," he says at last. He indicates to his men to turn around and exit the city.

✿

Bin Mas'ud always seems to find himself on the scene for some of the most dramatic events. He is the only Hashemite to witness the exchange. Always enterprising, he hijacks a camel and rides out of the northern gate.

He catches up to Sa'ad, who recognizes him. Bin Mas'ud directs them to the Shi'ab to unload the cargo, which can be smuggled into Mecca to help the starving survive.

✿

While the aid trickling in does allay the hunger for a time, the Hashemites reach a dire point during the first year of the ban. An entire family will eat one meal per day, then be reduced to one meal every other day. The situation becomes so bad that Hashemite children wait outside luxurious events like weddings for uneaten food to be thrown in the garbage, competing with dogs for the scraps. Slaves are ordered to chase the children away in favor of the dogs.

Though the Meccan lords take pleasure in their cruelty, the Hashemites will not bend. Not only do the Hashemites stay united under Talib's leadership, but more adopt the Prophet's practice, making the lords even angrier.

In one of the Notables' ever more frequent meetings, Sufyan takes his familiar position as first among equals. "The ban didn't silence Muhammad; it only ruined our reputation among the Arabs. The last pilgrimage was a massive funeral, not a celebration. And Muhammad got only sympathy and attention."

That produces a flurry of loud cross talk as Lahab commands the floor. "We need to reinforce the ban, cut off any hand that violates it."

"How many hands and heads do we need to cut off in this case?" Sufyan asks.

"We can't cancel the ban now, if that's what you're suggesting," says Jahl. "We will look weak and defeated, and no one will respect us ever again. Muhammad and Talib will have won."

"Yes, the ban must stay in place, no matter the cost," Sufyan agrees.

"No matter what we do, things will never go back to normal with the Hashemites," Jahl says. "Our relationship will never be restored. They are weak now, and they can't fight all of us united."

All eyes turn to Jahl.

"Are you proposing war against the Hashemites?" Sufyan asks.

"No," Jahl answers. "Only Muhammad."

"You can't kill Muhammad without provoking a fight with all the Hashemites, especially now, when they have nothing to lose!" Lahab exclaims.

"Listen!" Jahl commands. "Let me finish. We gather the top fighters from various Meccan and non-Meccan tribes. Each one with a spear surrounds Muhammad asleep in his home, and each strikes a fatal blow. His blood would spread among many Arabian tribes."

Sufyan takes a long moment before reacting. "You surprise me sometimes, Jahl—very clever. The Hashemites will not be able to fight all of us united in the blood debt."

"This is it!" Lahab insists. "Cut the head off the snake!"

"Why didn't we think of this from the beginning?" Sufyan wonders.

"I've been saying kill him from the beginning!" Jahl responds.

"It perhaps would not have worked two years ago. Now, circumstances are in our favor and against theirs," Sufyan says.

"Wait a moment," Lahab says. "If we're committed to killing him, we must make the most of it. Kill him in public. Capture him in his bed, tie him up, and bring him to the foot of Hubal in front of the Kaaba, and there the assassins will do the gods' work."

Everyone can imagine that. Hundreds of witnesses. No doubts he's alive. Brilliant.

"What if he has bodyguards?" Amr asks.

"Kill them all!" Lahab answers.

The Meccan leaders unanimously adopt the plan, the final solution to the Muhammad problem.

Once they receive approval from key allies, they need only to select the assassins and decide when—and how to keep the plan secret. The very fact of how clever it is makes it more difficult not to "confidentially" share it. The decision is made to kill the Prophet during the coming new moon, the darkest night of the month.

As the fateful day arrives, the assassins gather. They are given final instructions by Jahl and Sufyan. Their order is to get Muhammad out of his bed, tie him up, drag him outside his house, take him to the Kaaba, and execute him at the feet of Hubal. In the darkest hour before dawn, as the holy city dwells in deep sleep, a dozen black-clad warriors approach the back wall of Muhammad's house. They have strict instructions to only deal with Muhammad, to not harm any of his family. They scale the wall and drop down into the court. Following the precise directions they have been given to the Prophet's bed, they silently proceed toward their victim.

The assassins make it successfully into Muhammad's room; no women or children are in their way. They hover over his bed and prepare the rope, spears at the ready if he resists.

Then they yank the cover off.

Staring up at them is not Muhammad, but Talib!

Talib knew that if Muhammad were to be killed, it would mean the end of the Hashemites. So, he has decided to confront death himself.

But the assassins have their orders, and they choose to leave rather than seize or harm the respected elder.

Alone once again, Talib closes his eyes. When a close friend of Hamza's from the desert tribe of Saqr, a strong ally of Mecca, revealed this plot, Talib had to finally accept his hope that his cousins would show some compassion as time went by were naïve. Starvation, death, and disease will not satisfy their hatred for Muhammad. They will only grow more aggressive. Muhammad is correct in his rebellion against such a corrupt and selfish generation of leadership.

It is no longer safe to stay in Mecca, and the leader of the Hashemites has decided they must leave.

FOURTEEN

EXILE IN THE WILDERNESS

As sunlight begins to fill the shadows in Mecca's streets the next morning, Muhammad and Talib lead the refugee families with their loaded camels. The exiles take what they can: basic household utensils, blankets, clothing, tents, tools, and their sheep and goats. Hamza takes down his swords, bows, arrows, and armor, then loads them onto his two horses.

The procession, now amounting to more than two hundred souls, passes through the northern gate into barren scrubland under the watchful eye of Malik and a squad of guards. Malik's sharp eye notes who's leaving and thus who's not.

After some hours of trekking, the walls of the city growing ever smaller in the distance, the exiles arrive at Talib's Shi'ab. The barren piece of land features small hillocks with caves, scrub bushes, and an abandoned well. The priority in this inhospitable land is basic survival. The disheartened travelers spread out under the encouraging supervision of Talib and

Muhammad. Those with tents set them up. The caves offer good shelter, and Muhammad and his family set up in one.

In the first weeks of the journey, the number one priority is food, the shortage of which has been made severe by the ban on any trade with Mecca. Hamza and other hunters bring back what wild animals they can. They quickly develop relations with outside merchants, especially with the agricultural exporting town of Taif, which of course asks for higher prices, but they arrive with laden camels expecting to be properly paid.

The animals the exiles brought also must be fed, and they are slaughtered little by little out of necessity. This eventually includes animals that are traditionally used for breeding to produce income. Even a crying Bin Mas'ud has to kill his beloved sheep with his own hand.

With leadership, ingenuity, and faith, these former city dwellers make it through their first year in the wilderness. Their number has grown from two hundred to more than four hundred, with new arrivals joining them from Mecca, where the ban has made their lives unsustainable. The increase in population has only doubled the extreme difficulty facing the refugees.

While the settlement still has the look of a camp, more solid structures have been built with branches, stones, bricks of clay, and dung that are housing the exiles. Some have used the particular rock formations to shape a shelter, if not a home. Smoke rises from a number of fires as the women cook. Children run about playing as the men work on building and improving units and digging around the one small well.

At night they gather around a fire and listen to Muhammad, who through his faith and their faith has kept the group and everything connected to it together. However, as they go deep into the second year, the situation looks more and more unsustainable. They face real starvation, and even water has to be rationed from the overdrawn well and firewood must be gathered from ever farther away. Sa'ad has managed to bring some aid from Yathrib, but the journey is long and what can be brought by camel is small in relation to the increasing need.

On a small hillock, Muhammad, Bakr, and Hamza stand, surveying the scene below: a dire picture of an isolated, starving community. Men, women, and children sit listlessly on the ground. The only sound that carries on the breeze to them through this eerie silence is the sound of coughing. A woman carrying water collapses. Her family goes to her, but she appears lifeless.

"I have no money left," confesses Bakr.

Muhammad and Talib acknowledge that they, too, have run out of any buying power. The reality is that there is no way to produce any sort of income on this barren land.

"I've been able to sell some of what I have at home, but they've confiscated the rest," Bakr says.

"Maybe there's finally sentiment building against the boycott," Talib suggests.

"No, they don't care," Hamza says. "Out of sight, out of mind."

Talib breaks into a fit of violent coughing. Muhammad and Hamza support him, helping him into his cave.

Muhammad returns to his own cave to find Khadija lying on their bed, covered with a blanket and surrounded by anxious family. Muhammad kneels next to her. Her face glistens

with sweat. She weakly coughs. Muhammad feels her temple.
Fever. Not good. He looks around at his family. Only yesterday,
she was fine. Ali holds out a bowl of water and a cloth, which
Muhammad takes and lovingly wipes her feverish brow. Khadija makes an effort to smile, then winces with pain. Muhammad smiles and grasps her hand that is searching for his.

⬡

The next morning, Muhammad, Ali, and Zayd dig in the dry,
hard, rocky soil. They are on a slight rise amidst a field of
Companion graves. Stones delineate the size of the deceased,
many of the stone ovals the size of children and babies.

That afternoon, the white, shrouded body of Khadija is
lowered into a fresh grave. Muhammad, his daughters, Ali,
and Zayd stand closest to the grave. Just behind are Talib,
Hamza, Omar, and Bakr, and behind them gathers the whole
population of the camp, in tears and crying out lamentations.
Behind them, visible in the distant haze, are the far walls of
forbidden Mecca. Khadija will never see again the city to
which she contributed so much.

"Be comforted, for God has prepared an abode for her
in Paradise." Muhammad attempts a reassuring smile as he
places his arms around his daughters.

As dirt is thrown over the shrouded deceased, a worried
Bakr confides in Hamza, "Khadija can never be replaced. For
twenty-five years, she was everything for him. She supported
and calmed him in the hard times, like now. I worry for him—
and us—as half of him is now gone."

It suddenly grows dark. The assemblage looks up to see a
dark dust storm bearing down on them, blocking the sun. A
fierce wind with a high-pitched howl presages the coming of

sand and dust as all break for cover. The great storm finishes the job of filling in the grave and covers the entire camp with sand and dust.

※

That night, Talib finds Muhammad deep in prayer, but Muhammad, aware of his presence, follows him outside. They sit across from each other, a small fire between them.

Sword-carrying guards are visible nearby in the flickering firelight.

Talib coughs, then tries to stifle it.

"Uncle, you should go to sleep," Muhammad says.

"I'm fine," Talib insists. "It's just the smoke."

The two men stare at each other for a long moment. They both know Talib is not well.

"This has lasted so much longer than I thought," Talib says. "And we have been forgotten."

"What are you saying?"

"We must find another place."

"I agree. What about Yathrib? Sa'ad has always offered us a refuge."

"Yathrib is too far, son," Talbib says. "I want to stay near home. Not to mention, Yathrib has its own conflicts. Sa'ad is a generous and honorable man, but on his last visit, he said the unity was threatened and the Jewish tribes were fomenting conflict between them. We can't afford getting caught up in their war."

"Where do we go, then?" Muhammad asks.

"Taif. They have kept us fed. They are not that far. Their leader, Suhail, owes a starving friend a warm welcome and a meal."

"What makes you think they would risk a profitable trading arrangement to honor your friendship?"

"Mecca depends on Taif, not the other way around," says Talib. "If they take us in, Mecca will have to accept it."

"They provided some food as long as we paid them, and now we have no money. Suhail has no friends when it comes to profit."

"Nephew, we are dying here. Tell Suhail that Talib is counting his last days, and ask him in the name of our long friendship. Go as my emissary."

Muhammad nods, looking down at the few dim fires of his beleaguered people. The situation could not be direr, and major action must be taken.

FIFTEEN

TAIF, THE LAST CHANCE?

M uhammad decides to make the five-day journey to the prosperous fortress city of Taif on foot. The fact that they have no animals to transport them, neither camel nor even donkey, is a testament to their desperate poverty. To make this desert journey on foot is running considerable risk for even the young and fit, but for a depleted, middle-aged man like Muhammad, the odds are very much against him even arriving in the city. His companions tell him it would be foolhardy to go alone, especially in his weakened state, so Muhammad asks his son Zayd to join him.

While it's still dark in the cool, early morning before dawn, Muhammad rises, grabs his shepherd's staff, his leather waterskin, and a handful of dates, and rouses Zayd from his slumber for their last-chance mission. The stars and a half-moon provide enough light as they set out toward the Hijaz Mountains where Taif, the second greatest city after Mecca, majestically sits. Muhammad's long experience has taught him the many lessons for survival in the cauldron of the Arabian Desert, where temperatures average 120 degrees Fahrenheit during the day before cooling off at night. The life-threatening risks from heat-related conditions are mainly from dehydration, when the body loses more fluid than it takes in, and heatstroke.

If on foot, one must travel as lightly as possible; carrying heavy amounts of water is a disadvantage. Back in the day, Muhammad would travel two weeks in one stretch to the next water source, where often the well would be depleted or its water undrinkable. For many years, regardless of water availability, he practiced taking in just enough water to stay alive. Whether in deprivation or abundance, his discipline is to never abuse God's gift, for greed turns man into easy prey in the mouth of death. Often, he would restrain from water intake for two to three days, then break his fast with a few sips to last two or three more sunsets. This practice would carry Muhammad throughout long stretches to the next water source.

This could be one of the most extreme physical and spiritual practices Muhammad has adopted in search of his own truth and the universal truth—living on the edge and pushing the limits to conquer the self and to conquer the harsh environment into which he was born. To deprive the body of water, the very basic source of life, requires superhuman willpower and discipline. Only strong travelers with self-mastery can manipulate the physical laws at this level. It is never about physical strength. It is about the traveler's ability to rise above biology, his ability to regulate his breathing to stay calm in the extreme heat, to manage his fear, to manage his limited water source, as well as his food intake. Strong warriors like Omar and Hamza might not make it to Taif in their weakened state. But Muhammad is much stronger in that other dimension beyond the physical. Self-discipline is a fundamental pillar of Muhammad's practice. He does not see the desert as his enemy but as his greatest teacher.

Traveling some at night and resting in the middle of the day, the duo makes it through the first two days. Muhammad, who has so often led camel trains over this road, knows of some springs along the way. Most are zealously guarded by the local tribes, and "stealing" water can be a capital offense. With only a few drops left in their waterskins, Muhammad begins to feel the symptoms of dehydration—dizziness, headache, and, most ominously, he's stopped sweating. They approach where the Prophet remembers a spring to be, but the only evidence that a water source once existed are few stone markers.

Muhammad sinks down. This can't be. After all this, such an ignominious end?

A shadow covers them. Muhammad looks to the sky, where pregnant, dark clouds gather, blotting out the punishing sun. A sudden howling gust of wind bowls them over. Thunder booms, lightning slashes across the sky. This awesome display of nature climaxes with a curtain of rain coming at them. Muhammad and Zayd stand with open arms and open mouths, celebrating this gift from the heavens with joyous laughter. Quickly soaked, they fill their waterskins. These summer storms are brief and rejuvenating, the air filled with a sweet, earthy aroma. The Prophet and Zayd pray their thanks. Refreshed, they take to the road headed for Taif, planning to travel as far as possible in the cooler air.

⁂

An ancient city with three thousand years of human culture, Taif was founded on an ideal hilltop location, which affords both a moderate climate compared to the searing desert below and an advantage over invaders. The city is famous for its circular basaltic stone wall, which further protects it. Blessed with food, water, and security, the tribe of Bani Thaqif, Sons of Thaqif, have accumulated wealth and power, albeit with a slave-based workforce, and fostered a rich culture.

Muhammad has traveled many times to the fortress as a trader, but this visit is different. They have nothing to offer. Yet this is Arabia. At any moment in the precarious desert, a traveler can find himself cut off from water and food, and so for ages those who seek refuge are honored for at least three days, regardless of age or status—that is, as long as their swords are sheathed and no blood debt exists between them. And how could one of the wealthiest communities in Arabia deny them a life-restoring meal and a sip of water? Whether the lords of Taif will welcome the surviving members of his shunned tribe who otherwise face certain death is another matter.

As they make the steep climb up the great mountain, Muhammad and Zayd revel in their surroundings, nature's verdant bounty of lakes, green pastures, trees and flowers, and magnificent rock formations a paradise sharply contrasting with the drab hell they've been living in. The Prophet drops to his knees at a spring, plunging his hands into the cool water and drinking deeply before washing himself, a long-deprived luxury, especially for a man so committed to cleanliness. Refreshed, he prays his thanks to Al-lah.

An old shepherd woman approaches the Prophet and, noticing his emaciated body, correctly deduces that he has come on a long desert trek out of the depths of Arabia and is starving. She quickly milks a sheep and brings a pot of fresh milk to the two men.

"Peace to you, Mother," Muhammad greets the old woman.

"Peace to you, son. How long have you been traveling?"

"Five days, Mother, five days."

She studies him, musing that five days is too little time to transform a human body like that. She's still holding the pot, on her face an expression of concern for the skeletal figure before her. "Forgive me, please—please drink."

It's been ages since they've seen fresh milk. Muhammad gratefully takes the pot and hands it to Zayd.

"Father, you drink first," Zayd says.

The Prophet insists that his adopted son drink first. They laugh—another thing they've not done in much too long—at the absurdity of arguing over who goes first. Then they share the delicious milk.

The woman goes back and milks another sheep, bringing more refreshment as the two drink their fill. Muhammad studies the sheep with an expert eye and chats with her about his time as a shepherd when he was a small boy. He tells her how he loved his sheep for providing wool for their clothes and milk for their sustenance.

Basking in the unfamiliar sensation of being satiated for the moment, the two travelers lie down under the shade of a tree to rest.

Once they have been refreshed, they continue over the rocky switchbacks, past the terraced plots of an agricultural cornucopia that during the year produces wheat and barley, along with fruits including limes, apricots, oranges, olives, figs, peaches, pomegranates, watermelons, quince, grapes, almonds, and dates. Some fruit trees offer their bounty, but slaves are out planting, and the pair resist the temptation to snatch a fruit. A heavily laden daily caravan passes them on the steep, winding road heading down to Mecca. No army can climb up the narrow paths to Taif without being annihilated before even catching sight of the wall.

Muhammad approaches the northern of the three gates, which leads to the famous Okaz Market. Ten years earlier, he entered the city on the back of a camel, a lord of Mecca leading a caravan of as many as two hundred camels loaded with fine goods and rare products. Then, everyone noticed him and welcomed him and his exotic cargo, the classic comparative advantage trade, agricultural products to infertile Mecca and fine goods to agrarian Taif, making both city-states prosperous. And now? If anyone notices this figure, they see only a beggar, a hungry nobody looking for food.

The visitors move cautiously through the loud, bustling market with its sellers and buyers, money changers, guards, slaves, and masters. Stalls offer a wide variety of foodstuffs, clothing, pottery, live animals. Muhammad can only think of the market in his beloved Mecca, so full of life, a crossroads of their known world. It reminds him of his prestigious past. He recognizes some of the merchants he befriended in the past, but no one recognizes him as he and Zayd move through the smoke-filled market. The aroma of cooked meat from the grills teases their hunger pangs as well as emphasizes their sense of powerlessness, as they have no means to purchase the most basic of items.

They emerge from the market and head south toward the heart of the city along with dozens of traders who rush to pay respects to the shrine of Al-Lat, the stone goddess of Taif that towers over the city. The Prophet leads Zayd toward a large mansion where in the past he had been received as an honored guest by the city's leadership, which consists of three brothers. This is one of the wealthiest, most powerful households in Arabia. The Meccans approach a group of boys playing a game with different-colored stones. The biggest boy angrily tries to grab a stone from a smaller boy. A look from Muhammad makes him stop. Zayd and Muhammad walk up to the mansion's massive carved wooden door. The lead guard stationed at the door holds up his hands to block the visitors, though neither of the two carry swords, evidencing their peaceful intentions.

"I'm here for Suhail, Son of Amr," Muhammad tells the guard.

"Who is asking?"

"Muhammad Son of Abdullah."

"Where are you from?"

"Mecca."

The guard hesitates. "Before I bother him, I must ask if Suhail knows you."

"Yes, he does." Suhail was one of Muhammad's longtime clients, to whom he delivered jewelry, silk, and other luxury items.

The guard disappears for a time, then reappears. "Come with me."

Behind the main gate of the mansion they follow the guard along stone-paved pathways through a magnificent fruit tree garden. Some slaves draw from a well to water the trees; others trim the rarely seen roses, which the mountain climate allows them to grow. Female slaves carry white linen sheets toward the mansion's entrance. The guard leads Muhammad into an ornate drawing room brightened by colorful Persian carpets. A statue of a scowling Al-Lat stands prominently in a corner of the room.

Muhammad and Zayd wait for some time, as several slaves come in and out, never leaving the Meccans alone. Finally, Suhail, dressed in white silk, enters. He regards the two bedraggled, starving figures with some irritation at the interruption to his day. It's only when he looks into Muhammad's eyes that he recognizes him.

"Muhammad?"

"Suhail."

Suhail, taken aback, can only ask, "What brings you here?"

Muhammad gets straight to the point. "I am here on behalf of a dying Talib."

Suhail registers the words, his reaction more suspicion than compassion.

"Mecca is determined unjustly to annihilate our tribe. I just buried my wife. Talib is dying. Many have perished. This evil has to come to an end. We are in desperate need of food and refuge."

The Taifian leader takes a moment to absorb all this information. He knows of the ban and knows the respected Talib's protection of this recluse has cost him everything. His worst nature comes to the fore. "Food and refuge? You make me laugh! Has the once noble Hashemite, too arrogant to bow to our gods, come today to beg for food and shelter? God truly changes the fortunes of those who slander him!"

Muhammad does not respond.

"In the past you offered us fine products and we paid you in gold and silver, but now what are you offering us to give you refuge?" After asking this rhetorical question, he continues, "You are just a beggar now. Talib is dying. The Hashemites are not a ruling party anymore! So why would I, Suhail Bin Amr, risk losing my profitable alliance with Sufyan and the lords of Mecca to help you?"

"Our people are dying of disease and hunger. This is against long-standing Arab traditions, against virtue."

"Your people are dying because of your arrogance and stubbornness. This is punishment of the gods for not submitting to them." A perverse idea comes to Suhail. "I will give you grain and refuge on one condition."

Muhammad waits, not speaking.

"If you bow to Al-Lat."

"Since when does a noble Arab ask his starving guest to bow before he helps him? I will not bow to a stone—not in Taif, not in Mecca, and certainly not for food."

Muhammad's response only makes Suhail angrier. "Why don't you ask your all-knowing, all-present god to feed you? I don't see him with you, or does he only exist in that crazed head of yours? Go back empty-handed to your dying uncle. Tell him, 'The Banu Thaqif refuse to help us because I refused to bow.'"

"Or that you cared for a stone more than you cared for a longtime friend who is now dying?"

"You are truly a disgrace to your people. Men like you should suffer alone."

"Thank you for receiving us. Peace."

A livid Suhail steps toward the Prophet, getting in his face, shouting, "A beggar who insults our goddess in our house should be stoned by whomever wishes to throw a stone at him!"

A guard, hearing the shouting, rushes in.

"Take this beggar to Al-Lat, make him bow. If he will not accept our lady . . . stone him!" Suhail commands.

The guard grabs the weakened Muhammad by the back of his neck and frog-marches him through the garden into the busy street with a frightened Zayd, carrying his father's staff, following behind.

Other guards join in the spectacle, and a curious crowd forms, with children, passersby, merchants, and pilgrims caught up in this humiliating sight.

The guards reach the foot of the shrine and force a resisting Muhammad to kneel, then push his forehead to the ground.

Finally, the lead guard lifts Muhammad to his feet and speaks to the crowd. "This son of a jackal has insulted Al-Lat—you have seen it! Who will have the honor of casting the first stone?"

Zayd is the first to react, pulling his father away toward the nearest gate out to safety. The crowd has not yet been riled up enough to become a mob. But the boy who Muhammad earlier stopped from bullying throws a stone, which strikes Zayd in the back. The other boys grab rocks and begin throwing, triggering the bloodlust of many in the crowd who add to the volley of stones.

Muhammad tries to protect his son, taking many of the hits as they hurry to put distance between themselves and the mob. When the Prophet takes a direct hit to his temple, he cries out in pain. This only produces triumphant shouts from the stone throwers. Near blinded by the blood from the wounds on his face, Muhammad trips but is held up by Zayd. A fall would prove fatal. Moving as fast as they can, they move out of range, most of the rain of stones now falling short. The boys chase after them, hurling stones on the run. The only direction open is toward the wall, but there they would be trapped.

Zayd guides Muhammad to the lowest part of the wall. Stones continue to hit them, propelled by curses. Zayd helps Muhammad up onto the wall. There is a path and a ledge some twenty feet below, and the stone wall offers handholds. Muhammad grasps the top of the wall, his feet searching for a toehold. His grasp slips and he slides downward, searching for a hold, but lands hard below. Rolling with his fall, he finds himself under the outcropping of a large rock. The stones still rain down, but the outcropping protects him. He's half-conscious, bleeding from the temple and from his other wounds, his clothing torn.

The boys peer over the wall. They don't see the wounded Prophet, but they spot Zayd and launch a fusillade of rocks in his direction.

Huddling against the sheltering rock, Muhammad looks up into the heavens. His expressive face shows a deep sadness as tears well up in his eyes. Why has Al-lah forsaken him? Has he not been his faithful servant? He turns his head and sees at eye level a tiny, yellow desert flower that has managed to blossom out of a small fissure in the monolithic rock. His gloom transforms to a faint smile. Lightning flashes across the cloudless blue sky. A deafening clap of thunder seems to shake the mountainside.

The thunder spooks the boys. They throw a few last stones before retreating back to continue playing their game.

Zayd is injured, but less seriously. He rushes to Muhammad to check his wounds. Realizing it's better to put some distance between them and their persecutors, the young man helps his dazed father up and supports him down the steep path, past the lake and the fruit trees. They limp over to the spring, which only a few hours before had provided such a hopeful rest stop.

The old shepherd woman is still there making sure her flock has enough water. Shocked to see the two bloodied men stagger down to the spring, she rushes toward them. Together with Zayd, she lays the dazed Muhammad down to rest under the shade of the tree. Then she fills a bowl with water, takes a cloth, and sets about cleaning the Prophet's wounds. Zayd drinks his fill and, thinking ahead, borrows a sheepskin bag from their shepherd friend and heads back up the mountain to fill it with fruit and dates for their return trip home. On his way back down the mountain, he feels dizzy and realizes he's had a shock and will need some days to recover. He knows what lies ahead, and what could be a better situation than recovering and gathering strength right here with this caring nurse, who has provided them with water and healthy food? There is no reason to rush; they are not being pursued.

Copious draughts of water and fresh, delicious fruit eventually clear Muhammad's dizziness. With night approaching, the two men easily fall asleep. The shepherd has very thoroughly cleaned the Prophet's multiple wounds, and the good news is that no bones appear to be broken. The bad news is that the Prophet is in considerable pain all over his body. Zayd is well aware they only made it to Taif through luck—notably, one rare and unexpected rainstorm. Now, with their hopes dashed, wounded and exhausted, they will need a monumental amount of luck and faith if they ever hope to see their family and companions again.

Muhammad and Zayd sensibly rest and recover for five days, eating and drinking their fill. Finally, they thank their generous and caring benefactor and set off on the return journey. Shi'ab, in their still weakened and wounded condition, might as well be as far away as Jerusalem.

In the middle of the second day, Muhammad has great difficulty continuing on. Zayd often helps him, and Muhammad is very aware that without his son, no amount of willpower could keep his wounded and depleted body making its way through the extreme desert conditions. Through the wavering heat in the far distance, they see what looks to be a single figure astride a camel, slowly approaching from the direction of Taif. When they realize it is not a mirage or a hallucination, Muhammad and Zayd get to their feet. The rider is a tall

Bedouin, his face covered against the dust and heat. He looks down on the derelict pair.

Muhammad is the first to speak. "Peace, brother."

"And to you." The rider uncovers his face. "You come from Taif?"

"Yes. We had business there."

"Obviously it did not go well." The stranger smiles, observing Muhammad's wounds, which have now dried to a dark brown.

Muhammad manages a dry chuckle. Better to pass through death's door with a laugh.

"Where are you headed?" the stranger asks.

"Close to Mecca," Zayd answers.

"Come up here." He motions to Muhammad. "I will take you part of the way. You, young man, can walk." He gestures at Zayd.

Zayd helps his father up and they set off at a good clip, much faster than their slow walk.

By the third day, the Good Samaritan, grateful for company and stimulating conversation, becomes a follower of the Prophet and vows to help. No other man he has ever met spoke in his ear such magnificent poetry. Not only that, but they exchange jokes, which lightens the monotony of the trek. Little does this Good Samaritan know that his simple act and his desire for company on the journey will save a movement.

SIXTEEN

ANOTHER GRAVE

B ack at the Shi'ab, the close Companions sit outside Talib's cave around a few dying embers. The old man has
been in bed since Muhammad's departure, drinking water but
refusing to eat. The elder's coughing has stopped, his skin is
glowing like an infant's, and his face is peaceful as he dwells
in deep sleep. He uses the few words he can get out to ask
about Muhammad.

"We must get word to his brother Abbas," Bakr says.

"Make sure no one, and I mean no one, in Mecca knows
about this," adds Hamza.

That next evening, Abbas arrives with two family members. They kneel around Talib's bed as he gasps for breath. Ali
kneels next to him. Hamza, Omar, Othman, Bakr, and others
keep vigil at a distance. Talib has propped himself up with
considerable energy, happy to see his brother. The brothers
exchange smiles and clasp hands until Talib, who has gone
through so much in his long life, sinks back down and lets go
of their hands.

Talib looks at Ali. "Muhammad . . . Ali, my son."

With that, Ali breaks down and the tears begin to flow as Fatima comforts him.

The death rattle takes hold of the chief of the Hashemites.

The survivors all look at each other, seeking to absorb what was expected but never accepted.

The sudden void is a heavy blow to those close to Talib, especially Ali, his son.

The group meets the next morning to decide what to do. Talib's body, wrapped in a white shroud, still waits in the cave for burial.

"Let's wait for Muhammad's return," suggests Omar. "He should be here any moment."

"We don't know when he's coming back." Hamza's tone carries the unspoken words "if at all."

"If Talib's death is known in Mecca, they will declare open season on Muhammad," Abbas reasons. "For now, we should bury Talib, keep his passing a secret, and pray that Muhammad returns soon with good news."

Ali has a different idea. "We must wait."

"Son, we can't," says Bakr. "Not in this heat." As though to emphasize his point, he wipes the sweat from his brow.

"We've waited all day, son," Othman adds.

Hamza chimes in with his opinion. "Honoring him is burying him now."

All the camp residents are present as the last stones are laid around Talib's grave, which is situated next to Khadija's.

The mood is one of despair, and no Muhammad is with them to speak words of comfort or hope.

The camp calculated that the journey to Taif would take twelve days. Seventeen days have passed when a boy on the hill above the caves of the Shi'ab spots two distant figures approaching. This must be them—their prayers have been answered! The boy cries out that they've come back. The residents, in the grips of lethargy and despair from malnutrition and the recent deaths of the Prophet's wife, Khadija, and his protector, Talib, stir with this spark of hope. They struggle to rise to greet the returning travelers. As Zayd and Muhammad walk the last few meters into the camp, they are surrounded by the Companions, whose spirits plummet when they see the state of the wounded, wraithlike Prophet. Omar and Hamza quickly move to support Muhammad, a woman lays out a blanket, and they place him gently on the ground.

Still barely conscious, Muhammad sees the deep sorrow in the faces of those around him. When he realizes that Talib has not come to greet him, he looks toward the cave. The mourning cries of women are unmistakable. Muhammad does his best to scan the faces of those around him, looking for confirmation. No one is capable of uttering a word, just as he is incapable of asking the question. He finally casts a pleading look toward his best friend.

Bakr gives a negative nod, and like someone pulled Muhammad's heart out of its place, he shrinks, his life force fading, bringing him to his knees. Facing heavenward with tearful eyes, he prays with a crying voice: "O Al-lah! I seek refuge in the Light of your Face, by which all darkness is dispelled and the affair of this world is set right, lest your anger descends upon me. I surrender until you are pleased. There is no power and no might except by you."

Muhammad bows his forehead to the ground and weeps as every soul in the camp follows his lead.

This year has been the most challenging of the Prophet's journey, taking him from wealth, prosperity, status, and success into poverty, starvation, isolation, exile, homelessness, cruelty, rejection, stoning, the passing of his wife, and now the death of his uncle. Blow after blow has rained down—how much can a human handle?

No mountain can carry his burden of sorrow and grief.

Muhammad falls back, passing out, alarming those near him.

When he returns to the edge of consciousness, he is safely in the cave. He recognizes his children, only to fade out of consciousness again. Fatima listens closely; he is breathing, and all are hopeful that he is simply getting some much-needed restorative sleep. The daughters attempt to attend to Zayd, who tries to push them away as he insists that Muhammad is the important patient. Hamza, Omar, and Bakr meet outside the cave, leaving their beloved friend to the ministrations of his daughters. All they can really do is to regard each other, not wanting to put into words their shared fears that this extraordinary man is on the last lap of his life journey.

Muhammad is not one more obscure hanif with a handful of local followers whose death would hardly be noted. He was well known on the caravan routes and by pilgrims to Mecca who met and heard him and never forgot the encounter. Stories about him and his opposition to slavery and female infanticide circulate in Arabia, making him a controversial but known figure. The power of his wisdom and truthfulness has attracted the leaders of far communities, his firm stand against Mecca's brutality has gained the respect of the far Arabian tribes that have less Meccan influence, and support has grown for him among Mecca's enemies.

Fatima puts her hand on her father's temple, withdrawing it as she realizes he is burning with fever. Muhammad has slipped into a coma, a fatal sign in his severely weakened state. Whatever the high level of consciousness achieved, it depends on the vessel to house it—which, ideally, is a reasonably healthy body. His companions surround him in silence, sharing his pain, feeling his struggle, but helpless to bring him back.

As the hours, then days, pass, the Prophet's survival looks increasingly less likely. The entire camp can only pray. They have overcome so many obstacles—surviving hunger, burying family—but now it is different. Everything they have fought for is contained within the dying body of their beloved leader; if he dies, then they have lost everything and Mecca has won. What a lost cause! What a cruel defeat! Sad instruments of mourning sound from different parts of the camp, signifying the Hashemites expressing their sorrow, pleading to the heavens to restore and rescue their master. Losing him is something no one is ready to accept nor understand.

SEVENTEEN

DESPAIR

Muhammad's closest companions are becoming physically weaker and are mentally challenged to come up with a solution to this impossible situation. Sitting around a small fire outside the cave for some warmth in the cold desert night, they share their feelings, violating their unexpressed rule to remain positive. Reality is reality.

"Is this how I will die, the death of a starving camel in the open desert?" Hamza wonders aloud. "I was born to die with a sword in my hand."

"Brother, drop this talk," Omar chastises him. "No one is dying, and we will overcome this. Muhammad will not die; he will not leave us without guidance."

Bakr, shedding tears of deep sorrow, cries out into the night. "My best friend and my lord, please stay!"

Ali looks at his father lying unconscious on his back. He can't help but think that this situation looks identical to the situation with Talib. If they are all going to die, he wishes to die now so he doesn't have to witness the Prophet's death.

After their morning prayers one day, Omar and Hamza step outside the cave to witness the cruel sight of two young boys struggling to drag their mother's dead body away from their tent to honor her in death by putting her under the ground. The boys collapse, lacking the strength not only to move her, but to dig a final resting place for the woman who gave them birth. Hamza and Omar, with whatever waning strength they can muster, join them to help, gathering shovels and dragging the corpse near a bush to lay her to rest. The dry soil is rock-hard.

"The spirit is strong, but the body weak," says Hamza. "We'll have to dig just enough to cover her."

The once mighty Omar, the strongest man in Mecca, saves his breath to work on digging. Taking turns, the two, both dehydrated and exhausted, manage to dig a shallow grave, lay the woman in it, and cover her body. At least she will be spared the vultures and the jackals.

The Shi'ab has truly become the Valley of Death. Is this not the end of a community when it is incapable of burying its dead? As Hamza and Omar climb back up the hill to guard the Prophet's cave, they agree they must make one final effort to honor the Prophet and all those who died here.

Calling all the camp together that night, despite weakness and illness, they commit to an all-night prayer vigil to lift up their master, calling on heaven to intervene. After all, Muhammad is the one who taught them the power of prayer, that God is eternal and never dies, that truth shall prevail.

They pray and weep to the heavens to purge the evil out of the Prophet's body. At the same time, all surrender to their fate, accepting their end. Many gave up positions and status to follow their master, but they have bonded in unity and compassion, a human bond beyond the material. Even in the face of death, they remain united and compassionate toward one another. If they live, they live together. If they die, they die together. Not a single person defects or leaves; they are one people under one banner.

At the first light of dawn, the Prophet opens his eyes, breaking the spell of the feverish coma, and regains consciousness. Looking around him, he sees his daughters sleeping next to him. Ali, Bakr, and Othman are also resting nearby, while Omar and Hamza are passed out in a seated position at the cave's entrance. They have all just returned from the vigil and have fallen into a deep sleep. Muhammad, unaware of the lost days, surveys his wounds, now healed, though that triggers memories of Taif. He gets up, careful not to wake the sleepers as he steps past Hamza and Omar into the first light of dawn.

It's a new moon, the beginning of another lunar cycle, the darkest night of the month, when the stars are the brightest and most visible, so close it seems he can reach them. Muhammad feels no sense of hunger or thirst, as though he has been well nourished. He walks through the camp. There is no movement, no one is up readying for the morning prayer; even the guards are asleep. Can it be everyone has given up, surrendering to death? He must be in the midst of a nightmare; this cannot be real. He's unaware that all have prayed through the night for their Prophet and now have collapsed in what might be a final sleep for some.

Muhammad goes back up to the cave. He gently shakes Hamza by the shoulder and with his deep voice calls to him,

"Hamza! Hamza! Time for the dawn prayer!" Hamza opens his eyes briefly but goes back to his dream.

But Omar wakes, sees the Prophet, and leaps up, spreading his arms wide. He shouts to the heavens, "The Prophet has risen! Thank you, God!" His voice comes from such depths, it echoes off the hillsides of the narrow valley. This jolts Hamza to open his eyes and see the Prophet standing tall, looking totally empowered. The lion in Hamza awakens.

Soon, those who faithfully watched over Muhammad emerge from the cave. The camp begins to stir and the residents look up toward the caves, where there stands the Prophet, the first rays of the sun lighting him up in his white gown like an apparition. The first reaction to this resurrection is that it must be an illusion. But as he is joined by others and embraces his daughters, the people realize it is indeed the flesh and blood Muhammad. Though the flesh is much wasted away and the blood needs replenishing, he is still their Prophet. The word *miracle* passes from one person to the next, and indeed, considering what the Prophet has been through, it is beyond human explanation.

Muhammad descends to his followers and assumes his position to lead the dawn prayer as they all gather, many of whom were dying, in this life-affirming ritual. Some are in tears, some still cannot believe it's their Muhammad, radiating the strength he has always possessed. It defies their known experience. A joyful Bakr voices his concern that they don't have the requisite water to purify themselves before prayer.

The Prophet smiles. "Purify intentionally without water, and we will all pray together."

As Muhammad looks out over those assembled, who regard him with a mix of disbelief and amazement, he realizes how much they love him. It was not only hunger, thirst, and disease that brought them to the point of surrender; it was their fear of living without him. With a smile, he addresses them.

"Oh, people of little faith—what if Muhammad were to have died or been killed? Would you just give up? I am here. I am with you. Whether with or without this flesh, we are together. We will always be! Death cannot separate us. Come, let us give all our being to the dawn prayer, which begins a new day."

Toward the close of the prayer, a few light drops of rain begin to fall, and those praying can't help looking up into the gray skies. As the prayer ends, the sky that has been waiting politely now opens up with all its glory of pure, heaven-sent rain. Some open their arms to welcome the downpour; others rush to tents or caves to set out every available pot to catch the precious rain. The hard soil of the valley soaks up the water and the dry spring regains life. Another miracle.

Muhammad goes to Khadija's grave, where he is joined by Bakr. With sadness, Bakr points to the fresh grave next to Khadija's, and the Prophet drops to his knees to mourn his mentor, Talib.

EIGHTEEN

THE HIJAZ—THE GREAT MIGRATION

For Muhammad, this is a time for deep thought and prayer. Their current situation is untenable, and he must find a way out if they and what they stand for are to survive. He realizes that the experience in Taif where he went unarmed in good faith is a turning point, and he is lucky to be alive.

The Companions sit together after evening prayer. No one speaks, all deep in thought pondering their post-Talib situation.

Finally, Bakr breaks the silence, stating the obvious. "We can't keep Talib's death a secret forever."

Hamza looks at Muhammad. "Right, and once they know there's no protection for you, there's nothing to stop them from an all-out attack."

"Pilgrimage is only two weeks away," Muhammad responds. "Do you think Sufyan will agree to attack, violating the sacred months?"

"They know we will not hand you over." Bakr shakes his head. "An attack that will lead to a massacre just outside Mecca during pilgrimage is unlikely."

"In any case," says Hamza, "we will up the number of guards, especially at night in case they use assassins again with one target in mind."

"We have to leave here as soon as possible, find a place of refuge," Bakr adds.

Othman is next to speak. "I say Jerusalem or Abyssinia."

"Jerusalem is too far," Muhammad counters, "and we still have work to do here in Arabia. Our friends in Yathrib have offered us a refuge; let Yathrib be our home for a while."

"Mecca will never allow us to establish a base in Yathrib," Bakr argues. "And it's impossible to migrate to Yathrib without being noticed."

Muhammad shakes his head. "Not if we migrate gradually, in small groups and during the pilgrimage, blending in with pilgrims traveling back north."

❁

Back in Mecca, Talib's death does not stay secret for long. Mourning of such a leader cannot stay contained within walls and behind closed doors. As the people prepare for the annual pilgrimage and its promised income for Mecca's coffers, a rumor spreads in the remaining Hashemite community. Arwa the witch, Lahab's wife who is obsessed with Muhammad, notes some Hashemite women crying and ferrets out the reason for their tears. She welcomes the long-awaited news with jubilation. Two men she has long wanted dead—one is now decaying in his grave, and the other is a dead man walking.

Lahab calls for a meeting in the Kaaba, his domain. Inflated with righteousness and pride, he can hardly contain himself. Arwa wants to be the one to break the news to the Notables, but her husband wants to take the credit with a nod to his gods. This was the person who delegitimized him among men, and Talib has paid the price for his wrong decision to encourage and protect Muhammad.

Lahab draws out the suspense, sitting on his throne as the invited Notables settle in waiting.

"What is it?" Jahl demands impatiently.

Lahab pauses for a long moment, then announces the news. "Talib is dead."

Boom! It's as though lightning has struck the temple.

The response in the room is mixed—for some, a tinge of momentary guilt; for Lahab, relief; for Jahl, revenge at last. Yet no matter how each of them feels, they all agree on one thing—they want Muhammad's head on a spear.

"What say you?" Lahab asks Jahl.

"I am very thirsty, and nothing will satisfy my thirst like Muhammad's blood," Jahl responds.

"Just in case you forgot, we are in the sacred months," Lahab reminds him. "And pilgrimage is around the corner."

"We can't wait this long!"

"Damn!" curses Sufyan. "Even our own gods play in his favor."

"No god, or sacred month, can save him this time," reasons Jahl. "Every law has an exception."

"Do you expect his companions to just hand him over?" Lahab questions.

"They won't, which could result in a very bloody event," Sufyan admits. "If it were Muhammad alone, that would be one thing. But annihilating a well-known Meccan tribe during the pilgrimage season would undermine the whole system Mecca has created, and it would be a victory for the traitor."

"I don't care what Arabia would think!" Jahl cries.

"Calm down," says Sufyan. "Rage blinds you. Have patience. Time is on our side. We will bring him back and publicly execute him."

A slave tending the Kaaba has overheard the conversation and now tells a woman slave of the Notables' intentions. She goes to the stables looking for Abbas, the Prophet's uncle, to report the lords' plan. Abbas makes sure no one sees them.

The situation has grown more difficult, even for powerful figures like Abbas. He is being constantly watched with suspicion. But this is a risk he has to take. He waits for the late hours of the night to travel to the Shi'ab.

Abbas first encounters his brother Hamza and describes the plan to him, ending with the obvious conclusion. "You must take Muhammad and leave as soon as possible. The only thing preventing them from killing him is the upcoming pilgrimage. You have to get out as fast—and as far away— as possible."

"How much time do we have? How sure are you that the pilgrimage is preventing them from attacking us?"

"Sufyan was adamant about not violating the sacred month, and he still has the strongest voice. He promised that with the pilgrims gone, they would bring Muhammad back to Mecca to publicly execute him, and also promised to kill anyone who tries to stop them."

"So we still have time. We can send out small groups."

A few days later, the camp appears in its somnolent state as a large group winds up its prayers. The prayer leader sits up. It's Muhammad, a trace of bruises still on his face. Distant cries sound from a far edge of the camp. Guards who were praying grab their swords, and there is a general movement toward the shouts. From out of the haze of the desert, more movement is observed. Then the guards make out a camel—and more camels. Coming into camp is a heavy-laden caravan of more than a hundred and fifty camels and some seventy armed guards.

Hamza remarks to Bakr, "I told you Al-lah would bring a miracle."

The whole camp greets the newcomers as their salvation, especially when, to their surprise, they exchange the Believer greetings. Dismounting from the lead camel is Mosaab, who abandoned his wealthy family in Mecca, despite his mother's protests, to follow the Prophet. Beside him, Sa'ad, the Khazraj leader, and Wehab, an Awes leader, also dismount. Mosaab and Muhammad embrace.

"Welcome, brothers," Muhammad greets them.

"Oh Muhammad, messenger of God," says Mosaab, "I bring you good news."

The camels, laden with foodstuffs, are being unpacked.

"I see that," replies Muhammad. "Our hunger and gratitude are great."

"Messenger of God," says Mosaab, "I speak of more than the dates of Yathrib, but rather truly good news. You sent me to Yathrib with those thirteen pilgrims, to instruct them in The Way. And with the beauty of your teachings, we are now seventy-five strong."

"Praise be to Al-lah!" Muhammad cries.

Muhammad then embraces Sa'ad, who cannot quell a tear. Sa'ad looks around at all the residents of the Shi'ab, who appear happy, but their miserable circumstances and emaciated bodies are all too evident of the dire situation.

"Lord, as we spoke about before, you are invited to settle in Yathrib," says Sa'ad. "We are here to accompany you on the long trip to the oasis, which can be a home for all."

Muhammad's expression shows gratitude as both look out over the refugees.

"I would urge you that we leave as soon as possible," encourages Sa'ad. "We have supplies and armed guards. The roads are full of pilgrims, and this should be a safe time to travel."

Muhammad nods in agreement to the heaven-sent Sa'ad. "Let us celebrate tonight and on the morrow prepare to leave."

From a nearby hill, Meccan eyes, posing as shepherds, watch every move. Malik hurries to Mecca to report to Sufyan.

Sufyan gathers what Notables he can on his terrace. Below, pilgrims fill the streets and worship their deities at the Kaaba.

"A massive Yathrib caravan just arrived at the Shi'ab," Sufyan warns the group. "He's plotting something."

He has Malik provide details, such as the numbers of camels and armed guards.

"O mighty Hubal," says Jahl, "this is the worst timing. Our hands are tied here for the moment." He looks out at the festive crowds below as though to confirm it.

"What are you still doing here?" a frustrated Sufyan says to Malik. "Go back and stay with your men, and keep your eyes on him the whole time! He's probably escaping right now.

We can't allow this, pilgrimage or no pilgrimage. Where the hell is Khalid?"

When none of the Notables respond, Malik says, "I'll find him."

❁

The next morning, the Meccan observers on the hill see the camp come alive, the people obviously preparing to move out. Malik sends a runner back to report this major development.

Those below gather their few belongings and load the camels. The spies focus on the object of their prey—Muhammad, who is dressed in white. He walks up and down the line of the caravan with Sa'ad, encouraging everyone. Arriving at the head of the line, a white, aged camel awaits the Prophet, who checks the water supply on board.

Sufyan and Jahl dismount from their horses and climb up to Malik's position.

"Dammit!" Jahl curses. "Is that him? He's leaving!"

"Calm down," implores Sufyan.

"Calm down? He's escaping as we watch!"

"Our force is almost ready; he won't make it very far. We'll intercept his caravan and capture him."

"I don't like it—if he takes refuge in Yathrib, we'll be in trouble."

"He'll never make it, trust me." Sufyan does his best to reassure the distraught Jahl.

"What about the warriors from Yathrib and all the Hashemites? This could be a war with Yathrib!" Jahl is still riled up.

Khalid joins the duo. "We're ready."

"How many?" Sufyan questions.

"All five hundred," Khalid responds.

Sufyan turns to address Jahl. "They have at most two hundred men. They will surrender him rather than fight a hopeless battle. They're not fanatics like Muhammad's followers."

Jahl remains skeptical. "And if they don't?"

"We will kill anyone who gets in our way," Khalid says with a shrug.

Sufyan, despite his confident words to Jahl, is worried about a bloodbath. No problem with the Hashemites, but the Yathrib tribes are another matter. Starting a war with them could mean losing Mecca's key caravan rest stop. He's only too aware of Muhammad's charismatic power over the gullible, and they could well resist handing over the Prophet. Sufyan tries to remain confident that they can avoid unnecessary bloodshed and loss of life by assuring them they only want one man. Having convinced himself that Khalid will be successful, Sufyan returns to Mecca to oversee the pilgrimage.

With impressive alacrity and burdened by few possessions, the caravan sets off in the early afternoon. At the head of the column rides Muhammad on the rather old camel, flanked by his daughters and Sa'ad. As all their animals have been sacrificed for survival, some walk or ride the camels brought from Yathrib.

Khalid leads five hundred mounted warriors, who catch up to the slower moving caravan in the late afternoon of the next day. He splits his army into two wings, basically surrounding them to prevent anyone who might attempt to escape out of the noose from fleeing. Khalid gallops at top speed to the head of the caravan, racing past some two hundred sword-carrying fighters, including Hamza, who travels at the head of the Hashemite procession, and the tough fighters from Yathrib. The ground shakes with the movement of so many horses as Khalid successfully intercepts the lead camels, bringing the caravan to a complete halt.

Khalid breathes heavily, as does his black horse. Drawing his sword, he points it at Muhammad on the white camel. "Dismount."

The rider dismounts slowly next to his camel.

"Uncover your face!" Khalid demands.

Ali uncovers his face, revealing a broad smile.

Hamza greets Khalid with a sarcastic laugh. Others can't help but laugh at Khalid's disappointment and embarrassment.

Khalid reacts with rage. "Find Muhammad! He's certainly hiding among the women. Find the coward, and kill anyone who gets in your way!"

Khalid's force lines everyone up and systematically searches every individual in the caravan. He himself walks along the row of faces. No one has attempted to make a run for it.

After this exhaustive search, the only thing Khalid can see is his own failure. From astride his horse, he threatens his longtime rival, Hamza. "We will find him—he is somewhere. When we find him, we will torture him, we will behead him, and finally we will nail his head to the Kaaba!"

Hamza, however, is still smiling with the memory of Khalid discovering that the rider on the white camel was not Muhammad but Ali.

Angrier than ever, Khalid wheels his mount around to ride back toward Mecca before the coming nightfall.

NINETEEN

WHERE IS MUHAMMAD?

In a distant part of the desert, two familiar figures walk briskly south. While the rest of the group is headed north to Yathrib, Bakr and Muhammad are traveling south with the plan of hiding out in a cave on Mount Thaur, close to Mecca. The goal is to stay near as their enemies look far. At this point, the two have no idea if the Ali ruse was a success or if it ended in frustrated bloodshed. Though both men carry swords, traveling alone like this still entails considerable risk, so Zayd is following behind them with a flock of sheep to cover their tracks.

They arrive before nightfall at one of the deep caves Muhammad knows well from when he has gone there to pray and meditate. He tells Zayd to leave the sheep with friendly nearby shepherds and go to Mecca and find out, if he can, what happened to Ali's group—and what the plans are to pursue Bakr and him. "Then come back with food and water," he instructs. "We won't leave the cave."

❈

Word of Khalid's debacle travels through Mecca faster than the fastest horse. Sufyan's distraught wife, Hind, rouses Sufyan from a peaceful nap, and he rushes out to see Jahl rein up outside the Kaaba. Meccans who have heard the news and are expecting an announcement about the death of Muhammad are headed for the Kaaba. Sufyan pushes his way through the gathering crowd to confront a humiliated Jahl.

"You missed him, is that true?" Sufyan asks.

Khalid hangs his head as he admits, "He wasn't there—he deceived us!"

As the crowd rapidly grows, the situation threatens to get out of hand as rumors build on the few scraps of news available. Sufyan looks about and sees no sign of Malik and only a few guards. With hardly any time to call a council meeting, he needs to take action now to quell a possible riot. The words of Suhail of Taif echo in his head: *How is it possible for one crazy man to cause all this trouble?*

"You're telling me, Jahl, that Muhammad is out there somewhere still alive?" Sufyan turns his attention back to the situation at hand.

Jahl shrugs again.

Sufyan mounts the steps of the Kaaba, stretching his arms out wide, attracting the attention of the restive crowd, which quiets down for a moment.

"People of Mecca! Listen! Muhammad heads for Yathrib, where he has made alliances with its tribes against Mecca, against our gods, against our trade, against all the traditions of our forefathers, against everything they sacrificed for us to make our Mecca the greatest, the strongest, the richest city in all of Arabia! He plotted with Mecca's enemies, your enemies, in the dark of the night as we slept. With evil intent, this traitor seeks personal revenge to sabotage our greatness, our glory, to humiliate us among our Arab brethren! He must be stopped before he reaches Yathrib." Sufyan's inspired voice, that of a talented demagogue, carries beyond the last row of people. "He is not far from Mecca. Anyone who brings him back, dead or alive, will be awarded a hundred camels and given a special status, protected by the eternal might of Mecca!"

The mood of the crowd now shifts as patriotism and religion meld with money—an unbeatable combination anytime, anywhere. The Notables, just getting over their shock that Muhammad somehow escaped, are impressed with Sufyan's quick thinking. And, as he didn't consult them, they each decide he's responsible for providing the hundred camels.

Sufyan's inspiration unleashes bounty hunters throughout the desert to track down the Prophet and kill him. Among them are some of the best trackers in Arabia, who are mixed in with amateurs hoping to collect the reward. Many are motivated by the possibility of quick riches, others by fame and status. A few are out for revenge, as they believe the Prophet has bitterly divided their families. Very quickly, every possible route north to Yathrib swarms with mounted armed men. Woe to the innocent traveler mistaken for the fugitive Muhammad.

The wise Muhammad recognizes that sometimes in the midst of a crisis, the best move is to do nothing. And so the Prophet and Bakr settle into the cave, enjoying the silence and taking the time to reminisce. They have known each other since a young age and were part of a generation growing up in a

Mecca when very few dared leave the safety of the city to trade in the dangerous wider world. Of the few caravans that ventured forth, some were never heard from again. Bakr and Muhammad explored the Arabian Desert together, traveled to Damascus countless times, and learned of the wider world—its major powers and their religions. Bakr became a very wealthy merchant and Muhammad, with his wife, Khadija, prospered from the overland trade, making Mecca the major commercial hub in the north-south trade from Yemen to Damascus. However, Mecca became the hub of the slave trade as well, with its slave market a principal source of its wealth. And so Muhammad found himself in a society that honored those who murdered their daughters and admired those who held the most slaves.

The result of this rich life experience, along with taking a principled position against the distorted norms of their society, has led the two best friends here to this cave, their only possessions the shabby clothes on their backs. Now fugitives on the run, they reflect on their situation and how far they've come. They have to laugh—really laugh. There, in the semi-darkness of the cave, they pray five times a day, have profound discussions about what they've learned in their lives, and share stories of their adventures on the road.

Zayd returns on the second evening, bringing sustenance and news of the one hundred camels reward and countless bounty hunters searching the landscape. The young son reports that on his way to the cave, he saw no one who was looking for the fugitives. It appears they are all searching north on the routes to Yathrib. There is nothing to do but stay put.

During the third day, Bakr thinks he hears voices on the trail below. Not sure if his fear of discovery has him imagining this, he taps the shoulder of Muhammad, who is in deep meditation. Yes, there are people outside, Muhammad confirms. Are they travelers simply passing by or bounty hunters who have picked up the fugitives' trail? There are many caves on the mountainside. As they look toward the narrow entrance, they see that part of it is covered by a new spiderweb highlighted by the afternoon sun.

A fearful Bakr whispers to his friend, "Will they find us?"

Muhammad speaks in his normal voice. "Not with the three of us here in this cave."

"But Zayd is . . . Oh, I understand."

"Our third companion is God, the omniscient and merciful."

Bakr smiles and relaxes as the voices fade away.

On the seventh day, Muhammad determines it is time to move on, calculating that the bounty hunters will have given up, assuming either someone found Muhammad or the Prophet is already dead, a victim of the merciless desert. Descending from the cave, they head west toward the Red Sea, waiting for a few days at the home of an old, trusted friend of the Prophet's. They rest and eat well, then leave to travel west and then north up the coast road, heading for Qiba, a small oasis in the desert very close to Yathrib. After making sure the danger is completely gone, they begin their journey once again, one step at a time, with Zayd following behind with the sheep, their small hooves erasing any footprints the men have left.

❁

Not everyone coveting those hundred camels has given up the hunt, however. The man known throughout Arabia as the region's best tracker is the legendary Surakah, who could spot an eagle in the sky and find its nest. Concerned that he was already too late, he'd arrived in Mecca some five days after the announcement. There he gathered more information, then headed for the Shi'ab, where he saw the obvious tracks of a large caravan heading north. He also saw the trail of a flock of sheep heading southeast. Surakah observed traces of human footsteps, which was promising, but they could have been from any traveler, or even from a fellow bounty hunter.

Surakah's fame rests not just on his uncanny ability to read tracks but with his skill at putting himself in the mind of his target. *If I were the hunted, knowing that everyone will try to intercept me on the way north to Yathrib,* he thinks, *I would head south and take the longer, more circuitous route.* Following the trail, he comes upon a group of shepherds and learns that a young outsider had appeared there recently with a flock of sheep. The path leads Surakah to a cave, where he detects traces of two different sets of footprints. Drawing his sword, he climbs up and enters the cave. It is vacant, but in it there are the telltale pits of recently consumed dates. Someone has been here.

Climbing back down, he sees that the trail south is covered with fresh sheep tracks, which have not succeeded in erasing all traces of the now familiar footprints. *I've got them!* he thinks. They have maybe a one- or two-day head start, but as they are on foot and he's on a fast horse, he will catch up soon. He's disciplined and experienced enough, though, to not start counting his camels before he has Muhammad's head in his saddlebag.

On the morning of the second day, he catches sight of two men traveling on foot in a narrow, sandy valley. He muses that this must be them, even though the tracks of the flock of sheep lead off onto another trail. He decides to head down into the valley. Knowing what he learned in Mecca about his two targets, Surakah is counting on his superior skill as a warrior to kill both men and bring Muhammad's head back to Mecca. He will worry later about what to do with the hundred camels.

⁂

The Prophet, a lifetime desert traveler, can detect unusual movement from a long distance away. He has the ability to distinguish the sound of a horse's hoofbeats from a camel's, even from behind a hill, and he knows the number of camels in a single caravan from the sound of its march. Those are skills only desert dwellers and caravan leaders possess. He and Bakr used to identify a person from the sound of their footsteps when they couldn't see them at night or from behind a barrier. The silence of the desert was one of Muhammad's greatest teachers. Now the distant sound of a single horse pierces the silence, and, whoever the rider is, he's treading softly. The Prophet and Bakr head for higher ground, clambering up a rocky cliff overlooking the sandy valley. Both have drawn their swords.

Bakr speaks first. "I'm ready to kill today and be killed, but you must carry on . . ."

Muhammad holds up his hand for his friend to be silent, as they can hear their pursuer below.

From up above, the bounty hunter stops, looking down at the confusion of deep footprints, which leads him to look up. His horse's legs sink into the soft sand, forcing Surakah to regain his balance in the saddle.

"Muhammad, son of Abdullah! I know you are here! Show yourself!" His voice echoes throughout the valley. "This is Surakah Bin Malik, and I am here for your head! Surrender, or come out to fight!"

Muhammad takes a step toward the edge of the cliff right above him. The Prophet can see the man, but the hunter's gaze is fixed at a lower point. Muhammad kicks a stone off the cliff to get the man's attention. Surakah looks up and sees the Prophet smiling down at him.

"What the hell! Today is the day you die! What are you smiling about?" Has Surakah missed something? The man is behaving like he has an army behind him.

A powerful voice resounds from on high, echoing in the narrow valley. "I have surrendered a long time ago, Surakah. Have you?"

Surakah doesn't understand. His horse, sinking deeper into the sand, can't hold its position much longer.

"It's your turn to surrender, Surakah," the Prophet continues. "What are they offering you?"

Now this makes sense. Muhammad must want to bargain. "One hundred camels!" Surakah shouts.

"A hundred camels for what?"

Surakah's horse tries to pull its right leg from out of the sand, nearly throwing Surakah out of the saddle.

"Do you think a dead man's head is worth a hundred camels? By what law, Surakah?"

Surakah wonders if he should climb up there and silence Muhammad for good, but the man has a sword at his side and holds the high ground.

"And on what charge do the Meccan lords want my head? I haven't killed any of their tribesmen," adds the Prophet.

The now-panicked horse struggles to extricate itself from the soft sand. Surakah dismounts to help the animal.

"As men of the desert, Surakah, we know the shifting sands," Muhammad continues. "Lord in the morning, a slave in the evening. Weak today, strong tomorrow. Defeated this year, victorious the next. Do you put your trust in the moving sand, Surakah?"

A trace of panic crosses Surakah's face as he struggles to pull his leg out of the sand. Even Muhammad is surprised to see the desert pulling him down.

The bounty hunter manages to pull his leg out and place it on more solid ground. But Surakah feels all his resolve, all the tracker's excitement of the hunt, draining away. How can he kill this smiling man? This man is not human. No wonder he's been called a prophet.

"Go back to where you come from, brother. They promised you camels? I promise you the bracelets of Kisra!" Muhammad continues to speak.

Surakah is in awe at this man's confidence, faith, and fearlessness. A fugitive with a price over his head, facing a certain death, yet promising the impossible.

"Kisra? The Persian emperor?" The greatest emperor of their time!

"Yes! In this lifetime! They promise you animals, but I promise you eternity! Glory in this life—and the life after."

Surakah is confused and worried. Could Muhammad be a magician? A jinn? He is suddenly overwhelmed by fear, not of the quicksand, but of this mysterious man. He looks back up to the top of the cliff.

No one.

Did he imagine all of this? Was it a dream? The experience was unreal; never has he encountered such a person, nor can he suppress his admiration for such a fearless and honorable man. Now he understands why the Meccan lords want him dead, why his nobility is a threat to their existence. They want him dead for his greatness, not because he is the lowest of criminals who has violated their laws.

Surakah manages to pull his horse free and, mounting back up, guides it north, homeward bound. The challenging questions Muhammad posed in that powerful voice resound in Surakah's mind. He's left with the unexpected desire to one day again be in the presence of this man that some call a prophet.

❋

After two days' march along the route toward the Red Sea, Muhammad and Bakr make it to the friend's farm. The friend warmly welcomes them. He knows of Muhammad's expulsion from Mecca but does not know about the latest events and why Muhammad and Bakr have shown up at his home on their way to refuge in Yathrib. The friend provides them with two camels and some provisions, which Muhammad reluctantly accepts on the promise that he will pay him back.

The pair take to the road again, the journey more comfortable and less tiring astride camels. This time, the glistening Red Sea is on their left as they head north.

One morning, they see what appears to be a small caravan coming from Yathrib and heading south. Probably a Meccan caravan, which could be a danger, though, if it is indeed Meccan, chances are there would be a relative among it. With their faces covered, they meet up with the caravan, which indeed turns out to be led by a cousin of Bakr's, Talhah. Talhah's camels are laden with cloth and merchandise he bought in Syria and plans to sell to the wealthy in Mecca. He stopped in Yathrib and learned the latest news—that the followers fear Muhammad has been captured and killed. He's happy to find Muhammad alive and recounts how eagerly the Prophet's arrival is awaited in the oasis town. Before going their separate ways, Talhah gives each man fine, white Syrian garments, worthy of their awaited entry to Yathrib.

The next day, Muhammad and Bakr head northeast inland, away from the Red Sea. They cross the Valley of Aqiq and begin the climb up the black mountain that surrounds the oasis of Yathrib on one side. Like two bridegrooms dressed in their white djellabas, Muhammad and Bakr ride into the unknown.

TWENTY

YATHRIB WAITS

Yathrib lies more than 1,200 meters above sea level, surrounded on three sides by the arid mountains of the Hijaz Range, which features the majestic Mount Uhud guarding the north. With its abundant subsoil water, the oasis lake, and numerous wadis streaming water into the valley during the winter, it is an ideal place for human settlement, especially in the arid desert of Arabia. The first group to permanently settle there were Jews emigrating after the Roman general Titus brutally put down the Jewish Rebellion in 66 CE. The Jews were more advanced than the nomadic Bedouin tribes, as they had been in contact with the leading civilizations of the time, were literate, and had written scripture and a recorded history. The Awes and Khazraj, now allied with the Prophet, arrived later from Yemen, occupying the northern area of the valley.

In 622 CE, the groups inhabiting the valley were Jews and minority Christians, both considered peoples of The Book; the Awes and Khazraj, coexisting in a tenuous peace brokered by Muhammad; pagans, those known as Sabians; the Believers;

and the Hypocrites. When the Companion refugees arrived, these various tribes were spread out across the valley, sharing the oasis, growing fruits, vegetables, and cereals, though the area was best known for its date palms that covered most of the oasis, making it the most prolific date producer on the peninsula. The different Jewish tribes lived in multistoried fortresses and were the most advanced militarily, generally staying out of the various tribal wars. However, when it was in their interest, they would intervene, generally resulting in victory for the side on which they fought.

Yathrib itself could be considered a natural fortress. With the walls of mountains on three sides, the defenders enjoyed higher ground and only two entry points into the city. One of these was the northern area, a natural back gate to the oasis controlled by the fortress of the Banu Nadeer tribe. The other was in the south, with Mount Uhud blocking entry except for a narrow passage. Yathrib was similar to Taif, blessed with water and fertile land and occupying a strategic hilltop location. Mecca, without these advantages, was forced to build its own city walls and use its intelligence to make itself a trading power and a religious destination, built around the Kaaba with its own myth and its practical function as a storage center for the tribal gods and totems. And it also had to throw a monthlong party every year!

It's in the southern area that the refugees from the Shi'ab and the new enlistees from the Awes and Khazraj await the arrival of the Prophet. His closest companions sit under the shade of a palm tree, discussing what should be done. They know about the bounty, but no other news about Muhammad has come. Everyone is running out of patience. Maybe they will have to think the unthinkable—that Muhammad is no longer alive. What then?

"I wish I'd stayed with him," laments Hamza. "I fear they've captured him."

"No one knows the desert like the Prophet," says Omar.

Sa'ad speaks next. "Their delay depends on how much time they spent at their hideout."

"Letting the bounty hunters chase ghosts," Othman adds.

Sa'ad tries to maintain an upbeat tone. "Our men are sharing their homes with you, and those with two rooms are giving one. We will share with you everything we have. When the Prophet arrives, we will have the greatest celebration Yathrib's ever witnessed. Everyone waits to please their eyes with his presence."

"We are most grateful to you, Sa'ad," Hamza says. "Without you, we'd be dying a slow death back in Shia'b, probably mourning the death of the Prophet. I'm a hunter and a warrior, not used to sitting and doing nothing. Maybe Muhammad is not far away. Maybe he's wounded, with no food or water. I say we go out once more and search. I will not rest until I see my nephew."

That mobilizes the group and, with Hamza in charge, they round up camels and provisions. Given multiple routes to Yathrib from the south, the searchers head off on their different assigned routes.

Ali and Jaafar, who have been given the Red Sea route, spot two camels approaching from the south with their riders dressed in white, catching the morning sunlight. Concerned these might be bounty hunters, Ali and Jaafar ride cautiously toward them. When the two unidentified riders stop, Ali recognizes one of them as the Prophet and, applying the switch to his mount, gallops toward them, hollering with joy.

The Prophet loves no human being more than Ali—his adopted son, the first of the young men to follow him, his nephew, the son of Talib, the person who risked his life to help him escape Mecca, wearing his garment as the target for assassination. Here he is, the first face the Prophet sees as he approaches Yathrib. He couldn't be happier; the evil cloud has been blown away! They've made it! This has to be one of the greatest moments on the long journey from the cave on Mount Nur.

Ali tells Jaafar to gallop ahead and let them know the Prophet has been found and is on his way.

Ali calls out to the Prophet, "Please take the lead—over the mountain they all wait!"

Another group from a hill sees them, then runs to tell others. Soon, dozens of the Prophet's disciples surround him and march together with him toward Yathrib. The crowd keeps growing, coming from every direction to join their leader. Muhammad is the very air they breathe! The sense of triumph is higher than the peak of Mount Uhud, reaching into the skies!

A rider on a jet-black stallion flies like an arrow toward the Prophet. Hamza! As he races up, seeing the face of the Prophet, this man who never cries cannot hide his tears, so great is his relief. Most of the Companions are already in tears, all the pent-up emotions and sorrows of the past bursting forth. An overwhelmed Muhammad cries as well. Now they are united, no force in this world, not men nor jinns, can separate them!

As they approach Yathrib, the entire city stops what they're doing. Men and women, elders and infants, everyone goes out to meet the Prophet and his Companions. A great victory reflecting the power of their master! With women and children beating the tambour drums, the sound echoes off the mountainside. Kings crown themselves, afraid of the populace, while this man is crowned by admiration and respect for his determination and humility. The eagles in the sky glide over him in a celebratory aerial dance. Even those who don't know him and those who are hostile can't help but surrender to the moment. This is not the guest they anticipated, so glorious yet so down to earth.

The Prophet extends his arm to greet people on both sides and those on the rooftops who are beating drums and waving palm fronds, sending love and peace. In Muhammad's humility resides his greatness and power. Sa'ad and the men of Awes and Khazraj rejoice with a large and enthusiastic turnout. They've taken a major risk standing up to the superpower of the time, and for the moment it looks like their alliance with Muhammad has popular support. The power they're witnessing is otherworldly. The Jewish leaders send their warriors in full armor on horseback to honor and put this charismatic outsider on notice that they are a powerful force.

Surrounded by infinite love, a reward he did not expect during the hardships of Mecca, Muhammad can only rejoice in the fact that he has survived and, more importantly, his movement has survived. Even those with an infinite faith in the Prophet can only marvel at this turn of events—the orphan shepherd boy given the reception of kings. It is a moment that will live forever. The Prophet, deeply moved, cannot help remembering those dear to him who cannot share in this triumph—Khadija and Talib, those who died in the Shi'ab, those killed in Mecca for following the Prophet. With all he's learned about the nature of his fellow human beings, Muhammad knows this is no time to rest. This is a celebration of survival, not a victory over his enemies. What looked like a lost cause has now been reenergized in a relatively safe environment. He does not forget that there are still powerful men plotting to kill him.

Muhammad turns down Sa'ad's offer to rest after the long trip, and Sa'ad leads the Prophet and his closest Companions beyond the houses to a large piece of uncultivated land. Sa'ad indicates to the area with a wide-armed gesture. "We offer you and your people this land—as far as your eye can see, it is yours!"

The Prophet drops to his knees and bows his forehead to the fertile soil in a gesture of thanksgiving to the divine. His companions follow with this same gesture of gratitude. Those who walked out of town with the Prophet hang close by, anxious to hear what he says.

Muhammad takes a handful of dry soil. "This is more valuable than silver and gold. But without water and seed, it cannot bear fruit."

"The soil is fertile, but the water is far and our farmers are lazy," Sa'ad attemps to explain.

Muhammad hardly listens, as in his mind he is envisioning this empty land as a flourishing farm. "Our first work is to regenerate this land. God made everything come alive with water, which is the sacred source of life and every human being. We will dig channels, bring the water from springs."

"What about seeds?" Bakr asks.

"We have no stock at the moment," says Sa'ad. "All the seeds we had have been planted for this season."

The Prophet nods in response. "Whoever wishes to buy your dates, let them pay, not with gold and dinars, but with seeds—all kinds. We will multiply vegetable and fruit farms, and we will add thousands of date palm trees."

Everyone gets caught up in his vision, propelled by his enthusiastic energy.

"Companions from Mecca and Yathrib, you ask me how to worship?" the Prophet says. "Work. That is greatest form of worship, the way to honor these gifts before us—sacred work!"

As the days go by, the vision begins to become a reality as the Prophet himself, full of spirit, a leader by example, digs the soil to plant trees, carries rocks to clear land, and lays a foundation for a mosque. He digs the channel, bringing water to the land, directs the building of housing for the new arrivals, oversees it all. His skin glows in the sun, reflecting youth, strength, and vitality. It's like the wheel of time has been reversed, and it's now hard to believe he's in his fifties, working alongside his companions from sunrise to sunset, planting fruits, vegetables, trees, and grain, establishing food security for the growing community. Working together, eating together, and celebrating together, the fully energized disciples see their determined efforts turning this once-infertile land into a paradise. More important than the fruit of the earth is the fruit of common effort, which produces unity, love, and compassion.

Their hosts, the Awes and Khazraj, upon seeing this unfamiliar model of unity and leadership, cannot help but be impressed with these men and women of Mecca who work tirelessly under the heat of the day and speak little. They are strong like their master; they don't overeat, oversleep, or overtalk. It is a contrast to Yathrib's slow pace of daily life—too many are testament to the downside of abundance, becoming obese and disease-ridden. This unfamiliar productive energy is a pole of attraction for tribesmen, and many enthusiastically join the effort.

TWENTY-ONE

SALMAN THE PERSIAN

Muhammad has been working hard in the field since dawn, and now he heads back to the mosque for his midday prayer and rest. His spirits are high as he marvels at how the tiny seeds they planted only a short time ago are now green shoots emerging to seek the sunlight. He looks forward to prayer time, when he will praise the Creator for such miracles.

Taking a different path than usual, he comes across a scene that deeply troubles and saddens him. An emaciated man, tied to a tree, is being brutally flogged, his chest showing fresh stripes of blood and scars. This is a scene all too familiar in Mecca as well—a slave being whipped for disobedience. Muhammad approaches a young woman who looks very distressed, then looks inquiringly at her.

"Most of us slaves greatly admire him," the woman explains. "He's a Persian. Salman."

The flogger drops the whip and picks up a bowl of water, holding it to the tortured man's lips. The man turns his head away.

"At least they're giving him water," Muhammad observes.

"No, no," explains the woman. "He refuses to eat or drink. He says he was born a free man and he is free to die his way."

That impresses Muhammad; he has never before come across anything like this.

"His master is very angry, as he says he paid gold for him and the Persian owes him."

"Who is his master?"

"Salul. Many of his slaves wish Salman would just eat something, as the master is very angry and taking it out on all of us. But I admire his courage—I wish I had it. We were all born free, even if our parents were slaves."

Muhammad nods to her and heads back. Praying alone, his mind dwells not on the miracle of the seed, but the cruelty of human beings to each other. *Why*, he asks God, *have you created that in all of us?* As always, Muhammad asks himself what he can do to remedy an injustice. Back when he was a prosperous merchant, he was able to buy many slaves their freedom. Some, like Bilaal, are with him in Yathrib. But now the Prophet is a refugee with no money. Human slavery is the system across Arabia, if not across the entire world of the seventh century. So, it's either money or a slave owner choosing to free slaves.

Upon returning for the afternoon's labor, Muhammad decides to take the same path. As he comes closer, he smells the pleasing aroma of grilled meat. The source shows an even a more perverse and crueler tactic employed by the frustrated slave owner, Salul. A grill has been set up, where meat is barbecuing. Salman the Persian is being held down on his bleeding back as food is being shoved into his mouth. He resists, spitting it out. The slaves gorge on the meat; they have been instructed that Salman must be able see them.

The scene stays in Muhammad's mind as he works alongside his companions in the afternoon, growing healthy food. It does not leave him at evening prayer, nor when an excited Sa'ad surprises him, carrying a cloth sack.

Sa'ad greets him and hands him the sack. "Peace upon you!"

"Peace to you!" Muhammad takes the sack, which is heavier than it looks. "What is this?"

Sa'ad gestures for him to look inside it. Muhammad does and sees jewelry and gold coins. He looks questioningly at Sa'ad.

"Women of our tribe are donating this sum to build additional space for the growing number of Companions," says a very pleased Sa'ad.

Muhammad doesn't reply.

"You look hesitant," Sa'ad says. "Please—it is honest money that was given joyfully."

"This was most generous of them, and I am not concerned by how it was gotten."

"What is it then?"

"I saw today a slave being tortured. They were attempting to force him to eat, but he said he would rather die of his own free will than die a slave."

"Yes, that's Salman the Persian. Everyone is talking about it. A sad affair."

"The Creator of all is not concerned about building mosques or demolishing temples. It is abusing a free soul that can shake the very foundations of the universe."

Sa'ad looks puzzled.

"Demolishing this house of worship is less of an evil than letting this soul fall into the pit of darkness. Take this sum and give his owner a generous offer which he can't refuse."

"What about the many other slaves? We can't buy and free all of them!"

"We might not be able to free all slaves today, but we are able to free one, thanks to this generous gift," says Muhammad. "Begin with Salman—his time has come, and others will be next."

"What do I do with him if we are able to free him?"

"Feed him, heal his wounds, and, when he is stronger, let him decide as a free man to do as he wishes."

Sa'ad is still unsure. "As you want, but I will urge him to come here, to meet you."

Little do the two realize that this decision, made because Muhammad took a different path, one day would have an historic impact.

TWENTY-TWO

INTERNAL SUPPORT
AND ENEMIES

Yathrib's nature in its majesty has created a paradise ideal for human settlement, but with the diverse populations it is in seeming constant conflict and has proved difficult to rule by one leader or king. Muhammad wants to make Yathrib a united city of peace. He knows the bellicose nature of man, that even in a "paradise" there would be violent tribal conflicts, fights even over what nature has provided—water, fertile soil, groves of trees. A promising start was made when Muhammad reconciled the Awes and the Khazraj in a written agreement. But that peace undercut the power of two of Yathrib's most significant figures, whose power came from being able to throw their resources to one side or the other, working in concert secretly.

One of these men is the slave owner Salul, whose ambition is to become king of the Awes. The Prophet's arrival has derailed his plan. Rather than looking for one of their own, tarnished with the conflict, to be the leader of the unified tribe, they look to Muhammad. Recognizing it would be a mistake to directly confront the respected Muhammad, Sulal professes loyalty to the Prophet and awaits his opportunity. He has a force of three hundred warriors at his command.

The other is the Jewish leader Azora of the Banu Qay-nuqa'a. Secure in his fortress and commanding seven hundred of Yathrib's most feared and competent warriors, he has no problem being direct. A head taller than his peers, he carries himself like a hereditary prince, and his arrogance and ambition know no limits.

There are many, of course, who view Muhammad not as a personal threat, but as someone who can bring peace and prosperity to Yathrib. One is a wealthy Jew, Mu-Khairiq, well known for his generous giving to the poor—especially the orphaned, regardless of their ethnicity—which makes him trustworthy among his own people as well as other tribes. This man of authority and wisdom sees in Muhammad a savior who can end the suffering caused by Yathrib's endless inter-tribal wars. Mu-Khairiq is fascinated by the Prophet's qualities, especially his humility and modesty. The two, despite coming from different backgrounds, become true friends.

On his own initiative, Mu-Khairiq goes to Azora to discuss Muhammad. Azora escorts him to the synagogue inside their fortress, the most suitable place for a conversation between two wise men of the oasis. The fortress was built before Azora was born, and he has to stoop down to enter doorways not built for his height. Once they are settled comfortably inside, Azora looks to Mu-Khairiq to find out the reason for his visit.

"Our faith has much in common with Muhammad's, who preaches the God of Abraham and Moses—devotion, charity, selflessness, moderation, and compassion," Mu-Khairiq begins. "Unlike the pagans, idol worshipers who can't see anything of life beyond pleasure and objects of the senses, he is most sincere and practices what he preaches. A wealthy merchant who gave up his comfort for truth, he is the most rare of examples among our fellow men and one who remains totally trustworthy."

Azora, well aware of the friendship between the two men, knows he must tread carefully, as he cannot offend Mu-Khairiq, one of his tribe's main donors. He takes the approach of friendly debate, applying Jewish logic. "Indeed, these are the qualities of a righteous man, of which there are few walking our earth, but not enough to qualify him as a prophet. Certainly not enough for all our Jewish tribes to follow him!"

"I am not asking you to follow him, simply to honor his faith as he honors our books and our prophets."

"Judging by what he says, Muhammad doesn't know our books, nor our prophets. Mistakenly calling King David a prophet! If Muhammad were a king, or any earthly ruler, we would submit to his authority, but never as the sword of God. It would suit him better if they called him King Muhammad, instead of Prophet. His knowledge is borrowed, apparently given to him by strangers on the road. He is welcome to read our books to educate himself. But then again, he can't read, can he? If we were to follow and submit to every man who believed to have a connection to the Divine, our nation would have disappeared a long time ago!"

"So you are saying, if he is not Jewish, he must be a liar?"

Azora, concerned by his donor's tone, takes a different tack. "What is Jewish? Jesus was Jewish, had a bloodline all the way to David. Did that justify his claim to be the Son of God? Ridiculing our teachers and our traditions. His Jewish blood didn't make him an exception. Even if Muhammad was

Jewish with a bloodline to Abraham, he would not have the authority above the eternal laws of Moses."

"What if Moses rose from the dead?" Mu-Khairiq's tone is friendly. "Would you still argue with him? Arabia has waited so long for someone like Muhammad to appear!"

"I'll argue with God if necessary! Arabia has been waiting, but not for a man who simply proclaims himself a prophet."

"Muhammad did not proclaim himself a prophet; others called him that. He accepted the calling, which allowed him to fight Mecca's evil doings and teach humility, charity, equality, and justice. By our city supporting his effort, we would be united and prosper."

"My problem is not with those who worship idols out of ignorance," Azora responds, "but with those who create the ultimate idol-God in a live person and punish people for not worshipping him."

"He is not punishing people for worshipping idols," Mu-Khairiq counters. "He is preaching against idol worship and those who promote it for their power and gain, as is the case with the Meccan Notables. What about the commandment 'Thou shalt not make unto thee any graven images'? Isn't this what pagans do? Isn't this what Mecca's all about? Muhammad is aligned with the Ten Commandments more than you! You humbly declare that you worship the God of Israel, but it looks like you are rejecting him for reasons other than faith."

"He's poisoned you like he poisoned the Awes and the Khazraj! Muhammad's God is a punisher, avenger, torturer. Those are not the qualities of our God. Our God is playful, a friend, a wrestler. We wrestle with him and he humbly accepts the challenge. He doesn't see us as being below him; rather, he sees himself in us. This is the God we worship as we play, for life is play, not serious warfare, where man's purpose is only to worship, and if he doesn't, he will be punished in eternal fire. The relation between God and man is not a master-and-slave relationship. I think the Meccans in their ignorance are closer to God than Muhammad. His dangerous approach would only bring destruction and suffering to Yathrib!"

"It is hard to understand how you choose to side with pagans against a man who has lost everything to follow the one true Creator! Is this God's play, or is it your play?"

Azora stands up to his full impressive height. "If you love this so-called Prophet that much, then go to him, stick your Jewish forehead in the dirt five times a day like he does! For you both are possessed by the same demons!"

What can the visitor do but get up and leave the hall of worship?

Azora's response is more than a lost opportunity to bring peace to Yathrib. The Jewish leaders roundly rejected Muhammad's teachings as equal to Moses's. More basically, they object that he does not worship and honor the same God as the Jews. This rejection would remain an open wound between the two faiths, assuring the oasis would be divided, resulting in a perilous instability.

A distressed Mu-Khairiq goes immediately to his friend Muhammad to report back on his heated conversation with Azora.

Muhammad, seeing the agitated state of his Jewish friend, invites him to walk together and talk.

Mu-Khairiq tells Muhammad, "It saddens me to tell you what Azora hides in his heart toward you, but you must know. I will follow you! And I will fight those who fight you. If I die, my wealth and property shall go to you to help you accomplish what you have started. I see light and righteousness in you; your word is in alignment with truth."

Muhammad stops walking. So much was said in those few words—a warning, a pledge of loyalty, and a generous offer to help the movement. "This is your choice, my friend. If your rabbis don't want to believe, then this is their choice, too, for I don't force anyone to follow me."

Mu-Khairiq describes the whole conversation in detail as they walk along, oblivious to others. The Prophet, a man of noted calm, is becoming more and more riled up, and with each new Azora calumny, he offers a retort, setting up a kind of walking dialogue.

"Your rabbi preaches the Ten Commandments! What does he say about killing infant females, human slavery, usury? Or is he blind to all that? Is his sacred work just to keep the law safe in a golden trunk? What is the benefit of Scripture if it is kept hidden along with gold and silver from people? So my practice is not from God, but all the laws written by the hands of your teachers are from God? And he says we do not worship the same God, yet we both believe in the one God? How can there be many one Gods? Is his God a God only for Jews? Do only those who can read attain truth? What about those who hear and see? When he says that life is only play, is it? Is this man's only purpose on Earth?"

Muhammad's walking pace has increased, matching his rhetorical passion. He suddenly stops and smiles at his friend as he realizes he's allowed himself to get carried away.

＊

The palm dates of Yathrib not only made great food for the desert dwellers, it also made great wine, aged in huge clay jars and barrels for long periods of time. Entertainment before the Prophet's arrival was based on two things: sex and wine.

The majority of the people were mired in sloth and gluttony, enslaved to their desires. Many of those suddenly wanted to be followers of the path, to join those energetic and strong Companions coming from Mecca who did more and talked less.

It has fallen on Bilaal, with his powerful voice, to continue his role of calling everyone to prayer. For the evening prayer, the disciples purify themselves in the channel water, forming perfect lines behind the Prophet, focusing on letting go of worldly desires, surrendering self to the Merciful Divine. Hundreds of men and women attend worship.

One evening, way in the back of the gathering, two Yathrib drunks loudly argue.

When the Prophet finishes his prayer, he addresses the assembled. "A Companion should be awake in awareness. The wolves hunt the weak sheep, so a Believer should be pure in body and thought. A follower should be in awareness even as they sleep, not submitting to the senses, drowning in desire and chained to lust. My Companions are awake—they can't be drunk. Make a choice—is it the path of awareness or the path of confusion? The two paths do not meet."

The Prophet has never touched—and will never touch—alcohol in his life. Many of his Meccan disciples have followed his lead. He didn't make it a rule; there were barely any rules during the Meccan era. But now with so many accepting The Way, things are different. Many newcomers who join still drink and gamble, even coming to prayer drunk. Many want to follow the Prophet but don't know what it takes to follow the path; they don't understand that it could mean death and loss of oneself and one's possessions.

It will take lots of work from the elders to help discipline the beginners, to create men of high caliber. One out of a hundred succeed; the rest fail. Hence it becomes necessary to make rules to govern the people, to hold them accountable for their offenses. To surrender the old self, to work, to obey, to pray, to fast, to give, to purify body and soul. No sexuality outside of marriage, no partying and clinging to the objects of the senses. One has to spend his day in sacred work—farming, building, teaching. Those who know how to write teach writing. Nights are for silence, contemplation, and devotion. Companions are not to oversleep, overeat, overtalk. When Muhammad formally forbids alcohol, the next morning hundreds of wine barrels pour out of Yathrib households like rivers. No Companion will touch alcohol ever again.

The Prophet's focus is to build a strong generation that can transform divided tribes into a great nation. His solitude up on Mount Nur in the Hira cave, long periods of fasting, giving up sense objects, were his secret methods and weapons for reaching emancipation. True followers of the path cannot be enslaved and obsessed with the material; they can enjoy it with moderation but never attach to its experience, drowning in a sea of infinite repetitions. Having a strong and pure body is essential for spiritual growth.

As time passes, the number of Muhammad's followers grow as more and more seek his wisdom.

One day a man, limping as he moves because he is so overweight, approaches the Prophet, asking what he can do to remedy his constant pain.

"Begin with fasting," Muhammad answers. "One meal a day is enough, so your body can become lean and strong and enjoy the work. Fasting is what you need for now. When you are ready, I will give you a new task."

INTERNAL SUPPORT AND ENEMIES

The man hesitates for a moment as he imagines giving up all those tasty meals, but his pain speaks louder. "I will fast every day until I become as lean as Hamza!"

The comparison brings laughter and a broad smile from the Prophet.

Another day, in the evening after prayer, Salul's eldest son, Abdullah, is last in the queue of those waiting to speak to the Prophet. "My lord and master! I am carrying a heavy burden, and I cannot sleep."

"Is it your father?"

Abdullah is surprised that the Prophet would know this. "Yes, he is not being truthful. In your presence he pretends to be faithful, but with others he's just the opposite."

"I know. He thinks I took Yathrib from him, prevented him from becoming king. But this is a trap he made for himself, and now he can't break free."

"What can I do? He is my father."

"There is nothing you can do; every soul is responsible for its own doings. In the face of judgment's eternal fire, every soul will be concerned only with its own action. No son will carry his father's debt. Abdullah, we didn't come to Yathrib for territory; we're just passing through, the same way we're just passing through life. It is all temporary. If your father understood this, he would stop fighting for a mirage, something impermanent, something that truly doesn't exist."

It is one thing to deal with the obese; more serious are the hypocrites. Abdullah's heartfelt concern for his father, a powerful local figure, highlights a growing category of "followers" the Prophet is well aware of. They care not for truth or self-discovery, only power and status. For them, Muhammad is an adversary. They hate him for losing their power and pretend to be followers of The Way, attending prayers

and giving generously to charity. But behind closed doors they
gossip, spread rumors, sow fear, and incite the locals against
this outsider.

Worse, Salul makes trips to Mecca, where he not only
spreads lies about the Prophet but seeks to provoke the Meccans into attacking Muhammad's Yathrib. The Hypocrites
would eagerly join the Meccans and Salul's warriors.

The Prophet knows that hearts full of hatred are very hard
to change. He chooses to openly address the issue without
pointing out any specific person.

Muhammad stands before a crowd of his close Companions, refugees from Mecca—the obese, the Hypocrites, and
new followers from Yathrib. For a long time, he does not speak.

The expectancy of the crowd grows.

"Gossip," he says at last.

The crowd murmurs in surprise.

"Gossip is a disease. The cure? Silence. Selfless work and
serving others. Gossip, provocation, sedition—are the qualities
of hypocrites, worse than killing. To gossip is similar to eating
a person's corpse after killing them. It is not the quality of the
faithful to judge and point out people's shortcomings. Count
your words—they have power for good or evil. Don't let your
jealousy guide you into darkness. Even if a person offends you,
forgive them. If you don't know how to respond to them, be
direct with them, because talking behind their back will not
heal your wound, it will only deepen it. The more you talk, the
more you gossip, the more you slip. It permeates your being
until finally it suffocates you. Let your refuge be in selfless
work, and be humble.

"With power comes responsibility, but man is ignorant,
running after status and gain. Power should be given to those
who don't seek it. Those who are desperate to mount the

throne are driven by selfish desires. They don't aim to serve; they aim to be served, and by doing so they suffer and make many others suffer. The faithful are enough unto themselves. No matter how small or big the task given to them, they do it as a way of worship, not for profit and gain. To truly follow The Way is to drop all selfish desires. That is the true power.

"For the hypocrite, his tongue says he has surrendered, dropped all selfish desires, yet his actions reveal the opposite. Hypocrisy rots the heart and steals its joy, which is the opposite of truthfulness. If this path isn't your path, then it is better to be truthful instead of moving around like a rabid dog spreading disease, seeding doubt, conspiring and plotting in the dark of the night.

"What has man forgotten? Death. Yes, death. When man is reminded of death, he suddenly retreats and drops all desires, but then very soon he forgets again and goes on collecting objects and expanding territory, which are failing attempts to escape death. The truth is, death is a cup from which everyone will drink.

"Man is measured against two things: death and temptation. The perfect scale. Men are not weighed by their wealth or status, for no one is taking their gold to the grave, and no one takes their status with them after death. Death is the conqueror of men, but those who have conquered death live for eternity. My Companions, who have no attachment to anything—not even their physical bodies—feed on death, which feeds on men."

TWENTY-THREE

A VISITOR COMES
BEARING GIFTS

The Prophet sits with a handful of Companions in the
yard of the nearly finished house of worship in the shade
of palm trees. They're enjoying recently picked figs. Ali and
Jaafar argue about what destination they should direct their
prayers toward. Mecca or Jerusalem?

Jaafar declares, "Jerusalem was the destination of prophets and kings!"

Ali responds, "Mecca was the destination of the father of
prophets, Abraham!"

Who better to resolve their debate than the Prophet himself, who smiles at the young men's passion? They are both
right but missing the point. "Temples or buildings are just
symbols; they represent an experience, principles, a journey
of faith, the stories of those who found truth. Man is lost,
searching for truth, traveling outwardly looking everywhere,
wandering in the vast universe, searching for the source of his

soul. The journey continues until the person stops wandering, gives up searching outside. At that moment, the person finds his center, his temple, the throne of his being, realizing that all his search and long travel has led him back to himself, to his inner sacred temple. Abraham found it, and at that place marking the end of his search, Mecca was built, symbolizing the discovery of his inner truth—of God. This is why so many travel so far to the holy destinations, hoping to find what the prophets found, but if the person hasn't found the core of their being, they can't find Mecca, they can't find Jerusalem; they will find only buildings and crowds of other pilgrims. Therefore, young men, make your pilgrimage to God, travel inwardly, and know that once you find your inner being, you are very close to finding God.

"This is why pilgrims strip themselves of objects when they come to the Kaaba, letting go of their attachment to the world, temporarily hoping to find who they are. The diverse forms of life all meant to redirect the seeker back, to return to his center, to discover his inner truth, no matter how far he travels. Even if he reaches the moon, he will realize that the simple truth resides within him and it is not about distance or destination. A Companion should learn to concentrate as he travels through life. Wandering all over the place will not perfect man; what perfects man is concentration. Jerusalem or Mecca—it doesn't matter, because both represent the same truth."

One evening at the hour of the sunset prayer, a wealthy man arrives at the mosque with a lavish entourage. He is dressed in silk and is adorned with excessive jewelry. Behind him are a host of slaves. One helps him dismount from his camel, then bows to him. The lead servant shows him the way to the mosque entrance and other slaves follow, carrying a variety of expensive gifts. When he arrives at the mosque gate, the wealthy man observes he must take off his leather sandals, so he looks around for a place where he can sit and allow the lead slave to remove them.

Bilaal happens to be near the gate when the man arrives. Looking at the slaves serving their wealthy master in total, humiliating obedience reopens a wound for Bilaal, who was once a slave until he was freed by Bakr. Now one of the Prophet's most trusted Companions, Bilaal five times a day calls all to join for prayer. *Does this man have any idea who the Prophet is and what he stands for?* Bilaal wonders. Should he stop the man from entering the house of God? Should he rebuke him? What does he think he's doing, bringing all these slaves to the mosque? Does he really think the Prophet will give him special recognition for showing off his wealth and the number of his retainers?

Omar sees Bilaal emotionally struggling and reminds him that everyone is waiting for him to call for the prayer, which he then does.

Omar walks toward the man. "What are you here for, brother of Arabia?"

"I have come a long distance to meet with the Prophet and offer him many gifts."

A crowd on their way to prayer begins to form around this rare sight of such opulence. As Omar speaks with him, it's clear the man has no idea what has brought all these people together. He thinks of the Prophet as a tribal leader who would give him a front-row seat and status in the new rising power of Yathrib.

Omar refuses to let him in, while Bilaal explains the situation to the Prophet. The Prophet indicates he will meet with him after the prayer, so the man waits outside for the prayer to end. After everyone has left, except for a handful of Companions, the man is allowed to meet with the Prophet, who has asked Bilaal to stay close by.

The wealthy man is escorted to Muhammad and bows to him. "Prophet! I am so pleased and honored to meet you! I have heard of your miracles and your power, and I come to offer my loyalty to you." The man signals to the lead slave, and a dozen slaves bring in a cornucopia of gifts: dinars, gold, silk, weapons made of silver, a tray of silver coins. They bow to the Prophet as they lay these treasures at his feet. Not since the Kaaba have the Companions seen such a display of wealth.

Muhammad takes this all in. "Please rise! Man should only bow to God. What is all this for? What brings you here, and what do you want in return?"

"Mecca attacked one of my caravans, stealing a third of my wealth. I am here to seek their punishment and recover what they stole. I heard you are building an army, and I want to donate half of my wealth to your army."

"So, you are here for revenge? If revenge and hatred is your motive, then we cannot meet. What brought my Companions here—and those you saw who came for prayer—is our love of God, not hatred for the lords of Mecca. And what makes you different than any lord of Mecca? You seem to enjoy slaves, prestige, honor among men, gold and silver, dirham and dinar. What you hate about them is deeply rooted in you! How can you have victory over them if you are still in slavery to the same things as them? Our struggle is not against Mecca; it is not against a group of men. Our fight is against injustice, ignorance, principalities of aggression and abuse. If you are sincere in your search for justice, then you must begin with yourself! Free yourself from your obsession for the material and honor that envious men give to you because of your wealth. Once you have defeated your desires, your raging passions and your hatred, then you will have defeated what you hate about Mecca. One day we will end the rule of Mecca's lords—but not with hatred, only with the power of truth. The swords of God's army are in alignment with justice and truth, not with hatred and revenge. Take your gold and entourage and go back from where you came. There is no place for men like you among us. I wish you a safe journey home."

Muhammad departs with the Companions, leaving the man alone with his unaccepted gifts. The Prophet's decision makes no sense according to what this man understands about how the world works and what motivates human behavior.

The slaves await his orders, impressed with this man called Prophet. No one has spoken so bluntly to their master before.

As they load the camels for the return journey, one of the African slaves approaches Bilaal, and they realize they can connect in their native tongue. The slave slips back into the mosque. The lead slave decides to say nothing as the rejected caravan sets off on the long journey without him, confident his master will not even notice.

TWENTY-FOUR

YATHRIB ON THE RISE IN
THE FIRST YEAR

R umors about Muhammad spread throughout Arabia.
Some speak of a king in Yathrib, others talk about a
Prophet who performs fascinating miracles. So many desire
to come see this man, to meet him, to ask him something.
He may have a cure for their disease, or he may wish them
wealth and prosperity. If they follow him, they may get a share
of the wealth and land in this rising power. And so a growing number of pilgrims make their way to Yathrib to see this
superhuman who stood up to the mighty of Mecca. Each has
their own needs and wants—mostly material—but very few
are looking for true freedom.

In Mecca, the Companions were brought up in a city that
had an order, a culture, and a code of conduct. Yathrib is
just an oasis that attracted simple Bedouins, concerned only
with basic human needs. Back in Mecca, the Prophet would
stay up all night praying until his eyes became white as snow,
and when he met his Meccan Companions at dawn for the

morning prayer, they would lower their gaze out of respect. The new prospective followers stare at him, study him, waiting for a supernatural event or act. They've come for the quick fix, fasting and staying up all night in one posture. Concentrating on a God they can't see is not for them! And with everyone welcome to attend the prayers, the morning's silence and worship that Muhammad and his Meccan Companions enjoyed are often interrupted by curious Bedouins and confused, half-asleep tribesmen who don't want to be up this early.

After prayer, many gather around the Prophet to listen and ask questions.

A tall man asks, "Is it true that you can hit the ground with your stick and cause a river to erupt?"

Before Muhammad can answer, another man bursts out, "Is it true you flew to Jerusalem overnight on a white donkey and met all the prophets of the past?"

Hamza and Omar smile, but they are more annoyed than amused as they reflect upon how far popular imagination can stray.

The Prophet, however, understands this new reality. He's here to help these people, but he cannot answer all their questions. Truth is experiential, and they ultimately have to live it themselves. He could describe what life has taught him, which hopefully has some value, but public curiosity never seems to be fully satisfied. Still, Muhammad smiles at his questioners. "I am a man just like you! Why would you expect me to release rivers from Earth? Look around. Do you see any donkey with wings? When you find that donkey, bring him to me, and then I can tell you about the trip to Jerusalem."

Meccan disciples were purified by hellfire, coming out like pure gold—their presence, appearance, attitude, speech, action, and energy all in harmony with the Master. They

didn't need guidance because their core being had been transformed with high physical and spiritual endurance, power
over the material and senses. It is not enough to say, "I am a
follower." In many cases, the eyes of a person reveal the lie of
their tongue. Purity comes from within, begins with thought
and intention, and the eyes will always tell the truth of men.
Here in Yathrib, many desperate people are looking for salvation, emancipation, and freedom. The Prophet can't reject
them, but they have to purge their old habits to get to the
purity that is an essential pillar for spiritual growth.

With the passing of a year and its seasons, Yathrib is transformed and is now flourishing with green fields, thousands of
planted trees, new houses, and an abundance of food and food
security. Men are busy constructing and farming; women are
busy raising children and producing goods like clothing and
rugs. Yathrib is a rising power!

Many of the Companions follow the Prophet's modest
dress code, even though it isn't a requirement. They wear long
garments made of wool. No silk or jewelry are allowed for
the followers, as they are choosing to renounce attachment to
the material rather than showing off gold and silver. Men are
encouraged to give up their jewelry to advance the new Yathrib model, to buy seed and cattle, but most importantly, to free
slaves. When a new believer breaks a rule, depending on the
seriousness of the offense, the Prophet requires them to find
a slave and free them. In the meantime, the Prophet has cut
back on the market for new slaves, dealing with the problem
in steps.

Muhammad knows that the more Yathrib prospers, the
more those corrupt and brutal enemies will see Yathrib, its
model, and its author as an existential threat. Without a
doubt, Yathrib is an emerging power to be reckoned with in

Arabia. What Muhammad accomplished in one year, all the tribes combined couldn't accomplish in many years. It is a testament to the power of unity and leadership. And so it becomes clear to the Prophet that it is now necessary to create an effective defense force to preserve the movement and this new concept for a prosperous and just society. This defense force consists of a few hundred strong warriors, skilled in fighting, who have also conquered their conditioning and integrated into higher beings.

One evening, as Companions sit around a fire to fend off the seasonal chill, Muhammad shares his most recent thinking with his trusted Companions. "The sword without divine principles is a destructive tool, but in the hand of righteous men it is divine. Justice will not be able to thrive without protection, and the aggressors should not escape without punishment. They should be held accountable for their wrongdoings and stripped of their power. Only the righteous men who have demonstrated their power over the material world can rule, to bring Arabia's chaos into equilibrium. The sacred sword wasn't meant to conquer and destroy; it was meant to bring justice and security."

The Prophet looks to the quiet Salman the Persian, the most experienced Companion on war affairs and tactics, to speak.

Salman takes his cue. "We must make two assumptions: one is that the enemy, the Meccans, will assume we plan to attack their caravan, and, given the balance of forces, we must assume we will be largely outnumbered."

"What do you propose?" Muhammad asks.

"When we were outnumbered by the enemy," Salman answers, "we adapted the 'Ring of Fire' tactic in our fight. It is not known here in Arabia, certainly not to the Meccan warriors. Their fight depends on independent individual combat.

We will fight as a group and on foot. The Ring of Fire is a perfect circle, shoulder to shoulder, ankle to ankle, with fighters facing every direction. The outer ring of men have spears to prevent horsemen from breaking the circle; in the inner rings are the archers. So, the defense is outer, the offense is inner. The defense gives protection and stability to archers to concentrate, aim, and shoot. The Ring of Fire should not break at any cost; the power resides in moving like one body, keeping the core fire out of the enemies' reach with the ability of the ring to move in every direction and retreat to higher ground if necessary. If Mecca learns of this tactic, they will come prepared, and so it must be a surprise. No one should talk to anyone about this, not even Companion to Companion, in case an enemy ear is listening."

A stir of excitement sweeps over the group as they imagine utilizing this new tactic. They are now committed to battle. Finally.

"Hamza, Salman," Muhammad continues, "you must select three hundred from our best, from our Meccan Companions and our Yathrib Companions, those well established in faith and self-discipline. Train them in secret in this Ring of Fire tactic; drill day and night, because time is short, according to the latest message from Abbas."

"It's clear we will need special weapons for the mission if we use this tactic," Bakr says. "With Salman's advice, I'll take responsibility to properly arm our warriors."

"The tactic requires hundreds of spears longer than ones used here, as well as shields, body armor, helmets, bows, and thousands of arrows, hundreds of swords," Salman adds.

With renewed energy, all set about their tasks. Efforts with the followers had concentrated on pursuing discipline of The Way, employing the methods of fasting and prayer to achieve balance in life. Now, the Prophet and Hamza need these men to master the art of the sword, and especially the art of the bow and arrow. With Yathrib's hills and mountains, arrows shot from a distance are an effective defensive weapon.

They find the best-trained warriors among the three Jewish tribes, each living in their own walled fortresses with their own synagogue and economy. These men are well known for working with metals, especially producing weapons. The arrival of Muhammad, a newcomer to the oasis where he had ancestral roots, was greeted with some skepticism by the Jews. They are one ethnic group with its own religion based on one God, but except for a few like Mu-Khairiq, they could never accept a non-Jewish prophet. Still, seeing what he was accomplishing, they accept him as one of the leaders of Yathrib and make pacts with him, most importantly mutual defense pacts in the event of an attack on Yathrib.

The training of the three hundred in the Ring of Fire takes place in a hidden valley. It's the search for weaponry, especially among the Jewish tribes so expert in armory, that creates the rumor that Muhammad plans a military operation. The sense of urgency implies this is not the slow buildup of a self-defense force. The rumors distill down quite accurately to a Meccan caravan being attacked at Badr Wells.

The training in the hidden valley goes well, as the chosen disciplined warriors quickly pick up the Ring of Fire. Assigned their place, they quickly get to know their comrades on their left and their right. Salman sets up mock combats to see how solid the circle will hold under attack. A few times the circle breaks and one warrior falls down, which causes the line to go down like a row of dominos. This produces some laughter and no injuries, until Salman and Hamza call them to order and command them to straighten out that weakness.

Hand-to-hand skills are also honed. During the training, Ali shows tremendous physical strength. The twenty-five-year-old surprises everyone with his reaction speed, fearlessness, accuracy, endurance, and sheer power. Even Hamza, without doubt one of the greatest and most fearless warriors of Arabia, is challenged when he faces him in mock combat. Ali is a born warrior. Several swords break from the might of his blows, and a special sword is designed for him. Observing Ali training in the valley, Muhammad wishes Talib could have been with them to see the powerful man his offspring has become.

TWENTY-FIVE

TRAPS

For the lords of Mecca, the Prophet's long absence from the holy city has unexpectedly made his voice stronger, and his message is now heard by even more than when he was present in Mecca. What is more influential than a master? The absence of the master! A group of young Companions continue sharing the Prophet's teaching quietly, especially with pilgrims who carry the Prophet's message back to their tribes. The message also circulates in the slave quarters, to the point where Mecca faces a slave revolt.

With this crisis looming, Jahl calls a meeting at the prestigious Nadwa Council mansion, inviting Salul from Yathrib, the man who would have been king until Muhammad appeared, and Suhail from Taif, who ordered the Prophet to be stoned. Jahl, who nurses a profound hatred for Muhammad, is the self-appointed leader of the meeting, but it's Sufyan whose voice breaks through the opening chatter to present the dire situation their beloved Mecca faces.

"Yathrib is closed to our caravans," Sufyan says. "I've had to reroute them, and now we need to increase our guards, as

Sa'ad threatens to attack our caravans. It is unacceptable and cannot stand. And his influence among our desperate and confused youth is growing!"

"He sends his teachings written on sheepskin to the youth." Lahab dramatically holds up a tattered sheepskin.

"He is influencing many in Yathrib," Salul chimes in.

Sufyan, annoyed at the interruptions, continues his dismal summary. "Worst of all, they are inciting our slaves to rebel, to disobey; they are promising them an afterlife. Torturing and executing a few as examples has had no effect. What do you do when they say, 'Better to die than live as a slave'?"

Those present shake their heads at this crazy behavior, which not only defies hallowed tradition but violates the natural law of master and slave—not to mention their prosperity and comfort.

Not only has Muhammad been able to threaten the lifeblood of their economy, which is the caravan trade, but, ironically, he has more presence in Mecca now than when he was actually there.

If Abu Salul wondered why he had been invited to meet in Mecca, Jahl quickly provides the answer. "We have prepared a venom which you, Salul, will put in his food. He will weaken and be gone before another full moon. No one will know why he died."

This excites the group. All eyes turn to their guest from Yathrib.

Salul's first reaction is favorable. It would certainly solve his problem of thwarted ambition. He imagines doing it, but he quickly sees the difficulties. How to get access to him? Muhammad's closest Companions are already wary. And what if he were caught? That makes him involuntarily shudder.

Finally, he speaks. "Poison him? How can poison kill someone who doesn't eat?"

"What do you mean?" Lahab asks.

"The man fasts during the day. When he breaks his fast, he eats a handful of dates and waits till the next day. He turned down my invitation to stay at my mansion, rejected the gold I offered him! How can I possibly poison him? Where, when, and how? Poison is a great idea, but I don't see how it can work with Muhammad."

All take this as a *no*. Even the disappointed Jahl is not ready to try to persuade this reluctant assassin.

"Well . . ." Jahl muses. "We can't attack him at Yathrib; that would put our Jewish allies at odds with us under the Yathrib defense pact. They would consider it an attack on Yathrib, not on Muhammad."

"In my view, killing him will not entirely solve our problem," Sufyan says. "We must get rid of all of them, including his close Companions like the traitor Hamza. They would go to war against us, and his followers here in Mecca would rise up."

Sufyan's statement produces general agreement—both the tree and the roots must be torn out. A silence descends on the room as all brains work to come up with a solution to save Mecca.

"We must engage him in battle on open ground. Outside of Yathrib," suggests Sufyan.

"Fine," admits Lahab, "but how do we get the snake out of his hole?"

"He hasn't left Yathrib since he arrived," says Salul. "In the meantime, his Companions have been forming what they call a 'defense force' to protect him in case of a Meccan attack."

This gets Jahl's full attention. "A defense force? Tell me more."

"A few hundred men have been arming and training. They leave before sunrise and return after sunset—no one knows what they do! They appear to be led by Hamza and Salman the Persian."

Jahl takes a long moment to digest this. Spinning a web to entangle the Prophet. "What if we trick him to get him out of Yathrib? Draw him into a trap?"

"How?" asks Suhail of Taif.

"What if he learned that his secret Companions and Hashemites had been arrested and a caravan was taking them to Damascus to be sold as slaves?" Jahl brainstorms out loud. "The caravan would pass through Badr Wells."

Even the slow of wit get it. Of course Muhammad would come to their rescue.

"Behind the caravan there would be a massive army, surprising him on open ground."

"This is genius," says Suhail, "but what makes you sure he would be there personally?"

"When he knows that his uncle Abbas is among those to be sold into slavery, nothing will stop him!" insists Jahl. This plan has an added benefit. Muhammad's uncle has kept Muhammad updated on Mecca's moves and helped the Prophet escape the Shi'ab.

Even Sufyan has to admit the plan is brilliant. "Good thinking. That solves both our problems. We get rid of the troublemakers here. We should include the rebellious slaves; they will fetch double the price in Damascus."

"We will enlist a thousand warriors and crush him and his companions at Badr," Jahl vows. "He will never return to Yathrib, and we will reclaim our trading center."

"I will deliver the news of the caravan to him," Salul promises.

"No!" Jahl interjects. "You should not talk about this with anyone! Coming from you returning from Mecca, he will be suspicious. We will send the news with a third party, one of the caravans from the south traveling through Mecca on to Yathrib."

The room is in high excitement.

Hind is particularly enthused by the mention of killing Hamza. "This is the day Mecca shows its might and glory!"

Her uncle Shaibah chimes in, "This is our opportunity! To catch him outside the oasis. Don't forget the wine—this is a celebration!"

"I will bring Muhammad's head back and hang it on the Kaaba's wall!" vows Jahl. "Now, let's get to work."

The first step is to take hostages. Then they need to let both the arrests and the caravan known. Above all, the army must be kept a secret. The Notables act quickly to execute their plan before word leaks out. Malik and squads of guards move through the sleeping city, dragging suspected Companions from their homes and through the narrow paths of the city to the stables, which act as a holding center, where they join the rebellious slaves in chains. Some Hashemites are also brutally rounded up.

The once peaceful night is punctuated by the cries of the arrested and the sound of families loudly protesting. To the surprise of the prisoners huddled in the stables, Abbas is thrown in among them, taking some last blows.

The very next day, Sufyan invites a group of Yemeni traders on their way to Damascus through Yathrib to witness Mecca's effort to uproot the rebels. He explains to the guests that any Meccan who opposes the gods of Mecca, like these miserable souls, will be sold into slavery. Many are in chains and, seeing Sufyan, they cry out for water. He makes sure that the Yemenis see Abbas, and for those who know Abbas, it is a shock to see this dignified man so humiliated. Sufyan notes their reaction, knowing they will not forget this scene. He tells them he is preparing a caravan that will take these miscreants through Badr Wells to the slave market in Damascus. Sufyan is already imagining the deadly confrontation with his greatest enemy, Muhammad, and bringing his head back in triumph to Mecca as proof to all that the Prophet is finally dead.

TWENTY-SIX

BADR WELLS

Some weeks later back in Yathrib, after the last prayer, Muhammad's closest Companions remain as Bilaal shows in a traveler, who is still shaking off the dust of the road. Muhammad and the Yemeni trader recognize each other and smile. Caravan veterans, they often met on the trails over the years and exchanged stories and jokes.

Muhammad welcomes him, and the trader expresses his condolences for the losses of Khadija and Talib. "Muhammad, I wish I had a funny story or a good poem I've heard, but I bring you sad news from Mecca. The Notables have taken many Hashemites hostage along with those who follow you. They intend to sell them as slaves in Damascus. Abbas is among them, chained for slavery!"

This news, so hard to believe, comes like a bolt of lightning, striking the hearts of all those under the roof of their house of worship.

Hamza tries to speak but outrage sticks in his throat.

"The cowards!" shouts Omar. "Did you hear this or see it with your own eyes?"

"I've known Abbas since the day my late father introduced me to him. I saw him bruised and chained in a stable crowded not only with Hashemites, but rebellious slaves who preferred to die than work."

"Do you know when the caravan is set to leave Mecca?" Bakr asks.

"Sufyan said they'd be ready to travel with the next full moon, taking the route through Badr Wells to Damascus," says the Yemini trader.

"Badr is two days away," observes Hamza. "We have to stop them!"

"They've gone way too far this time," says Bakr. "They must be really desperate to take revenge on a man like Abbas and sell him into slavery!"

"We have to intercept them at Badr." Omar looks to the Prophet, and all follow his gaze.

Muhammad looks distant as he processes this startling news. These are his disciples, Abbas the third uncle he's losing.

Hamza impatiently breaks the silence. "A handful of us can stop this madness!"

Yes! A surge of determined energy takes hold of those present.

The Prophet speaks and all listen. "A small force will tempt Sufyan to fight. If he's outnumbered, he will surrender and there will be no reason for bloodshed. Send for the first generation of Mecca's Companions, and the first generation of Yathrib's, but not those who talk too much, eat too much, sleep too much, and lack self-discipline. Above all, take only those strong in faith. We will wait for Sufyan at Badr Wells."

At dawn, Jahl leads the impressive Meccan army out the main gate, waving their weapons and flying their red and black banners. Mecca has never seen such a large military expedition nor such a large caravan. When the stakes are high, overwhelming force is the only guarantee of success. Hind bids farewell to her father, Otbah, her brother Walid, and her uncle Shaibah. The populace cheers them on, but when the hostages pass, there are fewer cheers, as Abbas is a well-known and respected figure.

Countless camels are loaded with supplies, as any successful military campaign depends on well-planned logistics. A large number are loaded with casks of wine, as a victory celebration is anticipated. Given the length of the columns, it will not be until midmorning that Sufyan leads the hundreds of camels on the Damascus-bound caravan through the gate and into the desert. A contingent of guards rides alongside, always mindful that a fast-moving enemy could capture some booty and disappear back into the desert.

❁

From Yathrib, the Prophet leads his force of battle-ready foot soldiers through the desert toward Badr to carry out a lightning raid on the caravan to free the hostages. It is the second week of Ramadan, and the Prophet and his Companions are all fasting from dawn to sunset—no water, no food during the day, eating in moderation around sunset, and fasting on water throughout the night.

Up before dawn on the second day, the force from Yathrib arrives at Badr Wells at midday and takes up their position. There is already a queue of travelers—some heading south, others heading north—giving their camels their fill at the main well. A rider on horseback, wearing a green turban, appears on the crest of a hill. Rather than head for the water, the rider guides his mount up a higher hill that has a panoramic view of the Badr Hills. After taking a good look at the entire area, he spurs his mount to head back south.

After the morning prayer, the close Companions gather around the Prophet to plan the day. Muhammad scans the faces of those who have been through so much with him, then looks at Ali. "Son, ride south until you see the caravan, and hurry back so we can prepare. Sufyan has certainly sent out scouts. Maybe he will decide to avoid Badr and take the Red Sea route. We must know his intentions."

As Ali starts to get up, Muhammad has another thought. "Better two of you go."

With that, all the Companions begin to stand up as the Prophet gives one more command. "Sa'ad, you have the fastest horse—you and Ali go."

Within minutes the two have grabbed their swords, saddled up, and begun to gallop south.

⸎

Farther down the trail, an army of exhausted, thirsty warriors is on the move, looking forward to the promise of Badr water, only a day away. Behind them comes the caravan with its two hundred camels and dehydrated future slaves, only kept moving with constant lashing by the guards. Those who cannot keep up, along with those who expire on the spot, are left for the vultures.

Sufyan and Jahl ride confidently at the head of the army. From the north, a single rider trots toward them. It's the scout in the green turban, who wheels around to walk alongside them.

The scout announces, "They are there."

Sufyan and Jahl smile broadly to each other.

"Muhammad?" Jahl questions.

"I don't know," the scout replies. "I've never seen him. But there was a man leading a prayer, and I recognized Hamza."

"Though I didn't want to, I had to admit the jackal was clever, but now what a fool he is!" Sufyan says.

More smiles. Their plan has worked! The end of their tribulations is finally at hand.

⁂

An hour later, Ali and Sa'ad, moving fast to the south, see in the far distance the head of a column approaching. They quickly move off the track and head up a grade, dismounting behind rocks that are out of sight of the main path. They recognize Sufyan and Jahl passing below. This is not a caravan, as cavalry, foot soldiers, archers, and support camels stream by, seemingly without end. This is an army! They look at each other, both thinking the same thing: *Is this a desert mirage?* No, this is only too real. They hang on until the last warrior passes, as they want to report back a fairly accurate count. As they get up, they see another column of laden camels and then more hostages and slaves on foot. So, the caravan is headed to Damascus.

A half day later, Ali and Sa'ad lead their exhausted, frothing horses to the main Badr well, then hurry to join the Companions, who gather around the returning scouts. All but Muhammad, who is off by himself.

"It's a trap! It's a trap!" Sa'ad insists impatiently.

"A huge army on the move is heading right toward us!" Ali exclaims.

Their vivid description is met with silence as all try to wrap their minds around this totally unexpected move by Mecca.

The first expressed reaction is a laugh from Hamza. "Son of a bitch, I didn't think they were that clever."

"You have to give them credit," Salman admits reluctantly. "But now that we know, they've lost the advantage of a surprise attack."

"How many would you say they were?" Omars asks.

"At least a thousand," Sa'ad responds. "There seemed neither beginning nor end."

"We must return to Yathrib, where the Prophet will be safe. He wanted to avoid bloodshed by overwhelming the caravan with superior numbers, but now they are the ones with the overwhelming numbers." These words of wisdom and common sense come from the oldest Companion, Bakr.

The expressions on the faces of Hamza and Salman show that they disagree.

"They are exhausted, counting on surprising us," says Salman. "Now we will surprise them. The Ring of Fire is designed to fight superior numbers."

"We can't risk the Prophet being captured or killed," insists Bakr. "Look at him—he is barely skin on bone."

"There is a solution." All look to the giant Omar, still a formidable warrior. "Bakr, you return to Yathrib with Muhammad. We rescue our brethren."

That seems an acceptable compromise. Before anyone speaks, Muhammad appears, immediately sensing the heaviness of the moment. He looks to the returning scouts, Ali and Sa'ad.

"A large army is coming," Ali tells him.

"How large?"

"Close to a thousand. Heavily armed, cavalry, archers."

Muhammad takes this in.

Bakr breaks into Muhammad's moment of calculating. "My counsel is that we all return to Yathrib, where you—and all of us—are safe, and where we will avoid needless bloodshed." He sees that the others are about to object and then adds, "However, I seem to be alone in that view."

Muhammad asks, "What about the caravan?"

"It's following behind; our companions are there," says Ali.

"Abbas?"

"Yes."

"So we decided with these views expressed, the best plan is that you and I return to Yathrib," Bakr explains.

Muhammad regards his Companions. "If you are ready to fight and die on this ground, I, too, am ready to fight and die here. This is the war we knew was coming."

Though Bakr is disappointed, the martial spirit of the others lights up.

"How far are they?" Muhammad asks.

"About one night's journey," answers Ali. "They should be here around midday tomorrow."

"Then we have no time to lose. We must prepare," states the Prophet calmly.

Few sleep that night, and the group gathers at dawn for the morning prayer.

Salman, moving to form the Ring of Fire, rounds up the core force of archers to occupy the center, then the next ring of foot soldiers who can move anywhere if there is a breach in the outer ring, then the defensive outer ring of the men taking a knee, lining up their armored shields and pointing their spears at horseback level. It all goes smoothly, as with their months of training, all know their place, know their companion to the left and to the right. Hamza and Salman move among them, checking weapons and offering encouragement. Their leaders' desire for battle inspires the ranks. They also hide some archers to the side amidst the rocks.

They do not have long to wait. The first sign is the sound of distant drums, at first faint, then becoming louder, the beat matching the heartbeat of the combatants heading toward a violent collision.

The first sight of the enemy are two scouts who appear on the brow of the hill, one with the green turban who turns in his saddle to signal those behind forward. Next, Jahl and Sufyan appear, flanked by horse cavalry. The cavalry moves forward with colorful banners flying. Will they come all the way across the open terrain to probe the enemy formation with their long lances? No, they rein up, and behind them pour warriors as if flooding out from a spring—on and on and on they come.

The Companion warriors watch. This is not a battle exercise played out in a hidden Yathrib valley with mock combat against their brethren; this is what they've been training for—their first life-or-death combat. A murmur rises from the ranks at the awe-inspiring spectacle. There's a restless shifting in the line. The Ring of Fire is a fearsome weapon, as long as they fight as *one*.

Muhammad steps out in front to address them. "The enemy will underestimate our readiness. They think of individual combat, one-on-one—this is their strength. They are not expecting us to fight as one. They will drink wine to numb their senses during combat. They will slaughter and they will feast, and when they arrive at Badr, they will be heavy and exhausted. We will leave a passage for them to the wells to drink, and the more they drink, the heavier and less efficient their movements will become. When you see among them your torturer and your oppressor, don't let hatred guide you . . . When you see among them your brother, your father, and your uncle, don't let guilt guide you . . . Remember, our fight is not for honor or glory; our fight is beyond victory and beyond defeat, beyond fame and beyond shame. If you fight only to live, then you will die. If you fight only for victory, then you will be defeated. *Fight for nothing, and you will be fighting for everything!*"

The Prophet's voice is enough to inspire the troops, whose collective heartbeat has increased in anticipation of the battle. "We have God, they have idols," Muhammad continues. "We have the Truth, they have falsehood. We have faith, they have void. We will fight for justice, they will fight for revenge and booty."

What the soldiers are not fully aware of, but what Muhammad foresaw as a strategy, is that this impressive array of military power is dependent on the overconfident, exhausted, half-inebriated, seriously dehydrated Meccan foot soldiers. Now, their first line of elite Meccan infantry can smell water and see water, only steps away. One individual begins to run, and a horde staggers after him, fighting their fellows to get their heads into the water where they can drink, drink, drink.

Only moments before, Sufyan and Jahl were triumphant, ready to be honored as heroes for generations, as there before them was their nemesis, whom they had not seen in the flesh since they had driven him out of Mecca years ago. Now, these future heroes do not like what they're witnessing.

The cavalry does its best to block others from rushing to drink and to rout out those swilling at the well.

Among the Companions below, the murmur now has a different tone, one of confidence rather than awe.

Hamza says to Salman, "You were right. Their need for water is greater than their desire for battle."

The Ring of Fire has been positioned so that the archers are within range of the well, and they have zeroed in on that target. The archers inside the ring have notched arrows on their bowstrings, ready to fire.

Hamza looks to Muhammad for the order.

Muhammad, watching this disarray among his adversaries, replies, "Let them drink."

Salman repeats the message. "Let them drink! Remember! Shoulder to shoulder, ankle to ankle, even the air should not pass through!"

Some discipline returns to the Meccan force, and they line up, with a cavalry unit in front. Now, two forces face each other across an open, dry field, ready to soak up the blood of martyrs—all blood the same, regardless of tribe.

The drumming stops and an eerie quiet settles over Badr Wells. High in the noon sky, vultures begin to circle, riding the air currents that rise from the heat coming off the land. Below them is a massive army, arraigned against a circular knot of warriors. The slaughter appears as if it is going to be one-sided.

With the Companions set in a defensive posture and the Meccans in attack mode, it is up to the Meccans to make the first move. The waiting Companions watch as three familiar figures, Otbah, Shaibah, and Walid, step out from the front of the Meccan line. The Meccans have decided to follow an ancient warrior tradition, where three champions from each side challenge to the death their designated adversary in single combat.

Otbah shouts out loud, "Muhammad! Send out your bravest, your most courageous, to face us!"

Three of Yathrib's best fighters step forward from the ring with the Prophet's permission. When they get close to Otbah, he doesn't recognize them.

"Muhammad, what camel dung is this?" Otbah says in disgust. "Who the hell are you?"

"Sa'ad Bin Mu'ath, leader of Awes!"

"We have nothing to do with you!" shouts Otbah. "Stay out of this! We are here for our cousins. Muhammad! Send us our peers from Quraysh!"

The Prophet calls the Yathrib fighters back. Then he looks to Hamza. "The man has a death wish—go, give him his wish. Where is Ali?"

Ali steps forward.

"Let me go," insists Omar.

"No, you stay," the Prophet says, then calls for Ubbaydah, who steps forward.

"Don't talk to them. Fifteen years of talking is enough; today is the day you let your swords speak." Muhammad is rolling the dice, as he's putting his best forward with his son. He cannot afford to lose his warriors and suffer such a defeat before this battle, on which the fate of his movement and his life depend.

Hamza, Ali, and Ubbaydah head toward their waiting opponents. Cousins, brothers, fathers, friends—all who are present hold their breath. Silence returns as this deadly ritual is about to play out.

Hamza challenges Shaibah. Before the Meccan can regret the opponent he has drawn, one powerful sweep from Hamza's righteous sword kills Shaibah instantly, separating his head with a perfectly accurate blow to his neck.

This produces a collective gasp from those watching.

Ali then steps forward to face Walid.

A few experienced Meccan warriors chuckle, remembering Ali as an awkward youth. Walid smiles at his luck in the draw.

"I swear by Manat, I will walk over your body to drink my fill at Badr Wells!" He strikes a first blow to test Ali's strength, which Ali blocks with ease. Walid then strikes harder. Ali blocks again.

Walid now realizes he's in a real fight and, mustering all his strength, delivers a mighty blow. To the air. As Ali deftly dodges, striking like a cobra, he severs Walid's right arm from his shoulder joint. Walid's brain orders his body to strike again, only to see his severed limb, still holding the sword, lying on the ground as blood gushes from his shoulder. In shock and about to faint, he loses his balance as Ali strikes him at the hip joint, cutting off his left leg. Ali stands over him as Walid starts to crawl with one leg and one arm toward the water, leaving a trail of blood. All watch the drama, which ends with Ali striking a merciful blow, taking off Walid's overconfident head.

This action produces a horrified reaction from those watching, which only intensifies when Ali grabs Walid's bloodied head and runs toward the Meccan line, screaming. He throws the head of their top warrior in among them, setting off a panic. No one saw this coming. They all had known Ali as a young boy; for him to strike each joint so accurately shows a mastery even they have to admire, and a ripple of stunned shock waves go through the Meccan lines.

The third round is now at hand, and it can only be an anticlimax after the first devastating victories for the Companion warriors. Though not for all. Hudaifah, a loyal companion of the Prophet and Hind's brother, has just watched his brother and uncle go down. Now, he watches his father, Otbah, who proudly headed the Meccan challenge, step forward with less confidence. Otbah is one of Mecca's top lords, one of its wealthiest citizens who has made his fortune mainly from the slave trade.

Ubbaydah meets him, and this time there is no lightning kill, as the two antagonists appear evenly matched. Otbah, with a feint and a sweeping blow at Ubbaydah's right leg, slices it to the bone. The back-and-forth under the relentless noon sun makes them both sweat, and as Otbah readies the *coup de grace*, sweat falls into his eyes, stinging and blinding him for a moment, which allows Ubbaydah to strike a blow that cracks Otbah's skull. Both warriors tumble to the ground. A hush falls as all wait to see who is the victor.

Finally, Ubbaydah stirs. Ali and Hamza rush to lift their fallen comrade, and the three hobble back to their line. Three Meccan soldiers retrieve Otbah and carry him back to their line.

Seeing his father-in-law's lifeless body, Sufyan gallops back to the caravan to order the guards to join the main force. Every Meccan sword is needed now in the full-out attack. While Muhammad's side gains confidence in these striking victories, the Meccans' defeats produce a rage for vengeance.

The hostages hear the drums and cries from over the hill, and with the guards departing for the front, they allow themselves a moment of hope.

The drumbeats grow louder as the Meccan forces, led by the cavalry, dash headlong into a full-out attack.

Hamza orders the archers in the Ring of Fire to notch their arrows and await his command to fire. Charging headlong, the cavalry, followed by running foot soldiers, enter the kill zone, only to be met by a rain of arrows darkening the sky. Scoring dozens of kills, the arrows also strike some of the cavalry mounts, who fall, causing those coming in from behind to trip over them. The Companion archers then launch a second devastating round.

The cavalry reach the Ring of Fire, but their lances only strike the shields of the outer circle, and the long spears of the Companion front line bring down the attacking riders. One Meccan lance passes between two shields, and a Companion grabs it and pulls the rider out of his saddle and down to the ground.

Sufyan orders the Meccan archers forward to get in range of the enemy, just as the third volley rains on the Meccans, creating massive chaos and blunting their attack. The Meccan archers drop to a knee and fire off an arching volley; some arrows fall short, others strike harmlessly the raised shields protecting the Ring of Fire, but a few slip through, causing more casualties. The archers have turned out to be the decisive factor in the battle. The Meccan generals relying on the cavalry made the tactical mistake of not bringing their archers into range sooner. The Meccan forces are now broken into small, panicked groups, some fleeing, others staying to fight hand-to-hand when Hamza lets some of the second ring of swordsmen out of the circle to engage their enemy.

Meanwhile, some of the archers hidden among the rocks manage to aim directly at the horsemen, bringing them down. Bilaal spots his former master trying to rally the fleeing troops. Taking careful aim at a shifting target, he lets fly. The arrow strikes Umayah in the heart and protrudes out his back. The slave master looks down, appears puzzled at seeing the arrow, and keels over, dead before he hits the ground.

Salman and Hamza order the ring to move forward. The discipline of this war machine fighting as one is in total contrast to the enemy, who are now all fighting as individuals bent on survival.

Sufyan and Jahl watch the battle below. All is definitely not lost. Sufyan orders another volley of arrows from his archers who, for the moment, are safe. With the Ring of Fire moving, the bowmen, using the same angle and bowstring pull, overshoot it, with a few laggards bouncing off raised shields.

The Meccans weren't expecting this unified fighting style and, unable to breach the ring, they give up, retreating on the battlefield with their comrades in total disarray and searching the sky for another incoming rain of death. Horses and camels without their mounts wander about until some smart soldier jumps on one and heads quickly back to Mecca.

Muhammad, surveying the same battlefield, sees the limitations of the defensive Ring of Fire now that the Meccan cavalry is decimated and its troops are in full retreat. He gives the command to release his forces and go after the fleeing enemy, unleashing Omar, Hamza, Ali, and the rest to feast on the Meccans.

A determined Jahl spurs his mount and canters into the heat of the battle to rally his troops. Hamza and Omar are fighting back-to-back, covering 360 degrees. The Meccans are smart enough to avoid confronting this two-man death machine, so Hamza and Omar find that a wide, empty space has opened up around them as the battle rages. Hamza spots Jahl, with whom he shares a mutual hatred. Signaling to Bin Mas'ud, the one-time shepherd, and to a tall warrior, the three run toward Jahl. Bin Mas'ud grabs the halter of the horse, holding it while the other warrior swings his sword at the mounted Jahl. Leaning over to avoid the blow, Jahl falls off. Unhurt, he stands up, only to directly confront Hamza, whose sword already drips red with Meccan blood. Jahl holds his open hands out, indicating he has no weapon—or perhaps in abject surrender. As Bin Mas'ud joins Hamza, Hamza takes his sword and throws it to the man who conceived the "trap" and led Mecca's army. The sword lands on Jahl's foot, and he kicks it off. His hesitation is brief, as he knows he must pick it up to fight to save his life.

He recognizes Bin Mas'ud. "Little shepherd, you have climbed high."

Trembling with fear, he reaches down and picks the sword up. He wonders, as he so often did in the past, what his legacy will be, what future generations will think of him. He remembers as a child the pleasure it once gave him to kill a bleating lamb.

Within one minute, a shout rises from the chaotic clamor of battle. "Jahl is dead! Jahl is dead!" A chorus of voices join in the chant.

Little is more demoralizing to fighters in the field than the death of their leader, especially when many came promised some good sport, a hunting party. Now, they are the hunted.

The voices reach Sufyan, who can only recognize that the battle is indeed lost.

Hamza looks up in time to see Sufyan wheel his mount around and disappear over the crest of the hill to the south. Hamza leaps on Jahl's horse and gallops off, weaving his way through the chaos of battle, nearly colliding with a spooked camel, whose cargo of a large barrel of wine has slid down. The leaking wine mixes with the sand and blood on the ground. Only the thirsty land can celebrate for Mecca today.

Hamza spots Sufyan heading south amidst the heavy traffic of fleeing Meccans. Sufyan spurs his mount to a gallop. None of the fleeing Meccans streaming by pay any attention to them. Caravan camels, disoriented, wander about. The thinking warriors try to corral camels for the ride back to Mecca.

Hamza is suddenly distracted from his pursuit when he catches sight of Abbas among the hostages and the slaves. Hamza reins up beside Abbas and, dismounting, is mobbed as their liberator.

Back on the battlefield, those Meccans who cannot escape choose to surrender, drop their swords, and, placing their hands behind their necks, thrust their faces into the sand. Many who were able to flee have left their weapons and armor behind. Companion warriors move to claim the caravan booty, take prisoners, and embrace the rescued hostages, some of whom are family. Hamza organizes them. One group rounds up all the caravan animals with their valuable cargo, another gathers prisoners together, and a third is assigned to escort the severely dehydrated former hostages first to a Badr well and then to join Muhammad.

Muhammad walks through the carnage, helping to carry wounded disciples. When he sees the carved-up corpse of Jahl, he doesn't miss a step and simply mutters, "All you have created is nothing but idols and death."

The stench of death forces the survivors to cover their noses as the grisly tally begins. Seventy Meccans killed, including Notables Jahl, Otbah, Shaibah, and Walid. Seventy more combatants captured, dozens severely wounded. Fourteen Companions killed, eight from Yathrib, six from Mecca. The good news is that the hostages and the slaves have been freed. Muhammad greets them, especially relieved to embrace his uncle Abbas.

With the humiliating and costly defeat, Mecca's reputation as the supreme power of Arabia has been buried in the sands of Badr. The Prophet's message is loud and clear: if the sword is the only language the Meccans can understand, then so be it.

The Companions who gave their lives are all buried at Badr. Jahl and the rest of the slain Meccan warriors are left to the carrion-seeking beasts of the desert.

Hundreds of swords and other weaponry are gathered in huge piles, to be taken back to Yathrib. Meccan camels and horses carry the wounded back to the city for care. A long row of prisoners, hands tied behind their backs, sit on the ground awaiting their expected fate—the unforgiving law of the desert: the executioner's sword blade. Muhammad surveys the prisoners as though he knows them. They are uncertain whether to avoid his gaze or meet it with hope or defiance. Some say last prayers to their deities.

Then Muhammad commands, "Give them water."

This causes some surprise, not just among the prisoners but especially from those helpers from Yathrib.

"We don't kill those who drop their sword and surrender. If you know how to read and write, teach those who don't, and you will be free to go."

When the caravan wends its victorious way back to Yathrib, it is larger than the one Muhammad led to Badr.

On the southern edge of Yathrib, a large crowd awaits the return of the victorious warriors, as word of the triumph has already spread. Everyone loves a winner. Hypocrites are there to cheer. It looks like the whole population is out to greet them, glad for an excuse to celebrate. Jubilation reigns.

As the Companions approach, the Prophet reminds them to stay humble and not get carried away by the praise they receive, for the same group would have scorned them if the outcome had been different. "Stay truthful to who you are; this is far from over. We won a battle, not yet the war."

The women cry their high-pitched "Ulululululu" when the first warriors appear.

Anxious family members, women, and children rush to welcome their returned heroes, some searching the ranks for their own, as they know the battle must have taken its toll.

Sa'ad's wife and children gratefully hug him. Fatima anxiously searches the faces of those who are returning, and she beams with joy and relief when she sees Ali. She waves to him, and he dismounts to approach her. Salul does his best to hide his disappointment, melding in with the crowd and avoiding his returning son, Abdullah.

The crowd splashes water on the returning fighters.

From the tower rooftop of a Jewish fortress, Azora and other Jews watch the triumphant scene below with growing alarm.

The rabbi notes sarcastically, "Almighty Mecca."

"Mecca will not let this stand," Azora says.

TWENTY-SEVEN

THE ADVERSARIES
REGROUP

Mecca is in full mourning. Women grovel on the ground, throwing dirt on themselves, slapping their chests and heads. It befell Sufyan, with the fastest horse, to bring news of the defeat. No matter how he tried to slant it, it only got worse as more survivors trickled in and the roster of those killed and imprisoned grew. All are aware that the two great empires to the north—the Persian and the Roman—always assumed Mecca had South Arabia under their control and would guarantee the mutually beneficial slave trade; now, they would have their doubts.

A subdued Nadwa session is underway. Despite considerable opposition and with empty chairs for the martyred Notables, all have to recognize that Sufyan is the most capable among them, both on and off the battlefield. His exculpatory line is that he was only responsible for the caravan; Jahl led the army into this defeat by underestimating the enemy. Quite impressive the amount of blame the dead can shoulder. The shock and anger have passed with the realization that this is a time for unity.

Sufyan manages to steer the debate toward Mecca's revenge and reestablishing their primacy. "I will not underestimate our enemy. The profits from caravans will go to raising an army so large and so well equipped that we will crush—"

Hind screams, publicly interrupting her husband. "I will eat raw the liver of Hamza!" She slaps her cheeks. Hard. "And I will keep my promise, unlike you men who promised the head of Muhammad displayed at the Kaaba. Where is it? I don't see it. I don't see my father, my brother, my uncle!"

She wavers on her feet, faints, and crumples to the floor. The assembled gasp, then fall silent at the ferocity of this woman who has lost the main figures of her family.

Her son Muawiyah drops down next to her, embraces her both to comfort her and to contain her apoplectic rage.

Sufyan reaches down to help her up.

She swats his hand away. "Coward! Coward!"

❋

Mecca begins forming an army three times larger than the one defeated at Badr. With no attempts at deception, this strategy would simply be overwhelming military power attacking him directly in Yathrib. Reaching out for warriors beyond Mecca's own, various incentives raise significant numbers, especially among numerous Bedouin tribes and settled allies like Taif.

Sufyan and Khalid supervise daily at Mecca's military training ground, focusing not only on increasing skills, but also on integrating new recruits into the Meccan system. They preach discipline, as that was one lesson learned from Badr, when thirst won out over discipline and they couldn't hold the line.

One group led by Muawiyah works with swords one-on-one. Archers practice on targets and also send long-range arcing shots flying out into the desert. The cavalry synchronizes their movements in units of a dozen. The group throwing javelins is rather competitive until the gigantic slave Washi draws all eyes as he faces a target that already has two of his javelins quivering in it. This gets Hind's attention. Washi rears back and thrusts his javelin straight up in the air. The others react at this errant "misfire"—until they look up and see a pigeon stuck with the javelin plummet to earth. Contest over. Hind can only be impressed, and a seed has been planted in her vengeful mind.

Sufyan says to the two Taif brothers beside him, "Jahl was overconfident and didn't draw on our allies. He wouldn't listen to me, as our experience with Muhammad has been never to underestimate him."

"We should never have let him escape when he came begging to us," says one Taif brother.

"I was not in the battle of Badr, nor was Khalid there. We will not make the same mistakes."

Khalid missed Badr while away on a hunting trip. He returned to a Mecca already in mourning. Twenty-four men of his tribe had been killed, and no man burns for revenge more than he. "Our allies like you have gathered now from every corner of Arabia. We will bring the world back to order."

The brothers are impressed with what they're witnessing and promise aid with food, camels, and warriors.

❀

Military preparations are not the only challenge the Meccans face in overcoming Muhammad. They also are challenged by the Prophet's diplomatic skill in negotiating various defense pacts. And then there are Mecca's traditional allies, who are obliged to defend Yathrib regardless of Muhammad if there is an invasion of the city. Sufyan calls a meeting in Mecca with the Taif leader Suhail.

"A clever move, coming to Yathrib, making us indirectly his protectors!" Salul says. "You can't invade Yathrib with our support; we're obligated by the defense pact to fight you. On the other hand, if we touch him, we set off a deadly war with the tribes hosting him and his rabble."

"So first he manages to escape to the oasis, and now he's forcing our own allies to protect him from us!" Sufyan exclaims.

"You still believe he's just a shepherd?"

"A master manipulator—he never should have gotten this far."

"The person we once knew as a shepherd now rules the desert routes like they belong to him," Suhail observes. "His raiding parties are hitting fast and retreating back to the oasis."

"No hostile force in a hundred years succeeded in invading the oasis," Salul says. "We fought united, despite our internal conflicts, against any invader. Muhammad entered as a king without a sword, as Christians, Jews, pagans, and all opposing forces came out to greet him! Magicians are not capable of doing his tricks."

"How can we fight him without the tribes of the defense pact becoming involved?" Sufyan wonders.

"The majority tribes will surely fight on his side," Salul reasons. "It's hard to predict what other tribes like the Christians will do. Muhammad's presence has undone the balance we had."

"The solution seems simple," says Suhail. "We must force him and his protectors to fight in the open, outside of the oasis."

"This would be ideal, but how?" Sufyan asks.

Salul appears confident. "There is support to fight outside to avoid destruction inside Yathrib. Leave it to me."

TWENTY-EIGHT

THE REPERCUSSIONS
OF A MURDER

In Yathrib, victory is presenting a new problem for Muhammad. He suddenly has countless individuals and entire tribes wanting to join this new force, attracted to fame and power. Few are interested in the faith, only what they can personally gain by allying themselves with this new movement. Muhammad is only too aware that having them join without understanding the essence of The Way would dilute and weaken the movement.

At the same time, life goes on, crops must be harvested, babies born, elders die, and important events in life are celebrated. One such event is the marriage of Ali and Fatima, officiated by a beaming Muhammad. Three musicians play upbeat, joyful music. The men dance with Ali while the women dance with the bride. Abundant food is served to the revelers. The Companions are not the only ones to dance—or at least to display fancy footwork. There's an informal competition of whose trained animal is the most extraordinary.

Camels and horses walk to the beat of a drummer, showing off their dance moves. For a people who've been through so many trials and hardships with the losses of so many loved ones, it's a day of joy.

But all too soon, they must turn their attention back to Mecca. The Companions are aware of the inevitable attack. There is no attempt at secrecy this time. Reports from travelers come in, confirming Mecca's mobilization and training.

"How many men do you think they can gather if they make a maximum effort?" Bakr asks Hamza.

"Three to five thousand," Hamza answers, knowing that no way can the Companions come close to matching such a number. "It depends how many Taif will contribute, how many warriors they can draw from allied tribes, and how many they can enlist with gold."

"Mecca won't invade Yathrib; they know it's a big risk," says Sa'ad. "When an outside enemy threatens our oasis, we put our differences aside. Our forefathers were involved in vicious battles and blood feuds, some of which lasted for forty years, but when an enemy came to invade the oasis, they miraculously fought united!"

"This time is different," Othman insists. "Mecca is not launching a war against Yathrib. Their war is against us, and some tribes will not want to be involved."

"What about the Jews?" questions Omar. "They seem to be the most feared and effective warriors in the oasis."

"They're divided, with long years of animosity and hatred," explains Sa'ad. "They fought among themselves, they fought with us one year and against us the next. A hundred years of warring since we all arrived from Yemen. They are unpredictable—today, friends; tomorrow, enemies. But they

can't betray us, for everyone knows the punishment for treason is public execution. They might demand we fight outside
the oasis, especially if Mecca declares its war only against the
Prophet. In this case, we might have to fight them outside."

On that note, the meeting breaks up.

Salman goes to talk privately to the Prophet, not wanting
to alarm the others. "It will be a losing battle with all the odds
against us. Many will be killed, and their goal, as it always has
been, is to kill you."

"I won't be the first prophet to be killed at the hands of his
own people."

"Given that we're extremely outnumbered, our only chance
at survival is to fight them inside the oasis. We'll use the rooftops and the hills, we'll plant traps all over, and we'll use
fire. Back in Persia, I saw this tactic being very effective, and
the invader withdrew with heavy losses despite having overwhelming numbers. They were never able to directly engage
the defenders in a straight battle between two armies."

Muhammad mulls this over. "You speak from direct experience, brother Salman, but my concern is that this strategy
could unify the other tribes against the Awes and the Khazraj.
We would not be a united city fighting the invader; we would
be fighting Meccans and other Yathrib tribes combined. Those
tribes know the terrain well, so the internal enemy would
know where we placed our forces, where we laid our traps.
A greater evil. I pray the Meccans will think twice about the
folly of war, but knowing them, revenge and hatred cloud their
vision. I suppose we will have to fight, always with the spirit of
victory even when outnumbered, even facing defeat."

There are very real obstacles in the way of Muhammad's dream of Arabic unity and peace. Home to many ethnic tribes, Jews, Christians, pagans, divided and subdivided, the political reality of Yathrib is fragile. The conflict for the magical oasis is as old as the volcano itself, and any misunderstanding could spark a wildfire.

The Jewish Banu Qaynuqa'a tribe claims to have the purest Jewish blood compared to the other Yathrib Jewish tribes who migrated from Yemen. More importantly, they are the most experienced and feared on the battlefield—and the wealthiest. One morning, an attractive Awes widow goes to the Banu Qaynuqa'a market to sell her goods. Two Jewish men approach her to seduce her. She rejects them, but as she hurries to leave, they pursue her and aggressively harass her. One of the young men grabs her dress to stop her and pulls it off, exposing her body right there in the middle of the busy marketplace. Instead of being ashamed, her abusers find this entertaining. A fellow Awes rushes to cover the naked widow, but the two Jews grab him. They fight, and the Awes gets the better of them until the Jews, angry that their moment has been spoiled, take it to another level and stab the rescuer, killing him.

This incident sparks outrage across the oasis, opening past wounds. Most tribal leaders call for the traditional punishment for the murderers—public execution. The leaders consult with Muhammad as their spiritual guide for permission to carry out their desired punishment.

The Prophet by now is more aware of the inner conflicts in this little paradise, and he doesn't want this incident to trigger another tribal war, which could sabotage his unifying efforts and leave them more vulnerable to Mecca. So, he suggests a lesser punishment: blood money to be paid to take care of the man's children and widow. The majority tribe leaders don't like the Prophet's compromising suggestion but agree to it out of respect.

A delegation of majority tribes goes to Banu Qaynuqa'a fortress to bring their demand of blood money as a peaceful solution before the Jewish council. Their leader, Azora, arrogantly refuses. In the past, when disputes like this came up, the antagonists were conditioned to resolve them not by negotiation, but by the sword—the option that made Azora supremely confident. Why should he submit to these inferior tribes, which the Banu Qaynuqa'a have always dominated?

In response, the rebuffed tribal leaders demand blood for blood.

If the crisis is not contained immediately, an ancient war could be reignited, tearing Yathrib apart. Muhammad decides to go to the Jewish fortress to convince them to pay the blood money and thus save Yathrib from more senseless bloodshed. Ali, Bakr, Omar, Zayd, and Othman go with him.

After a considerable wait outside, the heavy entry door opens and the delegation faces the overbearing Azora, flanked by armed guards, two of which, unknown to the visitors, are the killers responsible for the crisis.

Rather than invite them further into the fortress, Azora directs a question straight to the Prophet: "What brings you here, Muhammad?"

"Your men made a mistake, we all agree on that, but I fear you are making a bigger one by refusing a peaceful solution."

"Was it your idea to make us pay blood money?"

"Yes."

"And who appointed you a judge?"

"The tribal leaders, seeking the harshest punishment, came to consult me, and I suggested the minimum punishment instead in order to break the cycle of useless carnage."

"You have no authority or say in this."

"Then who does?"

"No one! Especially not a self-proclaimed prophet, a self-appointed judge, a bandit who is outlawed by his own people—a traitor to the city that made him."

"No need to be disrespectful!" Ali says sternly. "The Prophet is extending his hand to help you out of this situation; he is not taking sides!"

"You say the Prophet!" Azora says. "The Prophet? By what authority?"

"By the authority of the Seven Heavens!" responds Ali.

"You know what the Scripture says of false prophets?" says Azora. "'From their fruits you know them!' They come to kill, corrupt and steal . . . What you did in Mecca, Badr, and now in Yathrib is the witness."

"You haven't seen the fruit yet; you see only the seed," says Muhammad calmly. "The seed must die in order for life to burst forth. This tree will grow and thrive beyond this temporary existence."

"Descendants of Ishmael, like you, can't be prophets!" Azora insists. "Kings and prophets are descendants of Isaac, son of Sarah, the true heir of the lineage! But you are ignorant of the true events, aren't you? Confusing Ishmael with Isaac. The Scripture tells us Abraham chose his favorite son, Isaac, to sacrifice at the altar—not Ishmael, as you mistakenly teach your disciples."

"Is that true?" Muhammad questions. "Abraham had to abandon his son Ishmael in the desert because of Sarah's jealousy. She wanted her son Isaac to inherent the throne! In this case, which son was actually sacrificed? And who is really confused? Hagar, the mother of Ishmael, was an Egyptian princess by origin, not a slave, while Sarah was only an ordinary woman. Was it her fault that Abraham chose her over Sarah? Or was it Ishmael's fault that he was born? He is the one who was sacrificed because of Abraham's shame. And who are you to prevent God from revealing himself, even to a descendant of a slave woman? Your righteousness and pride is an offense against him!"

"The truth lies in Holy Scripture, for only from Scripture can we know what is true and what is false," says Azora. "In a silver trunk here in our sanctuary, we guard Scripture. This, of course, means nothing to you, as you can't read!"

"By God, we didn't come here to be insulted!" interjects Ali. "If you can't restrain your tongue, my sword will cut it out, and you will never again speak!"

Bakr grasps Ali's shoulder to calm him down. Omar grips the handle of his sword, as the armed Jewish warriors behind Azora take a menacing step forward.

"Don't think your sword can scare us, Ali," says Azora. "Your victory at Badr was against tribesmen who didn't know how to fight! We are not Meccans born as merchants; we are Meccans born as warriors! In the day of reckoning, everyone shall know that we are the true men!"

Muhammad addresses him. "Enough said. You've made your choice. I leave you and your 'true men' to the judgment of 'lowly' tribesmen and the law of the desert." He leads his companions out of the fortress without looking back.

✳

While Muhammad's peaceful mission was being turned down, the leaders of the majority tribes lead warriors to the Jewish market to kill the offenders. When they are unable to find them, the leaders shut down the market. Mobilizing a large force, the tribesmen surround the fortress and demand the two killers be surrendered to them.

Derisively refused, the tribesmen settle in for a long siege, preventing Jews from entering or leaving the fortress and blocking any water or food from getting through.

From behind the high walls of the fortress, Jewish archers shoot and kill three Awes tribesmen. The sieging forces move out of range and, as days pass, they make two new demands: either they come out to fight, or they get out of Yathrib.

When the fortress runs out of food and water, the only honorable option is to come out and fight. The fortress can mobilize seven hundred warriors, but there will be no victory in such a confrontation. The new reality is that the unity of the tribes allied to Muhammad makes them the strongest force in both the oasis and the surrounding area.

Salul, a great friend and ally of Ben Azora and the Jews of Banu Qaynuqa'a, offers to mediate with Azora to convince him to surrender. The majority tribe leaders permit him to pass through the siege lines to reach the main gate. When he reaches the main gate, he calls out, "Azora!" Despite more calls, there is no response.

After nearly an hour, just when Salul is ready to give up, Jewish guards appear to let him in through a smaller door in the main gate. Inside the fortress, the well-fed Salul passes women and children slumped down in the listless lethargy of starvation. He follows the guards into the synagogue, where Azora sits on pillows next to the open silver trunk as he reads Scripture.

Salul, seeing how poorly his friend looks, gets straight to the point. "The situation is not in your favor, noble friend. Old and new enemies have gathered against you. It doesn't look good out there. If you fight, you will lose. If you surrender, they will behead you and every last one of your men."

"What choice is that? Of course I prefer to die fighting."

Salul studies his weakened friend. "Can you even lift a sword?" Salul takes out a piece of bread from under his gown, but Azora holds up his hand to refuse it and indicates it be given to the bodyguards.

"What if I convince the majority leaders to give you safe passage to leave Yathrib?" Salul asks.

"Hell no! I would prefer to be beheaded. Yathrib is my home, and no one can force me out of it!"

"You are outnumbered this time; their men are thirsty for your men's blood. They have been feasting, and you, along with your warriors, women, and children, have been starving. Why fight a losing battle?"

Azora can only shrug his shoulders. His end is near? So be it—his pride is much greater than his fear of death!

"Azora! Listen to an old friend—you will not have this opportunity again. Take your men and go to your cousins at Khaybar Fortress. Prepare, build an army, then come back to claim not only your fortress but the entire oasis!"

Salul's words paint an irresistible picture. Azora sees himself at the head of a mighty army, returning to rule over his birthright. Yes, a humiliation in the moment, but a much greater reward in the future.

"With your gold and silver, you can gather an army along with those here now who want revenge," adds Salul. "I will be waiting for your return, my friend!"

"What makes you sure they will agree to give us safe passage and not betray us?"

"Muhammad!"

"Damn Muhammad!"

"He will definitely be in favor of this suggestion against the majority tribes demands—and they listen to him."

Azora agrees to give this idea a chance, but he must convince his council. The young want to fight, which is suicidal, while the elders see the wisdom in migrating to their cousins at the magnificent Jewish fortress of Khaybar, seven days from Yathrib.

Salul, always the cunning manipulator, knows the tribal leaders won't listen to him, so he goes directly to Muhammad. The Prophet agrees with Salul's plan and encourages the majority tribe leaders to give Banu Qaynuqa'a safe passage out of Yathrib.

Hundreds of warriors, elders, children, and women carry their belongings north, leaving their fortress behind. Azora leads the column, and behind him two bodyguards carry the silver trunk. Thousands of Yathrib residents and fighters watch. None could ever have anticipated such a powerful tribe leaving in humiliation like this.

Under the terms of the capitulation, the impressive military equipment of the Banu Qaynuqa'a is confiscated and added to Muhammad's armory, along with the captured weapons from Badr. Their departure also means more land and housing for incoming migrants.

Like any balance of power shift that creates winners and losers, the losers plot revenge. And they attribute the chain of events to one man—the Prophet.

TWENTY-NINE

THE MECCAN
ARMY DEPARTS

As the sun rises over Mecca, Sufyan and Khalid, riding on horseback, lead the largest force Mecca has ever assembled to battle. Flags waving, drums beating, the populace lines the road, cheering them on. Two thousand foot soldiers and four hundred cavalry made up of Meccans, Taifans, and Bedouin allies, along with fifteen hundred camels and five hundred horses, march past. This time, elite assassins have been enlisted, motivated by the promise of ten Byzantine gold solidus coins to the hero who kills the Prophet. They are led by Waqqas, a well-known Meccan warrior who lost his brother and two cousins at Badr and is therefore highly motivated by revenge, not just the gold. Rewards are also promised for any who kill Muhammad's prominent Companions—men like Omar, Ali, Hamza, and Bakr. Badr widows and other women have come in support, most noteworthy the vengeful Hind, who is riding in a canopied howdah on a camel with her slave,

Washi, striding alongside her, his lethal javelin propped over his shoulder.

Sufyan and Khalid stop at the north gate, waiting for two hours before the last warrior clears the holy city to begin the twelve-day desert trek. The two leaders then gallop along the column, waving to their shouting troops as they retake their position at the head of the marching army. Defeat is not an option for the Meccans; this is an army that is well equipped, totally prepared, and, this time, well led. Victory in this battle can repair not only their broken pride but their standing as the premier power in South Arabia.

✻

News that thousands of Meccan warriors are on the march travels faster than such a large army can move. Two scouts are sent out to determine how many days the enemy is from Yathrib, while Muhammad calls an emergency war council at the mosque.

Muhammad's authority is more spiritual than political, and he believes in the shura, a group meeting with differing participants whose goal is to reach a consensus decision. He invites not only his closest Companions, but also Salul, Ka'ab, various tribal leaders, many young fighters, and others potentially affected by an invasion, such as farmers who have crops and livestock outside Yathrib. The issue is whether to fight inside Yathrib utilizing the tactics of urban warfare or to engage the enemy outside of Yathrib, like they did at Badr.

Salman favors fighting inside, which he believes is the best choice against overwhelming numbers. Others object.

Agitated chatter quiets as Bakr is finally given the floor. "The reality is that we are extremely outnumbered," he begins.

"If we fight them in the open, we will be annihilated. Our only chance to survive is to use the oasis as a base and to fight in the mountains, where we have the advantage in our knowledge of the terrain."

"And if fighting inside Yathrib would lead to your defeat?" questions Salul. "Who will stop Mecca from selling every last person to slavery? You?"

A tribal leader speaks up. "We were outnumbered at Badr, and we won on the open battlefield. God willing we will do the same this time!"

Sa'ad voices his opinion. "Yathrib has never been conquered, as despite all our differences, we always unite to fight an invader."

"I wouldn't be so sure this time," Ka'ab warns. "There are many who favor Mecca and are angry with the loss of business from the Meccan caravan trade that no longer comes." This, of course, is a direct dig at Muhammad and how his presence has upset the Yathrib status quo.

"I will fight with you but not at the oasis," vows Salul. "I, my sons, and two hundred men—we are all at the command of Muhammad!"

Salul's son, Abdullah, looks askance at his father, who before always advocated a defense based on barricading themselves in their fortresses.

A farmer speaks up. "Inside or outside, we have to bring in our crops and animals immediately. Each time invaders have waited outside, they have lived off our food, leaving us with nothing. We favor confronting outside." Given the urgency, the farmer stands up and leads his fellows out of the meeting to get on with bringing in the crops.

The most enthusiasm for fighting outside the city comes from the young Companion warriors. Some missed out on

Badr and the glory of that victory. One tall, muscular young man stands up and states the thinking of his cohort. "Either we gain glory in victory or martyrdom in defeat, earning a place in Paradise. I welcome both outcomes as we go outside and, like men, meet the enemy in the open field of battle."

The young cheer their approval. They constitute the bulk of Muhammad's army and, given Mecca's numbers, he depends on them.

Then Ka'ab speaks. "We are obligated by the defense pact to defend Yathrib, so we will fight as well. But not at the oasis." This is unexpected. The treaty with the Jews, skillfully negotiated by Muhammad, was that they would fight alongside the majority tribes. Their forces are crucial for the already badly outnumbered Companion fighters.

The enthusiasm of the young and the position of Salul and Ka'ab carry the day to fight outside Yathrib proper. But Muhammad, who favored Salman's advice to fight in Yathrib itself, comes up with a compromise of sorts. They will go to Mount Uhud just outside the northern entry to Yathrib and adopt a defensive posture on the high slopes with its rocky ground. Uhud is the highest mountain above the oasis and partly blocks the south entry to the oasis.

The meeting breaks up as the leaders depart to prepare for the imminent battle. Warriors work on their equipment, sharpen their swords, test their bowstrings, assure the straightness of their arrows. Each is aware that careful preparation could mean the difference for their own survival and the army's success.

Salman and Hamza stay behind to talk to the Prophet.

"We all know the Meccans have one goal in mind," says Salman, "and that's to kill you, to destroy the movement. I suggest you stay here at a safe location so all their efforts will come to nothing."

Hamza, who has been eager for battle, inside or outside, adds his voice. "This is a wise suggestion. What does the Prophet say?"

"If it is written for my companions to die facing evil, then I prefer to die with them," Muhammad responds. "But since when is cowardice considered wisdom?"

"But—" Salman begins to object.

The Prophet interrupts him with a hand gesture. Enough said. So be it. The dice have been thrown.

By midmorning the next day, the Companion force has been assembled, ready to march. Muhammad, dressed in full battle armor—helmet and chain mail, a shield across his back, his sword at his side and a bow on his shoulder—mounts his favorite stallion and leads the army of a thousand out toward the northern entrance to the oasis. By late afternoon, they've gone past the border of the oasis, with Mount Uhud looming some four miles ahead. There is no sign of the enemy. Muhammad decides to order camp, with a plan to sleep well and part at dawn in order to best establish their strategic position on Mount Uhud.

A scout returns to report that a vast Meccan army is camped only a few miles from the base of Mount Uhud. Upon hearing this, Muhammad calls a meeting with the leaders.

"They're waiting for us," warns Salman. "The battle will be tomorrow. We must move quickly to take the high ground on Mount Uhud."

"We will move out before dawn," says Muhammad. "Alert your men to be ready."

❋

The Companion camp rouses two hours before dawn. Salman has informed the Prophet of the bad, but not unexpected, news. By the time all are gathered to march out, everyone knows of the Banu Qurayzah betrayal, the first stab in the back on this fateful day.

At dawn, the Companion force and Salul's warriors arrive at the base of Mount Uhud. The mount is conical-shaped, pockmarked with caves, its slopes steep and its rock formations creating narrow passages, which allow for only a few attackers to pass through at once. It is, in fact, an ideal defensive position. The classic ratio when defenders are well dug in is three attackers to one defender.

Salman and Hamza quickly place their troops. The main force of foot soldiers occupies the first line of defense, taking advantage of the rocky terrain above the flat terrain at the base of Uhud. Salul's two hundred men occupy the left flank. Hamza is in charge of the center and right flank, placing Ka'ab's forces there. Above them are the archers, and above the archers is Muhammad.

Salman, the tactician, explains the plan. "The archers on higher ground, using rocks as shields, will protect the rear and the front, regulating the pace of the battle. When the attack intensifies, the archers' duty is to hit harder to break the wave of the offense, to slow them down or even force them to retreat—back and forth until they're exhausted. Their cavalry, the advantage they count on in open battle, will be useless on this steep, rocky slope. Given the terrain, we will be fighting a reasonable number at a time, taking away their numeric advantage. The archers have the heaviest responsibility, keeping the enemy at bay while the infantry fight with swords to prevent the enemy's foot soldiers from climbing up the mountain. If things get difficult and we lose many men, we retreat higher—the higher we go, the harder it will be for the enemy to reach their main target, the Prophet."

Hamza addresses the leader in charge of the archers. "Archers must not leave their posts for any reason, even if they see the main force being killed one by one. This will be a great test of discipline, yet with patience this monster will tire."

Muhammad climbs up the mountain with Omar, Ali, Bakr, Mosaab, and some twenty Companions charged with defending him. Others also follow, taking positions below like Muhairiq. They find a point high up that offers a panoramic view of the scene below, as well as being safely out of range of any Meccan archers. Before Muhammad, out of breath from the climb with his heavy armor, can find a boulder to sit on, the sound of distant drums echoes off the mountainside.

The first Meccans to come into view are three horsemen: Sufyan with Khalid on his right, and the son of Jahl on his left. Behind them come a wave of black-clad warriors marching to the cadence of the drums being beaten by the women behind them. They shout, "Amit! Amit! Kill! Kill!" The women chant the millennial message to their warrior men: "Fight bravely, and you'll have a place in my bed; flee, and there will be no love for you." Behind them, over the brow of the hill, the cavalry waits.

Sufyan raises his arm to halt the march as he and Khalid survey the situation. It's quickly evident the enemy forces are in a near-impregnable natural fortress.

Sufyan curses. "That wily bastard—someone has to be helping him! I don't believe the shepherd is capable of this."

"His name is Salman," says Khalid. "He's a veteran Persian warrior who was enslaved during a war and sold at Yathrib. Muhammad freed him. He's clever, with long experience."

"How do you see the situation?"

"The higher ground allows them to control the pace of the fight; also, their position allows only a part of our army to fight at once, which is a number they can handle. It looks very rocky and steep, and with our troops jammed in those narrow passages as they climb, the archers positioned safely above can make it a death trap. We risk big losses. I have to say, they chose the best possible location."

"This is unbelievable! We are five times their size, and you are telling me we can't even get to them?"

The two leaders look at each other. With thousands waiting behind them, a decision must be made quickly.

"How do we get the snake out of his hole?" asks Sufyan. "Do we wait them out? Starve them out? Invade Yathrib?" These options are rejected before the words are even out of his mouth. "We still have the plan agreed on in Mecca, as long as we can trust the rascal." Sufyan spurs his horse and the three leaders gallop dramatically toward the base of the mountain, reining up in a swirl of black volcanic dust.

Muhammad's group, positioned high up the mountain, thinks he has come to propose an opening battle of champions, like what happened at Badr. But Sufyan shouts, his strong voice echoing off the mountainside, "Awes and Khazraj! We have no quarrel with you. This is not your battle. This is a battle with Quraysh—only Quraysh!"

The young warriors shout loud insults in return. "Go back to Mecca!" "We're with the Prophet!" However, the left flank of the defensive line, led by Salul, rises up, abandoning their positions and coming down to the flat ground.

Abdullah intercepts his father. "You coward! I will kill you when this is over!"

"This is not our fight," laments Salul. "It's crazy—there's no chance against such a force!"

Some thirty warriors remain with Abdullah, but one hundred and seventy head back to Yathrib.

Sufyan and Khalid gallop back to their waiting line of infantry. With this sudden depletion in the defenders' ranks, they give the order for a frontal attack, directing more to the weakened left flank.

Hamza and Salman hurriedly move warriors from the right and center flanks to thinly cover the left flank.

With battle cries and swords waving, the black-clad warriors charge to the base of the mountain. The Companion archers on the hillside let loose a rain of arrows, but the Meccans have learned their lesson and the shields go up, protecting them. Once the first line of attackers starts up the hill, the archers can't shoot anymore, as they risk hitting their own men who are engaged in hand-to-hand combat with the attackers. Even though the Meccans make some progress up the weak left side, the defenders have the advantage, holding the high ground and blocking the narrow passageways, raining stones down on the climbing enemy. Little blood is shed on either side.

The order is passed down the Meccan line to withdraw. This first attack is a probe, designed to feel out the enemy's response and spot any potential weakness. The regrouped Meccans come again under a volley of arrows bouncing off their shields. The majority of the two thousand infantry and the women stay outside the archers' range.

Sufyan now orders a full-on assault, and the Meccan warriors charge forward crying, "Kill! Kill!" The battle breaks down into one-on-one swordfights, with the Meccans using their long lances effectively. Making progress up the hill in certain areas, one unit makes it close to the archers, who fire arrows at them at close range. But the Companions, in a sudden surge, drive the attackers back. On Hamza's right flank, they drive them all the way back onto the flat. A few of the young warriors leave their posts and go down to the flat to fight the enemy. But heavily outnumbered and shouted at by Hamza, they scurry back up to their posts.

Sufyan and Khalid must decide their next move.

"We're just banging our heads against a wall," Sufyan laments.

"I have an idea," says Khalid.

"Yes?"

"The challenge is to get them to come down to fight us on the flat."

"How do we do that?"

"You saw how some came down to fight."

"And then they went right back up."

"We attack again—but we choose to do it badly," Khalid explains. "Our defeated soldiers come down and many run away, leaving their equipment behind. The enemy, sensing victory, will come down and chase them."

"And what if they don't come down and chase us as we retreat?" Sufyan is skeptical of this plan.

"Then we're back where we were, with nothing really lost."

"What makes you think it can work?"

"I know human beings," says Khalid confidently.

Sufyan and Khalid explain the plan to their lieutenants, who then have to convincingly explain it to their units.

The Meccans launch their third attack, and after initial progress following the plan, they are beaten back. Once on the flat, many start to run away, shedding their equipment. A wave of triumph surges through the defenders' ranks. Khalid appears on horseback, as though to stop his fleeing Meccans. He is not far from Hamza, and for a moment they make eye contact. For Hamza, this is unfinished business! Khalid knows he is the bait playing to Hamza's weakness.

Hamza rushes down from his position onto the flat, where he begins cutting his way through to Khalid. Seeing their leader leap into the fray, hundreds of defenders pour down from the mountainside, believing victory is at hand as they engage the enemy. Finally, Hamza and his blood-soaked sword close in on Khalid. The challenge is there: *Get down from your horse, and we have it out one-on-one and resolve our unfinished business. This is a war, and there is no Muhammad to save your life this time.* But to Hamza's surprise, Khalid wheels his mount around and joins the many who are retreating. Cowardice from Khalid? Hamza, still in the midst of the confused battle, goes back to work.

The Companion archers are useless, as they cannot fire into the chaos without hitting their own men. They watch the battle unfolding below, with many Meccans in retreat, some even dropping their weapons. Not wanting to miss out, the archers rush down to join the battle, supporting their brothers in victory and picking up the booty, despite clear orders not to abandon their posts. The Companion in charge can only stop some of the archers.

Khalid joins Sufyan as they watch the chaos of the battle scene below with satisfaction.

Their plan is working! They order the "fleeing" warriors to regroup. Khalid rides off to head the cavalry, which is useless against the steep mountainside defense but highly effective on the flats. He waits for the signal to close the trap. The now undefended gaps on the "fortress" of Mount Uhud leaves open the number one goal of the whole expedition: killing Muhammad. Sufyan orders the team of assassins to climb up the mountain, corner the Prophet, and do their job.

Muhammad stands motionless like the mountain beneath him. He can see as clearly as the noonday sun the developing trap that has been set by the Meccans. He and Salman watch helplessly as Meccan infantry regroups and the cavalry readies.

Muhammad grasps his sword.

On the field of battle, the "fog of war" is made even more confusing as black volcanic dust fills the air from all the movement. The Companions continue to fight the few Meccans who are still engaged in battle, unaware of what awaits them. No one is happier to be in the fray than Hamza, the born warrior. Like an angel of death, he stands out with ostrich feathers on his helmet, moving quickly amidst the clanging of steel and the grunts of the combatants.

He is not aware that he is being relentlessly stalked. Hamza is a fast-moving target, but Washi does not miss, whether it's a lion in Abyssinia or a lion on the Arabian battlefield. He rears back and lets loose, sending forth his shot for freedom. The javelin strikes his victim full in the chest, the sharp point protruding out his back. Hamza falls backwards, the point of the javelin nailing him to the ground. Washi dashes up to the body, jams his foot on the dying Hamza. Some surrounding companions see Hamza go down, prompting Washi, now a free man, to quickly flee the scene with his bloodied javelin. The fighters are too paralyzed with disbelief to chase him.

The news quickly travels the battlefield. "Hamza's dead!" "Hamza's been killed!"

Muhammad watches this drama play out and sees his beloved uncle lying on the battleground, impaled with a spear.

He weighs his sword in his left hand. Now he has no other option but to fight.

Sufyan gives the order to close the two jaws of the trap. The regrouped foot soldiers sweep in as the cavalry charge in from the south. The massacre has begun! The demoralized Companions stand no chance, especially against Khalid's cavalry. A few panicked Companions manage to escape the trap amidst the confusion, fleeing back to Yathrib. A total Meccan victory lacks only the head of Muhammad on a pike.

While many of the Meccan women gather up swords, daggers, chain mail, helmets, bridles, saddles, and anything of value, Hind moves amidst the battlefield. Enemies with raised swords, realizing she is a woman, do not strike her. She spots Washi jogging away from the field of battle, his javelin bloodied. Excitedly, she moves from corpse to corpse until she finally stands over her ex-lover. She screeches such a cry of victory that the battle freezes for a moment. Those who survive will still shiver years later at the memory of it. Exulting, Hind stands astride Hamza and, gripping her knife in both hands, drives it deep into his javelin wound, tearing open his chest to reveal his organs. She slices out the largest, the liver, and thrusts it above her head. All watch as she crams the liver into her mouth, chewing victoriously. She is a woman of her word, fulfilling her vow. Blood pours down her chin and chest. She spits out morsels, stamps on them, and grinds them into the dirt.

The women gather around her, and she encourages them to do the same. They go about mutilating the fallen enemy and accessorizing themselves with body parts as if it were some sort of hideous fashion show. The Bedouin allies express disgust, as they believe this behavior dishonors their cause just at the moment of victory.

At the same time, dozens of Meccan foot soldiers move through the gaps left by Hamza and his men. They confront the second defense line of outmatched archers and, in deadly combat, a few manage to break through. Among them, the group of assassins led by Waqqas moves up the mountain, step by sword blow. Word moves through the Meccan ranks that there is a gold reward for the lucky man who kills Muhammad, not to mention eternal glory. Upon hearing this, some from the victorious field of battle head up the mountain for their chance at this lofty prize.

Companions who are not with Muhammad see the threatening situation developing and spring into action. Nothing else matters as they battle their way up the mountain to defend the Prophet.

Muhammad, surrounded by his closest Companions, stands unshaken. He sees the assassins climbing up toward him and holds his ground with an even gaze, his sword ready, as the wave of revenge, hate, and bloodlust grows ever closer. It is not easy to demonstrate surrender in all circumstances. As many are busy defending themselves, few are able to watch the Prophet's reaction in the face of death. His expression is unchanging; he's neither running backwards nor running forward.

Before the first assassin can reach within a sword's length of the Prophet, two arrows from Meccan archers some distance away hit Muhammad, one in the shoulder and one in the thigh. Rising above the pain, the Prophet maintains his tall posture. He may not be an aggressive and violent warrior, but his power over his senses, his ability to transcend both pleasure and pain, can defy even the most violent warriors. Muhammad no doubt has conquered death, even before his

God called him to do his work. The Prophet is certain that physical death is not the end.

The two forces clash. One assassin launches his spear straight at Muhammad, but Mosaab steps in, taking the spear in his chest, sacrificing his life for the Prophet. The Companions are in the battle of their lives, fighting against Mecca's top veteran warriors. Waqqas and another assassin close in on the Prophet as Ali and Omar fend off others. Muhammad blocks their sword blows with his own sword, but as he fights, a third assassin lands a heavy blow to his sword arm.

Muhammad confronts Waqqas as they make eye contact. There is nothing to say. Waqqas raises his heavy sword above his head and hits the Prophet with all his might. The Prophet blocks the blow despite his injuries, his body bending under the might of the blow. Waqqas hits him again, stronger this time. Again, the Prophet blocks, but is growing weaker. The third blow, to the side of his head, cannot be blocked by the weakened Prophet. This mighty blow is the fatal one, driving a ring of his helmet into his temple. Waqqas knows he has scored a fatal hit as blood gushes from the crack in the Prophet's helmet. On behalf of thousands, on behalf of Mecca, and on behalf of all the gods, Muhammad is finished.

The Prophet pitches forward. Only the shaft of the arrow sticking out of his shoulder keeps him from falling into Waqqas's surprised arms. The victor, covered in blood, pushes the body of the Prophet away, and Muhammad falls down on his back.

For a moment, all action stops as those present watch in stunned disbelief.

A cry sounds out. "Muhammad is dead!"

Waqqas steps back, his job more than finished.

The Companions, led by Omar and Salman, quickly form a defensive circle around the body of the Prophet. Facing the forming defense line, the Meccan attackers back off, having no desire to die now that the job has been done.

Omar cries out in his deep, authoritative voice, "Muhammad, the Prophet, is dead!" His cry travels as far as the human voice carries, only to be repeated over and over by anyone within hearing range. The words are triumphant to some ears, devastating to others.

Sufyan and Khalid raise their arms in triumph at the news.

"May Hubal be praised! The false Prophet is dead!" exclaims Sufyan. He is then distracted by the gruesome sight of his wife approaching him with a bloody smile. Hamza's body parts festoon her. Sufyan expresses his disgust. "Why Hamza? He was a noble warrior. What more explains your unhinged revenge, woman? He did not deserve this. You called me a coward, and now Muhammad and your Hamza are dead."

With this, Sufyan decides it is time to take another wife. It will only enhance his status, so risen he has become with this victory and the death, finally, of his nemesis.

Waqqas careens down the mountainside, nearly flying to claim his golden reward. Breathless, he stands before Sufyan and Khalid, his bloodied shirt telling his story more than any words ever could. Khalid looks to his fellow assassin, whose wounded arm confirms that the blood is indeed Muhammad's. He was a witness to the mightiest blow ever struck that will live as a legend forever. Sufyan just barely resists the temptation to touch the blood. By her expression, he knows his wife wants to rub her face in it.

Khalid turns to Sufyan to consult about what they should do next. Their troops are either scavenging the battlefield or returning to their base camp thirsty and hungry. In any case, they seem to have no interest in pursuing enemy survivors back to Yathrib.

"We could hunt and kill those Companions still alive," Khalid suggests.

Sufyan shakes his head in disagreement. "They're nothing without him. I'd call a day of ridding ourselves of both Muhammad and Hamza the best of all days."

❧

Above, inside the defensive circle, Bakr has dropped to his knees crying, "O Al-lah! O Al-lah!"

He removes the Prophet's helmet, causing more bleeding and . . . *pain?* The Prophet stirs, his consciousness having returned. Bakr cannot believe this. The Prophet is alive!

THIRTY

THE CONSEQUENCES
OF DEFEAT

Bakr and the companions cry now out of joy, not sadness. Bakr takes his scarf, folds it, and covers the Prophet's head wound, then places the helmet back on his head to stop the bleeding. He examines the two arrows, one in Muhammad's shoulder, the other in his thigh. The wounds are not fatal, but the arrows must be removed. The only way to do this is by pushing each arrow farther into the wound until its head has appeared. Then the arrow's shaft can be cut and the remaining part pulled out from the other end. A very painful process. Bakr calls to Sa'ad, the most experienced Companion, to operate on the Prophet. Sa'ad, with the help of Ali, manages to pull the two arrows out as the Prophet drifts in and out of consciousness.

As soon as the wounds are cleaned and bound and Muhammad regains consciousness, he insists on going to the battlefield. By now, the Meccans have departed, leaving the battlefield strewn with mutilated corpses. The reaction of the survivors to the horror ranges from retching to disbelief. They stop next to the body of Muhariiq, his Jewish friend and defender who has given his life. They make it to the flat and come across the barely recognizable body of his uncle Hamza. A flood of conflicting thoughts rushes through the Prophet's concussed brain. How many uncles he has lost on this journey! As a man of peace, he did not want this battle, but he knew they had to act in self-defense. That knowledge offers no solace. He scans the carnage of those who made the choice, in their case fatal, to follow him. If he had never come to Yathrib, they would all still be alive. And still this war is not over. It has only ended for the dead.

❋

The Meccans break camp early to start their triumphant return home. Sufyan makes sure to send scouts ahead to bring the news to Mecca and prepare a massive welcome celebrating the victory and the savior of Mecca, Sufyan.

The Companions, assured that the Meccans are heading home and that they will not be under attack, begin their sorrowful task of burying the dead and tending to the wounded. By the second day, Muhammad is more coherent and steadier on his feet, though when his Companions urge him to rest, he does consent to sit down. He consoles the widows who come to him, assuring them that Paradise welcomes the fallen, and he makes sure that camels, along with his own horse, are available to transport the wounded back for care in Yathrib.

The first arrivals back at the oasis brought the news not only of the defeat, but the death of Muhammad. The rumor spread quickly, bringing joy to those who had betrayed the Prophet and shock to his followers. When others arrive, reporting that

---

Muhammad was wounded but is still alive, some of the skeptical point to his horse as proof that the Prophet is dead.

For three days, most of the survivors and the women labor to clear the battlefield and dig graves. Sa'ad walks in silence with the Prophet, for what is there to say? Both men are deep in a profound sadness that is beyond words. Sa'ad had done what he could to stop his tribesmen, the bulk of the army, from rushing onto the battlefield. As they pass the dead, Sa'ad recognizes every one of them, close tribal and family relations. This is a world accustomed to war and violent death, made up of people who know that if a family member is off on a journey, they may never come back, and the family likely will never know what fate befell them. But this? Sa'ad has never experienced such catastrophic loss. Even with the evidence before his eyes, it is difficult to believe.

Muhammad chooses a spot that has a view of the desert road heading in the direction of Mecca to bury his beloved uncle as well as Mosaab. As Hamza's body is laid in the fresh grave, Muhammad has Omar place Hamza's helmet with its ostrich feathers on the warrior's ravished chest. The tears of all those present stand in for words.

On the morning of the fourth day, those who had stayed with the Prophet begin the long walk back. Muhammad, agreeing to ride a camel with Omar, does not know what awaits him in Yathrib. There will be no cheering crowds like after Badr. Victory has a thousand fathers; defeat is an orphan. And this was a resounding defeat. The plan was solid, but Khalid's bet on human greed won the day. He knows that the survivors feel terrible shame, as they had been in the maelstrom of the slaughter of their companions. Those who deserted their posts could be a major challenge to Muhammad's leadership.

That test comes just before the survivors reach the southern entry to Yathrib. A lone camel approaches, with a rider
and a body slung over the camel's back. The rider, Abdullah,
reins up in front of the Prophet. He kicks the body, which falls
hard to the ground. It's his father, Salul, his hands and legs
tightly bound. Abdullah slides to the ground and draws his
sword, the blade of which is still dark red with dried blood.
His first words come out with unchecked anger. "I swore I
would behead this coward! May you all witness justice!"

Differing emotions flow through those who have just buried their companions. Some feel he deserves it. Those who
deserted their posts feel the sword blade on their necks. Many
are shocked to witness a son treating his own father this way.
All look to Muhammad.

"Untie him." It's an order from the Prophet.

Abdullah struggles to untie the knots. Ali steps forward,
and with his dagger quickly slices the constraints. Sulal, as
unsure as everyone else about what will happen next, looks up
from the ground at the man who can decide his fate.

"Go," Muhammad commands.

Unsure of what that means, Sulal sits up.

"Get up—go," repeats the Prophet.

This produces a certain relief among those present, for
Muhammad is opting for mercy.

The patricidal son, who has worked himself up into a
vengeful frenzy—partly because this coward was his father,
with whom he must share the shame—looks confused.

Salul gets up, moves tentatively back toward the oasis, then
breaks into a run, scurrying back to Yathrib.

As Muhammad, his wounded head held high, leads the
survivors past silent residents lining their path, those who
despaired over his death now feel hope. Those traitors who

were elated at news of his demise are now wary. With Muhammad dead, Sulal saw himself becoming king, and the Jews saw themselves restoring their power, with perhaps the exiled Jews returning from Khaybar. Both planned to unravel what Muhammad had accomplished.

Muhammad dismounts at the house of worship. A now overcrowded wing has been set up to care for the injured. The women are all too skilled in patching up the wounded from the all too many battles. Muhammad, with Omar, walks through the area, offering encouragement as he calls many by their names. Some had no idea the Prophet was alive, so his visit is a welcome surprise. One of the caregivers wants to tend to Muhammad's wounds, but he defers with a lopsided smile.

The Prophet, accompanied by Sa'ad, Othman, and Omar, heads toward his modest home near the house of worship. He makes it known that he wishes to be alone and retreats into his shelter. The three Companions, although accustomed to Muhammad's need for solitude, look at each other, concerned about both his spiritual and physical health; after all, the Prophet has suffered a serious head wound.

Muhammad goes into deep mourning, plumbing the depths of his grief and reflecting on his future in this life—a healing process. It is a week before he emerges, restored close to his usual vigor, much to the relief of his Companions.

Muhammad's journey has had many points where his survival and the survival of his movement seemingly had as much chance as a condemned newborn baby girl. Now is one of those times. He himself is not fully recovered physically, and he is afflicted with headaches, a lingering effect of the concussion. His supporters bicker among themselves about who is responsible for the defeat, questioning each other's loyalty.

His Meccan enemies are riding high with their powerful army relatively intact. The widows of the Uhud fallen are left with children and no resources to feed them. His enemies in Yathrib see him as politically, fatally weak.

What will become known as The Way depends on one man, making it very vulnerable. None of the close Companions taking charge could pull the movement out of such a deep hole. Without Muhammad, tribal and family loyalties would reassert themselves. It is Muhammad who has the vision and the will to build a nation based on revolutionary principles, but the odds are against him being able to pull it off.

The Prophet's first action is to reestablish the discipline of daily prayers. His words to the faithful are about faith and looking to a bright future without recriminations about the past. As a leader, he juggles the three roles required to run a state: king, priest, warrior. As king, he makes policy decisions. As priest, he supports them with an accepted set of religious beliefs. And as warrior—and general—he defends the state against external and internal enemies.

The first urgent, practical problem he addresses is the sudden large number of widows and orphans in the community. In the existing culture, women and children require a man as protector and provider. Muhammad has been consistently a marriage conservative, disgusted by Mecca's licentiousness. But this is a case of *force majeure*, and the Prophet takes a radical step, as there is only one humane option available. He allows men to take more than one wife. In fact, in this pressing circumstance, he allows each man to take up to four wives. Though this does not make everyone happy, it does solve the problem, which is one close to the orphan Muhammad's heart.

In this patriarchal society, to prevent children from going hungry, they must have a male figure in their home.

The next problem is a labor shortage. All the enterprises he had founded, from farms to artisanal workshops to trade with their production, have gaps to be filled. So Muhammad, with his calm mastery, turns his attention to restoring the pre-Uhud balance to the Yathrib economy.

THIRTY-ONE

MECCA'S VICTORY IS SHORT-LIVED

Two days from home, Sufyan sends out two scouts to announce both their imminent arrival and the news of victory and Muhammad's death. When he and Khalid lead the proud army through the main gate, it appears most of Mecca is there to cheer the victors. This is the biggest news of their generation—the fallen from Badr have been avenged, Mecca's preeminence has been reestablished with an overwhelming victory, and, perhaps most significant, Muhammad has been killed. As Sufyan and Khalid bask in the cheers and adoration, they're secure in the knowledge that they won the battle through their own skill in the art of war.

Not all Meccans are out there to cheer. For the Sons of Hashim, this was not only Muhammad's defeat but also the defeat of their tribe. The Hashemites have lost everything. Their leader, Talib, died the death of a starving camel in the desert. All his efforts to protect his nephew were in vain. Hash-emite glory, pride, and honor are now only memories.

For the slaves, this is a particularly devastating setback. It took Mecca hundreds of years to give birth to its Prophet, the only voice from Mecca's elite to stand up for them as equal human beings. A flower that blossomed out of this dry and rocky ground may never appear again. Those who saw a spark of hope, especially after Badr, now know they will die as slaves. Those who were fortunate to hear him search their memories for his words, needing some succor to pull themselves out of the pit of despair.

Not every wealthy household greets the news of Mecca's triumph with applause. One unexpected response comes from Zainab, who is now living alone in her luxurious estate as her sons, Mosaab and Saif, long ago moved on. When news comes of Mosaab's death, her anger turns against the gods. Her daily repeated prayers to open her son's eyes and bring him back to her were just words lost in a bottomless well. In a blind, tear-filled fury, she demolishes the jewel-encrusted gods in her ornate living room, then smashes the inlaid furniture, startling the par-rots, who fly around in their cages, shedding feathers into the air. Three slaves rush in to restrain their owner and grab the now old leopard by the leash to pull him out of the room.

Zainab has no desire to live any longer. She refuses food in an attempt to starve herself to death. The last exchange she had with her son—which was about Muhammad, whom she cursed in her prayers—replays over and over in her mind. As her slaves gather around her in concern, she announces that they are now free. Two of the six, however, refuse to let her die alone and attend to her before she breathes her last.

Sufyan's first stop is his mansion home, where he shakes off the dust of the journey. The one person he wants to share the news with is Lahab, Muhammad's greatest adversary, whom he did not see among the Notables greeting the conquering heroes. Walking over to Lahab's home, he sees a slave leaving food and water at the keeper of the Kaaba's doorstep. From the slave, he learns that Lahab is gravely ill. His wife, Arwa, died a few days before, having become infected after her husband, the official guardian of Mecca's morality, paid one of his frequent visits to the red light district.

It seems a pestilence has broken out among the prostitutes and is now spreading to the slave quarters and the poorer districts of Mecca. The first symptoms of the disease are fever, chills, and horrible abdominal pain. One in five victims succumbs in an agonizing death. Understanding at the most basic level that contact with a sick person risks infection, infected prostitutes and slaves are being isolated from the still healthy.

The slave cautions Sufyan about entering the house. No fellow Hashemite has come to offer comfort to the dying man who betrayed them. But the slave reports that Lahab's fellow Notables call to him through the closed door.

Sufyan, excited to share the good news with his closest friend and distressed by this sad news, cries out, "Lahab! Lahab! I have brought you the long-awaited news! Muhammad is no more! Meccan swords killed Hamza and most of the rebel army! Today, Mecca's glory is restored! Praise to Al-Lat! Glory to Hubal! Honor to Manat! This is your victory! May the gods remove the spell over you, turn the magic against the magician. The dark force of evil that stood against value and virtue is gone. Gone forever! Celebrate! This is our day!"

While Lahab's fervent prayers to his false gods provided neither cure nor relief, ironically, the false news of Muhammad's death allows him to spend his last hours a happy man. Mecca was saved. Finally, relief from the lonely pain of his moribund body. When he dies, the stench and the disease don't allow a proper funeral for him. His corpse and belongings are set on fire in his own house.

At a hastily called Notables meeting, those present rise when the conquering hero, Sufyan, enters. Anxious to hear some good news, the Notables press Sufyan for details of the rout of their longtime foe. Sufyan is only too happy to oblige, giving proper credit to Khalid and embellishing the gruesome death of Muhammad as though he had been a witness. The audience vicariously revels in the vivid descriptions of battle, yet Sufyan senses that this historic victory is not receiving the exuberant response it deserves. What he perceives is the opposite, even a kind of panic. They react to anyone coughing by moving away.

Amr, anxious to speak, takes advantage of a Sufyan pause. "Sufyan, all honor to you and our courageous warriors. However, in your absence, two problems here have grown worse—much worse. The level in the Zamzam well is dropping. And the pestilence is not just striking the whores and the slaves, but now has hit even some of our number, like your friend Lahab."

The meeting descends into a free-for-all with everyone speaking at once.

"The bad water is causing the sickness."

"The gods are angry and punishing us."

"We must ration the water from Zamzam!"

"How can we have pilgrimage this year with so little water?"

"How can we even service passing caravans?"

Sufyan's strong voice cuts through the panicked voices that are now rising to shouting. "Brothers! Brothers! We are Meccans. We are from the greatest of cities. Just as we triumphed over the worst evil of our time, so we will deal with these challenges that Hubal has sent to test us."

That quiets the room.

Sufyan heads for the door. "I have not yet gone to the Kaaba, and I will go to Zamzam to examine the situation." Finally a man of action, Sufyan leaves the meeting as the sajvior of Mecca and the acknowledged leader of the holy city.

⁂

Sufyan's victory is short-lived, however. A small Yemeni-based caravan arrives from Yathrib. From the stables and the Zamzam spring, the news that Muhammad is still very much alive spreads rapidly through every neighborhood of Mecca. When it reaches the ears of the Notables, though they are ready to dismiss it as nothing more than a rumor, they invite two of the Yemeni traders to meet with them.

In a half-full room, Amr welcomes the two Yemenis, who are becoming ever more nervous as they are beginning to realize they did not understand the significance of the news they bring.

"Did you actually see Muhammad alive, or were you told by someone?" Amr asks.

The two visitors look at each other, wanting the other to answer. "Yes, we saw him," one finally says. "He was wounded, but he seemed alive."

At that moment, Sufyan hurries in, still unaware of why the meeting has been called.

"He was on a camel," the other trader says, "and he clearly needed help, as it was evident he was injured."

Now sensing what they have been summoned to report, the first trader adds, "I wouldn't be surprised if he died later. We left right after that."

All eyes turn to Sufyan as sweat breaks out on his brow.

"Sufyan, Sufyan! Did you see with your own eyes the corpse of Muhammad?" one Notable demands.

Sufyan's mind races over his options. He's trapped. "No."

The assembly deflates.

Sufyan looks at the Yemeni traders. "Had either of you ever seen Muhammad before?"

"No." The Yemenis do not want to get caught up in this Meccan drama.

"I'm not really sure who it was that I saw," the other trader says. "I know from talking to people that no one wanted to believe Muhammad was dead."

Doubt settles over the meeting.

Khalid steps in. "Brothers, Mecca has just won the greatest battle in its history. Muhammad is dead. Now is the time to celebrate. And after that, we can turn our attention to our problems here at home with the same spirit of victory. Long live Mecca!"

The Notables look at a relieved Sufyan. For now, he is the leader of Mecca.

Sooner or later, though, the truth will become known.

THIRTY-TWO

DROUGHT

The news of the great Meccan victory and the defeat of the Meccan rebels seeking a power base in Yathrib spreads far and wide, from Yemen to Damascus and beyond, including to the numerous Bedouin tribes in Arabia, whose survival often means being on good terms with the ascendant power. From the perspective of an objective observer, Muhammad and his movement were doomed to be forgotten in one generation, another challenger to established power ignominiously crushed. And yet. And yet. How is it that at every point in his remarkable journey, when it appears that all is lost, including his own life, the Prophet manages to come out ahead? Like an alchemist turning lead to gold, Muhammad always seems to turn defeat to victory.

None of the Prophet's close and very able Companions who shared the down times with him ever defected, despite efforts to tempt them with gold and prestige. They all have the baser failings, including the temptation of power, but they love

Muhammad and what he stands for and never waver in their loyalty. And he loves them in return.

By chance or divine design, as wells across Arabia began dying, Muhammad and most of his followers have found themselves in an oasis. Water is never far from a desert dweller's consciousness, and Muhammad, who experienced the failing of the Shi'ab spring, understands the devastating impact. The drought does have somewhat of an impact on Yathrib, but water is still abundant.

The Prophet knows his enemies have their eyes on Yathrib more than ever. The Banu Qaynuqa'a have never given up their goal of returning to their ancestral homes, and the Meccans have vowed that they will not rest until Muhammad and his subversive movement have been destroyed. It galls them all the more that while they suffer drought, this orphan shepherd is living with abundant water!

With each passing day, a power shift is taking place from the ancient city of Mecca to the oasis of Yathrib. No one would have predicted this after the defeat at Uhud—that Yathrib would become in effect an alternative to Mecca. Muhammad's leadership in encouraging this shift has been important, but nature is his determinative ally.

Meanwhile, lack of water in Mecca threatens the very existence of the holy city. The Notables are sinking into despair. Their power and money cannot buy them rain. And the longer the drought lasts, the greater the damage. Exchanging blame in anger has not produced rain, nor have desperate prayers to a variety of deities. If it weren't for Taif providing some of the very basic food items for payments in gold, the Meccans would have starved to death.

Facing reality, the lords of Mecca cancel the annual pilgrimage for the second year in a row. The vast majority of caravans requiring plentiful water are rejected, despite strong opposition from those whose business has been impacted. They must care for their own first. Word travels fast in the caravan community to avoid Mecca. The city's long-established reputation as a reliable trading hub has been ruined. Thus, two of the main sources of income for the Meccan economy have been summarily eliminated.

THIRTY-THREE

WAR CLOUDS GATHER

Over the months and following year, Yathrib becomes the number one destination for the tribes of the Hijaz. Not only is free water an attraction, but for the holy month, Muhammad institutes a pilgrimage along the model of Mecca's where all are welcome, regardless of tribe, religion, or servitude. There is no such thing as master and slave—all men are equal. Yathrib's pilgrimage offers all what Mecca, the high point of the year for tribes, had with its carnival atmosphere, except a sanctuary where the tribes could store their idols and totems. Muhammad himself and his teachings become an attraction, and the number of followers grows from people simply coming into contact with him. Many migrants stay, and Yathrib becomes a magnet for escaped or freed slaves. Muhammad preaches to surrender the self—its ambitions, desires, passions, and senses—to the only force worthy of being called the Creator. This is emancipation. The Prophet is building a nation.

Muhammad and his close Companions have not lost sight of the fact they are beset with enemies. Their world can no longer be viewed as bipolar—Muhammad versus Mecca and its allies. It's tripolar. From the moment the Banu Qaynuqa'a marched out of their Yathrib fortress, one goal has consumed them—to return to their homeland and take their revenge. Never did they consider, like other refugees throughout history, to resettle in their new surroundings at the magnificent fortress of Khaybar. Instead, the Banu Qaynuqa'a refugees have sought to convince their cousins to raise a massive army to conquer Yathrib, take back their property, and erase the humiliation suffered at the hands of Muhammad by seeing him to his grave. There is water under the Khaybar Fortress, which was the main reason for that site long ago being chosen, so the drought is not a major argument for them not to undertake a major offensive campaign. Though the influx of their co-religionists has strained Khaybar's limited resources, including drawing down its water supply. If truth be told, many cousins in the now overcrowded fortress would welcome the departure of their "guests," whom they consider arrogant when in fact their ancestry is less prestigious than their hosts.

All three cities recognize that the balance of power rests with who can enlist the most Bedouin warriors. The Bedouin tribes, who are Khaybar's traditional allies, have serious water issues, and joining such a campaign has its appeal. For both those who have been to Yathrib and those who have not, the oasis, with its water and dates, is a real-world Paradise. Led by Azora of the Banu Qaynuqa'a, Khaybar sets out to enlist Bedouin tribes as foot soldiers, with the promise of gold as well as land and water. The offer results in a potentially large force willing to commit. The Arabs have grown up with the particular desert equation of blood and water. How much blood would it cost one tribe, whose well has gone dry, to capture their neighbor's well? A major victory in the recruiting effort is a pact with the Banu Ghatafan, a confederation of bellicose tribes located northeast of Yathrib.

In a tripolar world, inevitably two opponents will join together and fight a third enemy, and Mecca and Khaybar are the logical allies to form a league. Muhammad and Salman recognize that both are actively courting tribal commitments, and that their own forces are seriously depleted after Uhud, especially in taking on both Mecca and Khaybar. Salman works hard building up their army with new recruits. With the great Hamza gone, Ali takes on his role of training the fighters in hand-to-hand combat.

Muhammad ventures out of Yathrib with companions to make mutual defense pacts with various tribes. Arabia is generally a lawless place, with marauders and outlaws disrupting both commerce and peace, and Muhammad also personally leads punitive expeditions to control them.

Time passes at a slow pace in these desert societies. Muhammad's enemies have their eyes in Yathrib and are aware that he is growing stronger. If they had acted soon after Uhud, it would have been a walkover. Now, two years later, while they still outnumber any forces Muhammad can muster, Muhammad has the military advantage of playing defense against an invasion.

The impatient Banu Qaynuqa'a treat retaking Yathrib and killing Muhammad as an urgent priority. They call for a meeting in Mecca during the forbidden months, inviting all the leaders who share the goal—whether motivated by water, revenge, or gold—of occupying Yathrib. They also invite tribal leaders who need convincing to go to war, which includes most Meccan Notables.

Meeting participants come into the holy city from every direction—north, south, east, and west. No previous gathering has ever counted so many top leaders. When all have arrived, Sufyan, as the host, calls the meeting, and Nadwa House quickly fills. All understand they are there for the common purpose of invading Yathrib and agreeing on a battle plan and the allocation of the fruits of victory.

Mecca's rationing policy and the discovery of two small aquifers have enabled the water needs of the population to be met, but not enough to host a pilgrimage nor service all caravans. This is a major blow to the holy city's prestige. Sufyan views a successful invasion of Yathrib as a way to put Mecca back on the map as the region's premier power. However, a depleted Mecca does not have the resources nor the manpower to repeat an Uhud, and they have little to offer in terms of a ready force for war. What Sufyan does have is his reputation as the battle-tested commander of a large, winning army.

After a few words of welcome, he gets straight to the point, addressing Azora with a question he already knows the answer to, since they spoke privately on his arrival. "How many warriors have you gathered so far?"

Azora stands next to Sufyan on center stage. "Six thousand, including foot soldiers, cavalry, and archers. Two thousand Jewish. Four thousand from Kinanah and Ghatafan."

That impresses the audience, and the two mentioned leaders take the opportunity to stand up.

The Kinanah leader states, "We have fifteen hundred, and a legendary unit that fought with the Byzantine Emperor Heraclius against the Sassanids south of Jerusalem."

The Ghatafan leader counters, "We bring the most, twenty-five hundred, and none have the poets sung more about than the exploits of these men."

"That is most impressive," Sufyan says. "As many of you know, after we invested all our resources in the battle of Uhud, the drought hit the Zamzam spring and we could not replenish our resources like we usually do with income from pilgrimages and caravans. We have managed to maintain much of our army, but some here hold they should only be used if Mecca is under attack."

Azora skillfully and gently opens Sufyan's wounds. "We will help you. This is not only our fight; it is mainly your fight. Muhammad is growing stronger, enjoying the abundance that doesn't belong to him."

The mention of Muhammad's name makes Sufyan shift uncomfortably as he wipes his perspiring brow. He's been riven with self-doubt since learning his victory was a false one, and that the orphan shepherd has once again gotten away. Should he gamble Mecca on one last shot? This time powerful tribes are with him, and there are allies inside Yathrib opposed to the Prophet. His enemies cannot resist such an overwhelming force. This time he will capture Muhammad, bring him back to Mecca alive and well, and publicly execute him. It is worth the risk.

Looking out at the crowded room, he sees some of the skeptical Notables he will have to convince. Addressing Azora, Sufyan asks, "When do you see yourself returning to Yathrib?"

"After the forbidden months. Our plan is to have all the forces meet at a staging area in the Falcon Valley, midway to Yathrib."

"You mean this year!?"

"Yes."

"That's not possible for us. It took us more than a year to prepare for Uhud, which was a third of the force, and the drought wasn't as severe as it is now."

"I agree with Sufyan," says Suhail. "We can't be ready in a few months."

"The longer we wait, the stronger Muhammad gets," Azora counters.

"I want him alive this time," Sufyan insists. "To do it right, it takes time, effort, resources, gold. We must convince our traditional tribal allies. I don't see this happening in a year or two."

Azora doesn't like the sound of this. How can he manage to hold a coalition together for that long? "Two years! Muhammad will die of old age! I say you can be ready in less than a year—with our help! We can provide all the gold you need and all the resources required to mount a major campaign. Yes, less than a year, and we will all enjoy the fruits of victory!"

Unsure, Sufyan looks away. His mind has already drifted ahead to imagining what a victory would look like. Uhud was strictly a Meccan operation. Now, there are many involved, all of whom expect some reward for conquering the oasis.

Suhail has anticipated this. "It's time to write an agreement honoring each one's interests."

Slaves move in and out of the room, serving tea, water, and fruit. One of them is Sawda. An Abyssinian woman whose parents were slain during a tribal war, she and her siblings were all sold separately. Now she is in Mecca, thousands of miles from home. Only seven years old when Muhammad was forced out of Mecca, she never met the Prophet, though she has heard much about how other slaves admire him. Having heard the endless plots to kill Muhammad—along with how the Notables ridiculed him for making slave and master equal—she decides to warn him.

Stealing a papyrus, she writes brief warning lines in Abyssinian, which she hopes no one here in Mecca will understand. If caught, it will be her head. She finds a slave at the stables from a Yemeni caravan carrying incense and spices that is headed to Yathrib and entrusts the message to him.

⁂

Two weeks later, the slave delivers the message to Ali, who brings it to the house of worship.

Ali hands the papyrus to Omar. "What is this? Greek?"

Omar turns to Bilaal. "Call everyone who knows a foreign language to gather after prayer."

Muhammad and the close Companions huddle together, though none can decipher the message. Othman suggests it could be Abyssinian.

The Prophet looks around, trying to find his Abyssinian friend, Bilaal.

Bilaal has climbed his usual palm tree to announce the call to prayer.

Omar goes out to meet him as he comes down from the tree. "Bilaal! Do you know how to read Abyssinian?"

"Read Abyssinian? Why?"

"There's an urgent message, and no one can make it out."

As they step into the mosque, all eyes go to Bilaal. Ali hands him the papyrus.

Bilaal studies it, squints, nods at the poor handwriting. "Yes, it's Abyssinian. It's been a long time . . . I think this is it . . . *The Prophet's life is in danger* . . . *Banu*—something must be *Qaynuqa'a*, or maybe *Khaybar*, or both. *Ten thousand warriors will attack Yathrib*—"

"Ten thousand!" exclaims Omar. "Are you sure? This has to be a great exaggeration!"

"Could this be some kind of trap or effort to scare us?" Bakr wonders.

"If the message was written in Arabic, maybe," says Omar, "but this has to be from one of our followers, and the messenger said it was a slave woman. I believe it, though it looks like we have a big war ahead of us."

"If the message was read right, it has to be from the Banu Qaynuqa'a, as they always wanted to come back. Surely they have paid many to fight with them." Sa'ad adds his opinion.

"Sons of hyenas!" Omar shouts.

Ali remains perplexed. "It doesn't make sense—a warning from an unknown person in Mecca about the Jews of Banu Qaynuqa'a."

"It makes perfect sense," responds Sa'ad. "The Jews of Banu Qaynuqa'a are building an army, and it's probable they met in Mecca, along with others like Taif. These are all of the Prophet's enemies."

"And we let them take their gold with them, didn't we?" Salman shakes his head.

Sa'ad sighs regretfully. "We did."

"If the letter is right and the writer actually heard the number ten thousand directly, that would be the largest army Arabia has ever fielded," observes Bakr. "But who can raise such a force in these years of drought?"

"Banu Qaynuqa'a can!" Sa'ad says. "This is the never-ending war between us and them, and now the Prophet is caught up in our madness."

"It's our fight together," states Omar. "Neither of us is fighting for the tribe. Our fight is against tribalism and tribal madness, as you call it."

Muhammad speaks at last. "Children of Evil. Our wounds are still wide open. May the almighty God return their vice back down their throats."

Muhammad's sharp eye lands on Salman, who has that distant stare the Prophet knows well. The Persian's brilliant, strategic mind is taking in this new information, processing it, and searching for a solution. A slight smile creases Salman's weathered face, as though he's hit on something. Muhammad manages to catch his eye. No words are needed; the Prophet nods, giving his permission to leave. Salman rises to his feet, grabs his waterskin, and heads out.

"If this is true, then the real question is when will they attack," Bakr says.

Bilaal thinks for a moment. "That it does not say."

Already on his way out, Salman turns back and says, "If they succeed, it will take them a long time."

※

Some hours later, Salman reaches the top of a hill that gives him a wide view of the oasis valley. Regarding this now familiar landscape from the point of view of a massive invading force, he confirms that the valley is secured by the steep cliffs of the Hijaz Mountains, except for two natural entry points. To the northeast is a long yet narrow passage that runs via a deep canyon, ending finally at the massive gates of the fortress of the Banu Qurayzah led by Ka'ab, the natural back gate to the oasis. It is seldom used, as any traveler has to be checked by the Banu Qurayzah, who often demand a toll. The

south entrance is a wide passage, the one used by regular traffic coming in and out of the oasis. The only possible strategy,
especially with this news of a possible army of ten thousand,
is to prevent any invading force from getting past the two
entry points, leaving them at the mercy of the desert. The wide
south entrance is the challenge. Looking down at the broad
entrance, Salman considers it from the point of view of both
attacker and defender.

Returning at sunset, Salman catches up with the Prophet
and confides in him a plan that is going to demand the total
support of every creature who breathes.

There is a feeling of anticipation among the faithful during
prayer, a sense that something is up. When Muhammad beckons Salman forward, the Persian takes his place next to the
Prophet to present his plan.

"I knew back in Persia of a strategy that was developed to
defend towns," Salman begins. "I've never heard it mentioned
here. The strategy is to dig a deep trench all around the town.
Especially when your enemies far outnumber you, this strong
defense gives you an advantage. Here we have the advantage
that there are only two entrances to our valley; high mountains and cliffs otherwise protect us. This means we can concentrate on our one vulnerable point—the southern entrance.
It is there that we will dig a deep and wide trench across the
length of this entrance. First, this will surprise the enemy, as
this is not the Yathrib they know and expect. The trench will
keep them in the desert, where there is neither food nor water.
With their overwhelming numbers and anticipating light resistance, they will not have brought sufficient food and water for
such a long siege. The fact there are supposedly ten thousand
means they come from many different tribes. As their animals

starve and die, they will question why should they, too, starve, and they will be tempted to defect. They came to fight us, as they believe Muhammad to be the great enemy. Yet they will find their greatest enemy is the desert."

There's an impatient clamor to ask questions about this strategy, which is new and unfamiliar to them. "The southern entrance is a long, long way between the two mountains. It will take years to dig it!" one individual shouts.

"All depends on our faith and willpower," responds Salman. "This trench is much smaller than what I know about in Persia."

"How deep and how wide is your trench?"

"Wide enough that a horse can't clear it, deep enough that a warrior falling into it can't climb out."

"They will bridge it," states Bakr. "What then?"

"We burn the bridges. The longer we can prevent them from crossing, the weaker they will get. Winning time means winning the war. Remember, we have water and they don't."

"What makes us sure the Jews of Banu Nadeer at the north entry won't betray us and let their cousins in?" Omar questions.

"Conflict of interest," says Sa'ad. "One tribe is from the far south, and the other from the far north. Each tribe believes they have superior Jewish blood. They have often fought each other, and every tribe acts according to its own best interest."

"That might be true," Salman admits, "but I don't trust them not to betray us; they have common Jewish blood. If they do betray us, remember that the north entrance is a long, very narrow canyon, which can be turned into a death trap, committing only a small force of our warriors."

"Did the strategy work in the case you know about?" Ali asks.

"Despite working like hell for a year, they had not entirely finished one stretch, and that gave the attackers an entry point. The lesson is that you have to finish."

All then look from Salman to the Prophet, who asks, "Any other vision, anyone?"

No one can think of any alternative except a suicidal confrontation.

"Then let's all dig." Muhammad ends the discussion.

THIRTY-FOUR

THE BIG DIG

That same morning, a group led by the Prophet and Salman go out to the south entrance and mark out the line of the proposed trench between the two steep hills. All can imagine a trench and how effective it could be, but if ever a project looked impossible, this is it. Some of the terrain is hard, rocky ground, some is more easily dug sand. Realistically, it looks like a lifelong project.

All living in the oasis must participate in this effort for the common defense of their homeland. The longtime residents of the oasis know the wrath the Banu Qaynuqa'a would bring down on those who they believe conspired against them. The fate that awaited them was either be slaughtered or be sold into slavery. Tomorrow, they will be offered a shovel so they can better their chances later with a sword.

The next morning, Companions, Christians, Jews, men, women, children, slaves, and freemen answer the Prophet's call. They mill about, congregating by tribe. Sa'ad calls all the tribal leaders together, Salman lays out the plan, and tasks are assigned. Salul and his men are given the hardest job. Most galling to Salul is that he's now taking orders from his former slave, Salman. Ka'ab and the rest of the Banu Qurayzah are placed equidistant from the two mountains. They strike a deal that they don't have to participate in the project on the Sabbath. While at first in skeptical awe at the distance between the two embracing mountains, the tribal leaders very quickly see in their mind's eye an army being held back, having to fight a losing battle against the desert.

The Prophet grabs a shovel and, with that act, more than a thousand eyes are on him. With a decisive thrust, he starts digging into the sand, tossing each shovelful to one side, the beginning of the future defensive wall on the Yathrib side of the trench. Surprisingly, many in the crowd cheer and the women ululate.

The herculean task has begun, and the valley is alive with the sound of tools at work and human beings in full exertion. The plan is to rise for prayer while it is still dark and then dig from dawn to twilight. Two main enemies face the people of Yathrib: the cold winter nights and time. They cannot control the weather, and they cannot control when their enemy chooses to attack. They do have control over the degree of their effort, yet if the League's armies arrive before the trench is completed, it will have all been in vain. They will have conveniently dug their own graves when the vengeful victors massacre them and dump them in an unfinished trench. All are aware of this wartime uncertainty, and continuing on requires strong faith, in addition to the motivation of fear over the fatal cost of defeat.

Friday night, the Banu Qurayzah contingent takes their break from digging, and Ka'ab, the leader, and his right hand, Eli the Councilor, head back to the Jewish fortress to celebrate their holy day. In the desert nights, the temperature drops low, and the two can see their breath as they speak.

"If a hell does exist, this is it," says Ka'ab. "Damn—the way my hands bleed. I can't feel them."

Eli says, "We must warn Azora and the cousins."

Ka'ab curses. "God damn Azora and his arrogance!"

"Put your differences with Azora aside for now. Muhammad sooner or later will force us out of Yathrib, like he did with Azora. He'll find any reason to condemn us!"

"We have made a defense pact with the majority tribes. We're defending Yathrib. If we don't honor it, we'll be punished for treason."

"Do you think that Sa'ad and Muhammad trust you to keep it when it comes to fighting your own blood, even though they know you hate Azora?" Eli asks.

"Yes, Muhammad doesn't trust us, and we shouldn't trust Azora," Ka'ab responds.

"The League needs to know of the trench plan; we have to send someone to inform them. I'd go myself, but I'd be missed and Muhammad would guess we're warning the enemy."

"The trench is a waste of time. Let Muhammad dig all the way down to Hell—the League will arrive before it's done. They will walk in."

"We have to send someone," Eli insists. "The new moon is approaching; they have to know what to expect."

"No way it can be kept a secret with caravans coming and going."

"Then it's just a rumor. We send someone with a written message; they will believe it."

"Do whatever you want, just don't get caught," Ka'ab warns.

"Muhammad's defeat one way or another is certain."

"Nothing is certain when it comes to Muhammad!"

THIRTY-FIVE

PREPARE, PREPARE

A week passes, then a month, then two months, as both sides prepare for the coming conflict. For those on the Yathrib side, bloodied hands have turned to calluses. The 640-meter trench has been dug half a meter deep, and the task now is to dig at least six meters deep. This is not that difficult when sand that is being dug can be lifted out in baskets to add to the growing wall. Those facing seemingly unbreakable rock envy the lucky sand workers.

From the start there was good-natured competition over what group got the farthest in a day, as well as the competition of who could come up with the best chant, be it bawdy or spiritual. A good joke could be judged by how fast laughter moved down the line, and another would usually come back to better it. There was always the sense of urgency that the attacking force could appear any day. Muhammad has formed a network, his "eyes" spies, with fast horses to gather accurate information, none more important than the date the massive force gathered by the League begins the march to the oasis.

On the League side, the question is not whether there will be a war; the only question is when. The Jews and Mecca are determined to attack before the forbidden months. Time is not on their side, and two of the smaller tribes have gone to war against each other. There's a risk that this could lead to cascading chaos as the two warring tribes call on their allies for help. At a meeting in Falcon Valley, it's evident to all the partners— the Meccan Quraysh, Taif, Khaybar, and the Ghatafan—that, given intertribal conflict, the unresolved problems of logistics, slow recruitment, and the challenges of coordination, they cannot pull off an attack before the sacred month.

It would be more than a month before word of the delay got back to Muhammad from his spies. The trench-digging project has reached its halfway point, and the effort faces numerous obstacles. The collective energy that has propelled them thus far is flagging, and those who have labored since the first shovelful of sand was dug are just plain exhausted. While the League delay is welcome news, it also means the exhausted workers cannot help but ease up. On top of that, a sandstorm hits, piling sand back into the trench. And a massive, intractable rock in the middle of the trench could prove to be a turning point between success and failure. The rock offers a solid bridge for attackers, so it must be removed. Even the repeated muscular efforts of Omar prove fruitless—rather than breaking the rock, the rock breaks him. Other men take up the challenge as workers lay down their tools to cheer them on. No one succeeds. That rock becomes a symbol of futile human effort. Dissenting voices are heard as morale sinks. This was a crazy plan to begin with, thought up by a crazy Persian. It's a waste of time. People begin to grumble that it would be better to meet the enemy in the open and fight honorably. *And die* is left unsaid.

The Prophet understands how the exhausted men and women feel. Do not his hands also bleed and does not he, too, lack sleep and fight fatigue? What the Prophet knows is that this is the only plan with a chance of keeping an overwhelming and merciless enemy at bay. How many times has he survived his enemy's efforts to kill him and his people, and now survival comes down to just one—albeit massive—rock!

Muhammad binds his blistered hands with a cloth, walks past Omar and others lying spent on the ground, and picks up a crowbar and a hammer. He makes seven marks down the center of the rock born out of the volcano millennia ago. He sets to work slamming the crowbar into one of the marks. All eyes are on him. What chance does he have compared to the stronger Omar and the young men recovering on the ground? Muhammad's eyes remain fixed on the task at hand, an exemplar of total focus. At dawn, when the others go back to their digging, Muhammad is still at it. All the Prophet's teachings up to this point—to surrender, to pray, to fast, to give—have been to teach them how to concentrate.

At midday, Muhammad steps back, grabs a hatchet, and walks off. A curious Omar drops his pickaxe and goes over to look at what Muhammad has done. He finds seven deep, narrow boreholes in the rock. The Prophet returns carrying pomegranate wood he has cut. He fills each borehole with water, then carves pieces of wood to snugly fit into the holes. What is he doing?

Next, Muhammad grabs a pickaxe, returns to his group, and begins the rhythmic blows to deepen the trench. He's back on the job. Everyone else returns to their assignments, and the familiar sounds resume. Dusk approaches, sunlight surrenders to moonlight. After leading evening prayers, Muhammad wraps a blanket around himself and falls into a restorative sleep. It's a brutally cold night, with everyone sleeping close together while some get up to make small fires to warm themselves.

On the third morning, after people have forgotten what Muhammad was doing, those who come near the obstreperous rock can't believe what they see. The rock is split into four pieces! Hard steel, concentrated effort, wet wood swelling, expanding along fault lines. Using nature to defeat a natural obstacle! For the Prophet, the greatest tool has been faith. New energy floods the tired bodies of the men and women. What was impossible yesterday has become possible today.

THIRTY-SIX

ESCALATION

Some of the principals of the League meet in a prearranged rendezvous in Falcon Valley. With the holy month imminent, they set a date immediately afterward for the invasion of the oasis. A dust-covered stranger gallops in on a camel. He says he brings an important message from friends in Yathrib. Escorted into the meeting, he hands a papyrus to Sufyan, who he judges looks to be most in charge. The Meccan reads the words on the papyrus, then hands it to Azora.

Azora looks at the messenger. "I don't recognize you. Why didn't Ka'ab himself come?"

"If he missed one day at work on the trench, Muhammad would have been suspicious he had come here."

"A trench?" Sufyan asks.

"Muhammad is building a massive trench across the southern entrance to Yathrib. They've been digging for months."

Amr bursts out laughing, joined by others. It's absurd to think any trench could stop an army of ten thousand united and determined warriors.

"Don't laugh," Azora says with a frown. "If you knew that main entry to the oasis, a deep trench running between two steep mountains makes sense. Never underestimate Muhammad nor his wily Persian."

A chastened Amr attempts to regain lost ground. "We can simply bridge any man-made trench."

"With what?" Suhail asks skeptically. "Dead bodies?"

"There are palm trees, I believe, outside Yathrib. Cut those, and you have your bridge."

"It's not that easy, Amr. That would require a lot of skilled manpower."

"I believe you give this trench more power than it deserves. I still think it's a foolish idea. It only shows how desperate they are."

"We need to properly prepare," says Sufyan, "and making bridges is not an easy project. We need lots of wood and iron. And most importantly, men who know the craft."

"Our men know steel and wood—that's how we build our fortresses," Azora adds. "We will go prepared. No trench can stop us!"

After more discussion about this new development, they reluctantly decide on another delay.

❁

Back in Yathrib, work on the trench continues with a certain urgency, as the holy month respite will soon be over. One of Muhammad's Companions happened to be in Badr when a caravan came through. From them, he learned that the League knows of the trench and has delayed the invasion to plan a bridge. The strategy game is on—move and countermove.

Muhammad, Salman, Omar, and Bakr have already thought ahead about palm tree logs being used as bridges and are ready to cut down the trees on the desert side of the entrance. Salman proposes lining the bottom of the deepened trench with flammable brush and branches. Flames would turn any attempted crossing into a living hell. This tactic also goes for the narrow northern passage, if the invaders get past the Jewish fortress.

The possibility of weaponizing fire opens Salman's fertile military mind. Igniting the brush would not be a problem with a flaming arrow, but the brush would burn itself out fairly quickly. The enemy would move back outside arrow range, then watch and wait, knowing there was no way the defenders could throw more brush and logs onto the fire. Salman's creative mind bounces around all the possibilities. There has to be another way to use fire to give them the advantage.

He is aware, through his travels in the Arabian Desert, of seepages of a black bitumen tar. He used some on his campfires to keep them going through the cold nights. No amount of water could put out their blue flame. Has someone ever used this tar as a weapon of war? He remembers hearing stories from long ago about an oil used by the Assyrians, who even had a catapult to launch fireballs. During his travels he also heard of a kind of "Greek fire" that was used in naval battles, again long forgotten, maybe not even true.

Salman sits down alone with the Prophet, who is repairing one of his sandals, and expresses the need for fire as a weapon to destroy the bridges. Salman describes his idea of using bitumen tar as a base to produce a highly flammable and portable liquid. He would like to devote his time to experimenting with it. Muhammad agrees. Within three moons, the trench will be completed to its full planned width and depth; it is better that Salman spend his time on this new potential weapon.

Salman, along with some bright young helpers, sets up his worksite in a secluded place. The experiment has to be kept secret so that in this "arms race," their opponents can't come up with an effective countermove. One of the first tasks is to go out to desert tar seepages with camels carrying casks and to fill the casks with bitumen, building up their stock of this basic element.

The tar works well for fire arrows, as it is viscous and, with some cloth attached to it, will stick to an arrow. It is not effective, however, to simply put it on a bridge. It has to be used in oil form. Laying the tar down on the bottom of the trench with branches and brush could prolong the life of that fire but would not be nearly as effective as a liquid applied directly to the logs of a bridge. Salman tries different methods and substances to transform the sticky tar to a liquid, even a thick one, but it needs to be thin enough to pour out of containers that can be carried.

Salman approaches the Prophet with his frustration. "My lord, the tar works well for fire arrows, and we are proceeding to build up stocks and train the archers to handle them. However, I have not been able to produce a liquid by mixing the tar with another oil. Olive oil didn't work, nor did rose oil. The closest we came was with wine."

Muhammad smiles slightly. "A good use for it."

"It has to be possible, as it's been done before."

"I remember an alchemist who lived in a monastery a day's ride from Damascus. We often spent nights there. The monastery was lit with an oil he had developed. I don't know what it was, but it definitely was not olive oil. Perhaps he has what you are looking for."

The Prophet wants Salman to stay with him, so he asks a few of his close Companions to join them.

Salman lays out the project he's been working on. "We need a caravan with empty barrels to travel north to this alchemist and return with what we need to produce this weapon."

"Travel now?" Bakr is perplexed. "In the midst of a war?"

"We have just enough time, as we are still in the forbidden months," Salman responds. "Our survival could well depend on producing this weapon."

"Bakr and Othman," says Muhammad, "your job is to get the caravan to the monastery." Bakr and Othman are the most experienced on the trading routes, and though rather advanced in age, are still fit for this mission. "Omar, your job is to get it there safely. Ali, you understand what Salman is doing, so your job is to find out from the alchemist what is missing to make this work. Unlike many alchemists I've met, this one is a divine master who knows not just the material but, most importantly, understands the spiritual—the essence and the unseen force behind form and matter. It's said he can turn lead into gold, if necessary. Tell him Muhammad sent you, his son, on this urgent mission. Be respectful in his presence, as you are in my presence. He would not give this knowledge for war. Explain to him what we have been through over the last twenty years, and how these lords of evil seek to annihilate us, continuing to kill and enslave the innocent. Tell him that Muhammad has exhausted all peaceful means to change their ways, but they have only become more intransigent and violent. The use of force is the last resort, but it means protecting the innocent from being killed or sold into slavery. Send him my peace, and don't exhaust him with your curiosity!"

Two days later, a caravan with thirty camels heads north toward Damascus. No one knows better than Muhammad the risks of these desert roads, and he has sent those closest to him on a quest that has only a slight chance of succeeding. Will he see them again? There is nothing to do but concentrate mind and muscle on completing the trench.

Weeks pass and the trench is near complete end to end, though Salman wishes it could be even deeper. In a felicitous coincidence, the very day Muhammad declares their many months of long labor a success, a familiar caravan appears. Omar leads the way as those returning marvel at the completed trench. Cheers erupt to celebrate the return of the Companions and the completion of the trench.

Looking at the smiles of the returned, Salman guesses their journey was a success and, drawing Ali aside, learns that it was.

The next day, tests with the components brought from the alchemist produce successful results. While closely guarding the secret, the race is on to build up enough stocks of sacred fire before the invasion.

THIRTY-SEVEN

NO TURNING BACK

The sacred months have passed, and the League with Banu Qaynuqa'a, Mecca, Taif, Ghatafan, and various small tribes committed to invading Yathrib gather in Falcon Valley. The leadership views it as an existential life-or-death battle and they've painted a picture for their thirsty warriors of an earthly Paradise, an oasis with plentiful water and endless date palms. They've pumped up the troops, telling them they will be part of the greatest battle in Arab history, and that their victory will be celebrated by the poets until the end of time. A well-justified overconfidence is the prevailing attitude.

At dawn, the order to march is given. Each tribe marches together. Their leaders on horseback ride at the front, then gallop back and forth to check on their contingents. Foot soldier infantry, archers, cavalry, and the whole logistical caravan with food, water, and tents are all anxious to get on with it. One group has gone ahead to set up the first night's camp.

Shortly after dawn, when it's clear this is the long-awaited day, a single horseman from Muhammad's spies races north toward Yathrib to sound the alarm. Three days later, he arrives in Yathrib and reports back to Muhammad.

Word travels quickly through the ranks that they are about to face the largest army ever amassed in Arabia. For many, especially those who survived the carnage of Uhud, there's no avoiding that sinking feeling in the pit of the stomach. Yet those who have been with the Prophet for a long time not only are inspired by his calm, but now know how to achieve that inner state of calm themselves, even in the moments right before the battle of their lives.

Each day brings the League's legions closer to Yathrib, their confidence and excitement growing as they believe they will quickly overcome the outmanned enemy and head to the water—more water than most have ever seen before. They've been told that the Yathrib natives hate Muhammad and that they will be welcomed as liberators, but they have no idea what awaits them. The news that their enemy has built a trench has not gone much beyond the leadership ranks. The logistics team moves ahead to establish the final base camp just outside the northern entrance, and by noon the hungry and thirsty warriors have arrived there.

The leaders on horseback ride ahead to reconnoiter the situation and plan the next day's attack. Casting their gaze ahead, they cannot believe what they see. Stretched before them is not the simple ditch they imagined, but a trench of such breadth and depth, it is frightening to look at. Beyond that is a high wall hiding they know not what. There is not a single human being in sight. Sufyan, Suhail, and Azora are paralyzed for the moment, fixated on this seemingly impassable obstacle. They exchange looks bordering on panic.

Sufyan pulls himself together. "It can be bridged. We came prepared for that." Though not with such a wide trench in mind.

He hears an alarmed buzz of conversation and looks behind him to see hundreds of warriors who have followed from base camp, unable to contain their eagerness to see the oasis. Instead, they've found this monstrous obstacle.

A whooshing sound comes from the sky, and a rain of flaming arrows streaks down on them. Panicked, those with shields raise them, only to have the wood and leather catch fire. They trip over each other to get out of range as the leaders gallop through them to safety. A second volley launches from behind the wall that protects the archers. In the chaos of every man for himself, the warriors attempt to stamp out fire and flee out of range as a third lethal volley, this time with no fire and thus longer range, pours down on the fleeing troops.

Those Companions who were in hiding with a good view revel in seeing the utter shock on the faces of Sufyan and Azora. Those who labored for so long on this trench, which at times seemed like a Persian folly, realize now that all their efforts were worth it.

When the deflated leaders of the League make it back to camp, Sufyan calls a council and, adopting a positive attitude, easily takes charge among the shaken leaders. "We came prepared for this; it's a simple matter of making the bridges a few feet longer. Imagine their disappointment when they realize in one bloody day that all their work—for months and years—was all for nothing. I want that Persian's head on a spear, but I think they will do it for us."

"There is much we can do before the bridges are ready," says Suhail. "That is a very long trench, and I'm sure they don't have enough men to cover it all. We don't know how many men they have behind that wall; we only know they have archers there. I propose we bring our archers forward and rain arrows down on them. That way we can take out some of their men while we learn more about their setup."

"I agree," says Sufyan. "Our men want to do something, and they came to fight. We must always use our great advantage in numbers."

Amr has an idea. "If we lay down eight or ten bridges, they can't cover them all. It might take longer, but it will divide their small numbers."

"We can build twenty-four bridges." Azora thinks out loud. "Each bridge consists of ten tree trunks, so two hundred forty trees, eight hundred men. I'll organize a group to cut wood and another group to carry the trees to our camp, where my people will make the bridges. Let's get on with it."

The meeting breaks up as each leader heads off to prepare.

On the Yathrib side, three small observational towers have been built, giving a view of the trench and the terrain approaching it. In addition, a few towers on top of one strategic hilltop have a view of the enemy cutting trees and constructing bridges in the camp. They also search for anyone trying to scale the mountainside cliffs.

One day, two young Awes tribesmen go to the top of the wall, carrying a large pot. That gets attention from across the way. What are they doing? One lifts the pot and pours water over the other to taunt the thirsty on the other side. They take a few swigs from the pot and then pour what's left on the ground.

Sa'ad curses them and orders them down from the wall. It's an unnecessary provocation.

Word on the other side travels quickly that the enemy have so much water, they can waste it on a shower. Frustration at the inaction takes hold on the League side, particularly among the cavalry, who imagined themselves conquerors tearing through the town of Yathrib.

At dawn, four horsemen appear and trot toward the trench, entering arrow range. Behind the wall, word passes quickly to Muhammad and Salman. Should the archers fire? No, comes the reply. Instead, they are to wait to see what the horsemen do.

Two of the riders reach out of their saddles and clasp hands. Letting go, the chosen rider on the massive black stallion spurs his mount forward and races full speed toward the trench, but at the last moment the horse balks, pulling up. The angry rider wheels the beast around and they gallop back to the others. This time, the rider concentrates, leaning forward, spurring and whipping his steed as they gather momentum. Just at the edge of the trench, they leap into space. The hooves of the forelimbs land on the solid ground of the far side. The horse is in a precarious teeter-totter balance, but his weight behind is too much, and, with a screeching whinny, horse and rider tumble backwards into the trench and out of sight. All who witnessed this second attempt while holding their breath now exhale. This reckless, if not stupid, attempt did prove one thing—no horse will be able to clear the trench.

Thousands of tents cover the valley floor, offering protection from the burning heat of the day and the bitter cold of the night. Wood and grass are piled up for cooking and heating. In one area, butchers slaughter and chop up camels as cooks prepare food for the massive army. A cloud of smoke from the countless fires sits over the camp, making it difficult for the hilltop Yathrib observers to see everything going on. A train of camels leaves camp for diminishing wells a half day's ride away and returns carrying water, having already drunk their fill.

Azora supervises the Jewish craftsmen from Banu Khaybar and Banu Qaynuqa'a. Teams are out cutting down trees, which are then carried to this outdoor workshop. The next stage is cutting the logs so that they have a flat surface on one side over which the attacking warriors will run. The flattened logs are then cut into three main pieces, which are attached into one long bridge with steel bolts, iron, and chains making them strong enough to support some fifty warriors at once.

The plan is to make twenty-four bridges in at least twelve days. The first attack will lay down eight bridges, holding eight in reserve. This operation requires a high level of coordination. Teams are rehearsing how to carry the bridges, jog to the edge of the trench, tip the bridge up on end, and drop it across the trench. There is general agreement to spread the eight out equidistant from each other, figuring that the enemy does not have enough fighters to meet attackers covering the whole trench.

Amidst the din of hammering and sawing, Sufyan admires the work, his flagging spirits lifting. "You're making good progress! It will be done sooner than we thought—maybe three more days?"

"More like four or five," says Azora. "We're not working tomorrow. It's the Sabbath."

"What! Every day counts—the wells we're sending camels to are running dry. We must break through to the oasis and the water now!"

Azora just shrugs.

"We can't lose a day!" insists Sufyan. "Aren't you allowed to fight on the Sabbath when it is a matter of life or death?"

"You go choose with the others where to put the bridges, and let me finish my job."

Sufyan suppresses his anger; unity must be kept. "We don't have time. I say go with eight bridges—forget those in reserve." He mounts his horse and moves on.

On the Yathrib side, the warriors have been divided into fast-moving units of archers, some with fire arrows ready to be lit, and foot soldiers armed with swords, lances, and battle axes. The pots of sacred fire are readied at points all along the wall. The major concern is communication—how Salman's orders can go quickly to direct the different units. Just as the League was blind as to what was going on immediately on the other side of the wall, so, too, are the Yathrib warriors hunkered down behind the wall. They have developed a sign language, and Salman, able to see the trench and battlefield, signals to his lieutenants.

Three nights later, those on the Yathrib side hear activity from the other side and see dancing torches flitting about in the blackness. The answer to that mystery comes at dawn. It looks like the League has assembled its entire force of thousands. Just out of the Yathrib archers' range are eight constructed bridges on the ground, with their team of porters lined up on each side ready to lift and carry. Behind them are heavily armed infantry, ready to run across the bridges. Between the bridges are the units of archers. Salman judges that the bridges widely spread out will head straight ahead. He places infantry and sacred fire units at those points of attack.

An ominous silence reigns.

An irresistible force is about to meet an immovable object.

A shouted order from Sufyan, and the porters lift up the bridges and, with a rehearsed cadence, jog toward the trench. Behind them march the infantry. The archers move forward to aim their arrows in range of the enemy.

And then the twangs of thousands of bowstrings cut the silence.

All hell breaks loose!

At the same moment, both sides' archers launch a volley of high-arcing shots that cross high in the air, some knocking enemy arrows off course. The Yathrib archers shoot flaming arrows, which fill the air with smoke, adding to the fog of war. Victory could well belong to the side with the discipline to stick to their plan and avoid a fiasco like Uhud.

An individual drama plays out on each of the eight bridges as they are rushed to the desert end of the trench. The volleys of arrows cause casualties on both sides as, aimed with no specific target up in the air, each falling hit is lucky but no less effective. More losses are on the League side, as they are clumped together in the open, though they have the numbers to afford the losses. The porters duck as much as they can under their bridge, which acts as a shield against flaming arrows that stick in the logs of the bridge above their heads.

A porter on bridge five is hit and goes down, and the porter behind him trips, setting off a line of falling porters, and the bridge tumbles sideways to the ground. Confusion reigns among a rain of flaming arrows.

Bridge six smoothly makes it to the edge of the trench, and, with practiced efficiency, the porters lift the bridge on end as the warriors behind prepare to rush across the bridge through the falling arrows. They let the bridge drop down, and it hits the far side solidly with its perfectly calculated length. So solid, in fact, that the blow causes the bridge to buckle and break at its midpoint. Two warriors have stepped on it to cross, and only one makes it back to solid ground before the bridge collapses into the trench.

Flaming arrows have landed at the bottom of the trench, setting the brush and branches on fire with flames and smoke shooting upward.

Bridge four is successfully placed, and the warriors start to cross. Salman orders a sacred fire unit into action and, backed up by archers on top of the wall picking off the crossing enemy, they pour liquid onto the bridge. A flaming arrow shot by an archer lands fortuitously, setting off a burst of yellow-orange flame. The warriors halfway across feel the extreme heat and quickly realize that this unexpected fire will bring the bridge down, and there's no way anyone can run through that wall of flame. Panicked, they turn to rush back to safety, knocking over a few comrades who fall screaming into the burning trench.

The same scenario plays out on bridges one, two, and seven, demonstrating how effective this weapon is and how totally unprepared the League forces were for it. With the enemy now aware of what they are up against, Sufyan orders concentrated, heavy direct archer fire on the units descending the wall with their pots. Sadly, this causes some Companion casualties.

Warriors stride along bridge three until their heavy weight causes the palm logs to bend down. A few warriors lose their balance and fall off the bridge into the trench. This sudden loss of weight causes the flexible bridge to rebound and move upward, shedding more warriors. On its way back down, the bridge snaps in the middle, and both bridge and warriors fall into the fire below. The quality of the palm tree–like bamboo gives it an unexpected fatal quality.

Salman, the slave turned general, surveys the flaming, smoke-covered battlefield with considerable satisfaction. Until . . .

At the far end of the trench, which they call bridge eight, League warriors appear on top of the barrier wall. They've established their first bridgehead! Omar leads a large group to meet the enemy dropping down from the wall. The first hand-to-hand combat of the battle. The overwhelmed League warriors on the Yathrib side are quickly dispatched as Omar and others beat back the attackers and go over the wall to fight them at the bridge. Omar steps onto the bridge and, with powerful sword strokes, knocks off the attackers, whose moving back causes a traffic jam, forcing more to fall off the bridge. A sacred fire unit arrives and empties a pot on the Yathrib end, and the warriors shout at Omar to come back. He makes it back just as the enemy warriors on the bridge, having witnessed what the fire tactic can do, hustle back to the desert side right before the far end of their bridge bursts into flame.

A quiet descends on the battlefield, punctuated by the crackle of flames and the agonizing cries of those still miraculously alive in the burning trench.

As the leaders on both sides look out at the trench, except for the smoke and fire, they see it just as it was an hour ago. No bridges cross the trench. Casualties have been relatively light, though heavier on the League side. It is a major setback for the League. Round two goes to the immovable object—Muhammad and Yathrib.

In their own way, all the participants attempt to absorb what they've just witnessed. Never before in all their battles and skirmishes have they ever experienced anything like this. It takes a couple of hours before Sufyan can round up the leaders to decide on their next move. Thousands of warriors brought to the front line await orders, while some tribes return to the base camp.

Finally, when the leaders gather together, the angry blame is spread around. Sufyan manages to bring the chaotic meeting to order. In a momentary lull, Suhail of Taif, in his deep, commanding voice, asks the question that is on everyone's mind: "Where the hell did that fire come from?"

"I've never seen anything like it!" exclaims Azora. "Why weren't we warned?"

"What do we do now?" Suhail asks.

Sufyan remarks, "We still have eighteen more bridges."

"Yes, but we can't use them just yet," Azora says.

"What do you mean we can't use them?" asks Sufyan impatiently.

Azora is frustrated with Sufyan's pressure to move faster. "They will burn the damn bridges like they just did! Haven't you seen with your own eyes what their fire is capable of doing?"

Sufyan tries to speak, but Suhail cuts him off before the meeting derails. "We need Ka'ab's collaboration. Opening the northern front will force Muhammad to mobilize a big part of his army away from the trench. Only then can we make our next attempt to cross the trench."

"This will take forever!" Sufyan objects to Suhail's suggestion. "A day's ride all the way around the mountain, with no guarantee Ka'ab will agree!"

"Azora, go to your cousin, persuade him to open the gate," says Suhail. "We can't risk losing the remaining bridges before we know what the hell is going on behind that wall."

Azora nods. He'll go.

Azora and a small group, mounted on the fastest of horses, depart quietly into the coolness of the night, riding toward the northern fortress that blocks the second entrance to the oasis.

After the meeting breaks up, a tribal leader from the Gad-fyan alliance bitterly approaches Sufyan.

"You arrogant Meccans!" shouts the tribal leader. "How could you so underestimate Muhammad? Lie to us? I'm not having my men die of thirst. We're willing to die fighting, but not like this. I'm pulling my tribe out—we're better off at home with our one dying well."

With that, before Sufyan can utter a word, the tribal leader goes back to his waiting men and they head for the camp to collect their belongings and load up their camels. The leaders realize just how fragile their massive army is.

This is just one example of the confusion and frustration spreading among the tribes. They have no one paramount leader like Muhammad to rally the troops, and the weakness of the tribal system becomes most apparent in perceived defeat.

Khalid has heard all of this, and he and Sufyan look at each other, the question hanging in the air without needing to be spoken. *What should they do?*

Sufyan speaks first. "I think our only chance is to assume Azora will persuade Ka'ab to agree to open the way. We should send the Khaybar Jews there now, though such a large force will take longer."

Khalid nods. "I agree. That's our last chance. I will mobilize them as fast as I can."

On the Yathrib side, spirits are high. Salman is the hero of the day, though all realize success came about with the collective effort of thousands of Yathribians. The first tasks are tending to the wounded and, sadly, burying the few dead. Many of the League fighters found their graves at the bottom of the trench.

The strategy nullified the enemy's overwhelming advantage in numbers, as even when they established a bridgehead, only a small group of warriors could cross the bridge at a time, and they would be met by a larger group.

The Jewish warriors from the Banu Nadeer who were in reserve at the trench depart to head back north to their fortress to celebrate the Sabbath. Some from the local tribes head home to visit their families, promising to return if the League makes another attempt.

The battle has gone into a lull, if not a stalemate. Both sides must reevaluate their strategy, as if looking at a chessboard. The Meccans have lost many pawns, which they can afford to lose—their knights are useless. On the Yathrib side, some pawns have been lost, and other pieces have been placed to defend the king, who has come out of this first battle not only safe but revered as an inspiration.

On the Meccan side, the strategy is to prepare more bridges and send a strong force to the northern gate, coordinating an attack from two directions on Muhammad's force at the trench. On the Yathrib side, the strategy is to send Omar with reinforcements to the northern canyon, where they occupy the hills and can decimate any enemy force coming from the fortress. At the trench end, they decide to stick with their strategy, which proved very successful in the opening battle.

Azora arrives on the afternoon of the following day and climbs up to the backdoor entrance to the fortress.

The Companion observers, well hidden in the hills, follow the arrival of Azora and his group. Uncertain as to whether to send someone back to Muhammad with this news, they decide to wait and see what develops.

Azora calls out to Ka'ab but receives no response, and the sentries on the top parapet move out of sight, hopefully to rouse Ka'ab.

After some time, as Azora's frustration grows, Ka'ab appears at the top of the fortress.

"Ah, it's you, Azora!" Ka'ab greets him. "You always bring trouble!"

"No trouble," Azora responds. "Open the gate and let us in; it is urgent, and we have ridden a long way."

"Go away! I can't give you what you want."

"What is it you think I want?"

"Forget about opening the gate for your army. You know I am bound by treaty."

"Open the damn gate!" Azora is growing angry. "There is no army. Just us."

Ka'ab steps back out of sight.

"Muhammad bewitched you!" exclaims Azora. "Let us in for the Sabbath—we are thirsty and hungry."

No response.

As Azora's horse moves back and forth near the gate, waiting, the small back entrance door to the fortress opens and Azora and his men are let in.

After the prayers, Ka'ab offers his fellow Jews food and drink. Azora then opens the conversation about why they both know he has come. "If we fail, you will be doomed to live with Muhammad's foot over your Jewish neck forever. This could be your only chance. Don't make the wrong choice all of us will regret."

"You had your chance, Azora. If you'd accepted the blood money, you would still be living here."

"I am speaking to you as a fellow Jew on this most holy of days. Open the gate, and I will be living here again."

"And I am speaking to you, Azora, as a fellow Jew. You made your choice. I've made mine, which in our tradition is to respect the law—and respect the treaty."

Ka'ab is resolute; there is nothing more to say. The long silence, in which Azora fails to find another argument, is broken when Ka'ab speaks again.

"We will provide you and your horses with water for your return."

❋

Back in Yathrib, an observer in the hills who has been watching the League base camp comes down to report that work on the next bridges is near complete and that a large force has been mobilized and is marching north.

"We have to go to the other side of the trench and burn the bridges on the ground before their forces reach the northern entrance," Ali says.

"If we can destroy their bridges on the ground," Salman adds, "it will ruin their plan of a two-front offensive, and we will be able to shift our defense to the north."

------------------------ **THIRTY-EIGHT** ------------------------

ALI TAKES THE
OFFENSIVE

The bridge manufacturing site has been set up just out of the range of Yathrib's archers, yet as near as possible to hasten transport and installation. Some hundred tents house more than seven hundred men, including the Jewish craftsmen along with the transport teams foraging for timber and preparing for the attack to lay the bridges down. A raid by the enemy on the site was not even considered, as it was clearly suicidal. They would not even get close and, on the off chance that they did, what damage could they actually do?

From a hilltop observatory, Salman, Omar, and Ali watch every move on the worksite during the day and especially at night. They count the number of warriors present at different times and take note of the pattern of the guards, especially at night; the illumination from the bonfires; and the safest points at which to cross the trench—all to determine the best hour to infiltrate. What none of them express out loud as they study the forces below is that having any survivors would be a true miracle.

Salman selects three men known for their bravery, skill, and ability to remain calm in a clandestine mission such as this: Ali, the Prophet's nephew Ja'afar, and Bilaal.

"Your success will change the course of the war," states Salman. "Victory or defeat could well depend on it."

Ali speaks next. "I suggest we cross during the last hours of the night, right before the dawn. Most of their army will be sound asleep then."

"Most of their warriors are Bedouins, so dress like them," suggests Omar.

"Right," agrees Salman. "Once you are in their camp, act like you're part of their army. Most of them don't know each other; they are Bedouins from different tribes. No one will suspect you came from the oasis as long as you fit in."

Ali smiles. "What about Meccans?"

"Most knew you only as a young boy," Salman says. "They won't recognize the man you've become. Cover your face from the cold night anyway."

A determined Zayd speaks up. "I'm taking part in this."

"Your brother is going," Salman disagrees. "One is enough."

"Three is not enough!" Zayd protests. "We need at least four. We have to carry the fire."

"Brother, please stay," pleads Ali. "We will get the job done. I promise."

Salman takes Zayd aside and speaks out of earshot to him privately. "The chances of making it back are slim to none. You know how devastated the Prophet was at losing Hamza. Losing two sons would kill him. Ali is enough; you must stay."

"Then convince Ali to stay. He has a wife—the Prophet's daughter. I'm the right one to go."

Seeing how resolute Zayd is, Salman unhappily relents. "All right, do as you wish then."

"Are you confident you have a perfect picture of the route to the target?" Omar asks.

"Oh yes," says Bilaal confidently. "We went over it all afternoon."

"Omar and fifty men will be ready to come to your rescue if the enemy is right behind you on your way back," says Salman. "Our archers will cover your backs on the way out. God be with you. And try to get some sleep. You'll be off in the middle of the night."

The Prophet joins the small group. "This is not the first time through the centuries that a faithful few have vanquished the evil of massive armies. Stay faithful! And remember that the Eternal, who never dies, is watching over you."

The Prophet then realizes it is not only Ali who is going, but his other son, Zayd, as well.

Now, the father in him speaks. "Are you going too, son?"

"Yes," Zayd responds.

The father in Muhammad awakens. It seems like only yesterday when he and Khadija rescued Zayd from the cruel slave master. He will always be that shaken little boy to the Prophet. Muhammad fixes his gaze on Zayd, a look that says *no* as he searches for words. Finally, he chooses not to say anything and instead gives a nod as a blessing. He then turns and walks away.

Zayd wonders he if will ever again see this man who has given him such an extraordinary life—a life he is only too happy to give up if this mission will save the Prophet.

❁

The last two hours before dawn, during the heaviest sleeping hours of the night, Ali, Zayd, Ja'afar, and Bilaal go to the edge of the trench, checking to make sure they have all their supplies—the fire brew, some water, and light, short swords. The stench from the trench is overpowering. As they have rehearsed, all descend the ladder set down on their side, tread over decomposed bodies and ashes, and then place the ladder on the desert side. Climbing quickly, they move into the night, the only light coming from a crescent moon.

A totally unexpected factor is to favorably help their mission. Wine was brought from Mecca for the projected victory celebration, and now the casks have been liberated by some frustrated, thirsty warriors. Half the camp sleeps close to their fires in the night, cold, while the other half drinks. At first, Sufyan made an effort to stop the drinking, but eventually put a positive slant on the behavior, rationalizing that his warriors needed something to lift their spirits. And so he allows the drinking, as long as they rapidly produce the bridges.

The raiding quartet move casually through the camp as though they belong there, carrying the alchemist mixture in leather bags. The firepits are dying out, surrendering to the dark. The intolerable stench is evidence of the lack of water— water they had counted on getting by storming into the pools of the oasis. The warriors have not bathed for weeks. The enemy has been forced to sacrifice many camels to get to their water reserve. Now, they have a surplus of meat when what they need is water. There are heaps of animal skins, bones, limbs, heads, and spoiled meat, as well as piles of animal and human excrement. Ali and his men think that the desire to flee this hell should be stronger than any desire to fight the doomed war.

As the four approach the construction site, they pass two enemies stretching outside their tent, who sleepily greet them.

"Peace to you, brothers."

"And to you," Ali replies calmly. "Sleep well."

Two Bedouin, each supporting the other to keep from falling and spilling their drinks, garble a giggling greeting to the four.

Before Ali can reply, one of the drunk warriors points to Zayd's leather bag. "Water? My mouth is burning!"

"No, no, this is not water," Zayd replies.

Before the warrior can ask the obvious next question, Ali hands him his real waterskin.

The drunk warrior drinks, and then hands the waterskin to his partner. "What tribe?"

Ali quickly responds. "Quraysh. We're Meccans."

The drunken warrior is impressed. "Protectors of the gods! May Hubal bless you brothers."

Ali nods his thanks and signals to his comrades to get going before the man can ask more questions.

Once the four arrive at the site, each moves swiftly with their planned tasks. Ja'afar gathers tools, putting the wooden ones on the log pile. Bilaal and Zayd collect prepared sections of bridge and move them onto the pile of heavy logs. All four then liberally pour the contents of their bags onto the wood, making sure they haven't missed any. As the four finish up, they're noticed by a passing group, one of whom waves, doing a double take at the tall, African Bilaal. But then they move on, assuming it's only a crew working round the clock.

Ali tells the three to start back to the entry point and, when they are safely far enough along, he will torch the log pile and follow them. What was previously thought to be impossible— not to mention a certain death mission—has appeared much easier than they thought. The path back to the oasis looks clear. Ali is taking the greater risk by staying behind, which the rest of the team accepts, as he is the leader. Ja'afar takes some prime steel tools, and Bilaal gives Ali his waterskin.

Ali crouches down behind the logs, calculating how much time his team needs to make it safely back near the ladder. When he figures they are safe, he moves quickly with his flaming torch, lighting the log pile and then the bridge logs that are under construction. A monster fire erupts, causing a wave of heat in every direction. Warriors emerge from their tents.

Ali's escape route is blocked. Running would be fatal. What to do? He pretends to throw dirt on the flames, a futile effort against the sacred fire. The drunk and half-asleep warriors join in, though it's not making any difference. All assume it was a firepit accident. The whole area is now lit up bright as day, attracting more and more from the camp.

Sufyan rides up on a horse. He quickly recognizes this as an act of sabotage. Despite the stench, he can smell the tar coming from the fire. He dismounts and questions those nearest. Soon he learns that a group of four were seen at the site, and, adding to his outrage, they claimed to be Meccans—Quraysh, no less.

Ali, wearing a mask to protect his face from the flames and from those who might recognize him, sees Sufyan studying the crowd and slips out of the gathering. This is too close. Moving into the darkness, he watches as, predictably, the furious Sufyan mobilizes horsemen, archers, and more or less sober foot soldiers, leading them as quickly as possible to head the saboteurs off before they can make it back to the oasis. Ali's exact escape route.

Grateful he has not started on that route, Ali "the Bedouin" calmly heads off away from the oasis. He passes a tent just as two sleepy warriors emerge from it. They look quizzically at him, but the fire is the greater attraction. Ali moves on into the shelter of night, pleased with his group's work.

As the dawn suggests itself behind the mountains, the returning raiders appear at the far side of the trench. They look back
for a sign of Ali but see no one. Hearing the sound of distant
hoofbeats, they hustle down into the blackness of the trench
and head up the opposite ladder.

The fire at the construction site is clearly visible from the
Yathrib side. The mission has been a success, and Salman
counts heads as each of the team appears.

"Where's Ali?"

"He's coming behind us," says Zayd. "He stayed to set the
fire, then let us get away."

All eyes peer across the trench, especially the Prophet's.

No one.

The hoofbeats sound louder.

Zayd, now hopeful rather than certain, says, "He'll be
here."

Within moments, four horsemen rein up at the trench.
Behind them come running a squad of sword-waving warriors.

Rarely has triumphant elation plummeted so fast. Ali could
not have survived. All sympathetic eyes involuntarily turn to
the Prophet, for this is his closest beloved son. Muhammad's
gaze remains steadfast. This is true leadership, not giving in to
the understandable human response during a critical moment
of an existential war. As though to demonstrate this, a rain of
arrows descends from the sky.

As the sun lights up the battlefield, Sufyan orders erratic volley after volley as his archers rush to take position within range
of the enemy. Acting out of frustrated desperation, this senseless
action only confirms how effective Ali's sacrifice has been.

Those on the Yathrib side seek cover or raise shields, while Salman orders a disciplined counterstrike from his archers. The Prophet, known for carrying his shepherd stick only to put it down to pick up a sword, now takes a bow strung with a flaming arrow from an archer. Standing to his full height with perfect posture and alignment, Muhammad draws the bow-string back. Showing a superhuman level of concentration at a time when he has lost his most beloved companion, he aims at those pursuing their evil goals. He releases the bowstring, and the flaming arrow takes to the sky, reaching its apogee before heading down into the midst of the disheartened adversaries. Inspired by their leader, the Yathrib archers fire away until Salman calls a ceasefire to this needless exchange. There's a more urgent threat to address.

Salman, self-consciously brushing away a tear, draws together Omar, Zayd, Othman, Bilaal, and Sa'ad, and they are joined by the Prophet.

"Ali is gone," Salman says sadly, "but the enemy is not. As we know, a major enemy force is about to arrive at the northern canyon to be let in by treasonous Ka'ab. We have won here; let us rain death on them there. This is how we will mourn Ali's martyrdom!"

The race is on to stop the League force before it makes it to the fortress and the open gate to Yathrib. Omar and Sa'ad line up their warriors and a spontaneous chant breaks out: "ALI! ALI! ALI!"

It echoes off the mountains and even reaches Sufyan's ears. Omar shouts, "Rise and march! Our heaven! Their hell!"

Hundreds of chosen warriors, filled with an immortal spirit and no fear of death, set off at a rapid jog toward a confrontation with the enemy at the northern entrance to the oasis.

For those who have fought these monsters bent on killing their Prophet and enslaving them ever since they left Mecca, this will be the final decisive battle of the long war—the final victory of truth over falsehood.

Sufyan returns to base, riding past the still smoldering wreckage of the bridges. The camp is in chaos as word of the debacle has quickly spread. Tribes are packing up to depart and take their chances in the desert.

Sufyan is quickly surrounded by several leaders, who pour a cascade of angry blame on him. He was responsible for security of the camp! How could he allow this to happen? Why didn't he control the wine-drinking? And why do the gods always favor Muhammad? They feel like fools for engaging in such a misadventure. The level of anger from the sword-carrying leaders reaches such a fever pitch that Sufyan begins to fear for his physical safety.

If ever there were a test of leadership, this is it. Raising his arms, Sufyan says in a loud, confident voice, "We are on our way to victory, as our forces are attacking the enemy from behind!"

This quiets his audience for a moment, as they're not sure whether to laugh or believe him. Their silence allows Sufyan to continue. "We came here to win, not to lose. Ka'ab has opened the gates, and thousands of our warriors are ready to sweep into Yathrib, taking it over. This is our day and our victory. The only enemy that can overcome us is doubt—do not let that into your hearts on this great day. Yathrib is ours and, just as we predicted, all our enemies will be buried in the trench they themselves dug!"

He goes on, building his case against any doubters. "Our enemy has very few warriors, only a small number watching the north as they counted on Ka'ab. We will keep the pressure on here and link up with our forces arriving in Yathrib through the fortress. Finally, we will have plentiful water—and the head of Muhammad!"

This appears to satisfy the disheartened leaders. For the moment.

❁

Up on Mount Uhud, the climbing Ali stops to rest and take a drink of water from Bilaal's waterskin. He looks about and realizes he's at the exact spot where Muhammad was gravely wounded. Now, he feels confident that that defeat is being erased with a resounding imminent victory.

Standing tall, Ali takes in the spectacular view. He can see into the enemy camp. Black smoke rises from the ashes of the bridges, and the camp is alive with activity. He sees some groups leaving the camp, heading south. When he looks toward the trench and Yathrib, he sees a major column of warriors from the trench heading into the hills above the northern entrance. It's too far to see the head of the canyon, where he knows enemy troops are expected. He must figure out how he can safely return to the fray. He is still on the wrong side of the trench, and he can see that enemy warriors are positioned just out of range along the trench.

THIRTY-NINE

MOTHER NATURE
HAS HER SAY

Back at the League base camp, smoke from the bridge fire and the campfires, which was rising up in the hot, still air, is now caught by the breeze, where it dissipates at a high altitude. Sufyan feels a cold breeze on his back and turns to see an enormous dark cloud approaching. The tents of the camp flap in the now cold wind as the warriors step out to batten down the tent flaps and stare in awe at the dark cloud filling half the sky and moving quickly toward them. Sufyan takes it as a sign of rain. Rain! This is their lucky day! He's confident the battle has turned in the south, and the coming rain will help them maintain the siege for as long as it takes. Sufyan spreads the word to put out every container that can be filled with precious rain. Hubal has finally answered his fervent prayers. Water!

But rather than water striking Sufyan, he feels the sharp sting of sand on his face. The mother of all sandstorms is bearing down on them, driven by hundred-mile-an-hour winds.

The sand blots out the sun, turning day to night. The end of the world is at hand.

Ali, despite having this spectacular vantage point, is equally blocked by the smoke from knowing what's happening on the northern front. He's struck suddenly by a strong gust of cold wind and turns to see coming from the south a massive black cloud, heading right toward Yathrib. As the wind grows stronger, kicking up sand and dust, Ali takes shelter in Muhammad's cave.

Azora has just caught sight of a major force far down the path. He recognizes it as his own force, on their way to the northern gate, and realizes the utter futility of it all. At the same time, he sees the dark cloud moving rapidly toward him. Not his first sandstorm. He searches for cover as the dark cloud of sand approaches and tries to block his nose and mouth, but he can't breathe. Suffocating, he drops to the ground—an unexpected end to a man who once wielded great power as the tribal leader of a powerful tribe. With his last breath, he has an image not of family but of Muhammad.

Now, it's every man, woman, child, and creature for themselves to find shelter to survive. Where to go? Run toward the sandstorm or away from it? Or just jump into the trench? Sand moving at this speed can quickly polish flesh down to the bone. The roar of the storm is deafening, the sand blinding.

On the northern front, the Banu Nadeer are well protected in their fortress. The residents of Yathrib can find shelter in their homes, if they make it back in time. At the trench, the Yathrib warriors and their leaders find refuge in the shelters built to protect them from the enemy's arrows. Huddling close to the barrier offers protection as the storm comes in from the desert and passes over the barrier wall. Once again, somehow fortune blesses Muhammad, for the bulk of the League force is out in the open desert. Some seven thousand men, along with their camels and horses, are totally exposed. Unable to breathe, unable to see.

Almost as quickly as it appeared, the storm passes over the oasis, creating a vacuum, a sand monster swallowing up all in its path. Now, there is a sudden stillness, the bleating of surviving camels the only sound until the traumatized survivors emerge to speak. The oasis is covered with sand, as if after a snowstorm. The great irony is that much of the trench is now filled with sand, making it easy for an invading force to cross. The trench has become the grave of their comrades.

One thing is clear.

The war is over.

The League has suffered a monumental defeat. While there were losses in actual combat, they are nothing compared to the toll the Grim Reaper has taken in the merciless desert. Killing the few surviving camels provides some water and food, but in order to live a bit longer, they sacrifice transport. Without sufficient food and water, the human body soon meets its limits under the relentless heat of the sun.

A handful of League warriors, who think their chances are better if they surrender rather than face the desert, simply climb, unarmed, across half-full sections of the trench. Some survivors report men driven raving mad before dying and rumors of cannibalism. Some survive through a lucky encounter with a caravan or nomadic Bedouins herding livestock. There's even a story, probably apocryphal, of a one-eyed man leading the blind.

In some settlements like Taif, and even Mecca, barely a small number of those who departed bound for glory and gold ever return. Some tribes have no one return, signaling their catastrophic military decline. For some, a whole generation of males has been decimated. Those who make it home are grateful just to be alive.

Most of the leaders, including Sufyan and the Taif brothers, manage to return, but they are objects not only of derision but of great anger at their total incompetence, which took husbands, brothers, and uncles away to ignominious deaths in unmarked desert graves. Defeated by the strategy of a Persian one-time slave and nature, these leaders now have no appetite for revenge. Even if they did, their once powerful city-states can no longer mobilize a significant armed force, other than for basic self-defense.

The mental blow is equally damaging. A one-time shepherd boy from Mecca stands supreme over Southern Arabia. How is it that he could not be defeated, when all the odds were against him? Muhammad obtains mythic status as an invincible and even supernatural figure. Does this not mean that his God, the one God, who is present everywhere, is more powerful than their totems and their statues, no matter how monumentally high they built them?

As Sufyan correctly predicted, this epic battle would be celebrated by the poets until the end of time. The story would travel quickly, even beyond Arabia. However, it was not the story Sufyan had envisioned.

FORTY

THE LAST SIEGE

Ali emerges from the cave on Mount Uhud to a sand-covered world below. Little remains of what was the League camp. He sets off down the mountain and makes it across the trench and through the sand, past damaged houses to his own home and his wife, Fatima.

She nearly faints, crying a torrent of grateful tears. "The Prophet and the others are repairing the roof of the house of worship—we must tell them you have survived!"

When they come to the Prophet, there is a celebration of great rejoicing, prayers of thanks, and more confirmation of the faith in the one God who guides all.

Weeks pass. The residents of Yathrib clear out the sand, repair damaged structures and wells, save what crops they can, and work to restore the oasis to its former glory. Tribes who learn of the great Yathrib victory—ones that were not connected to the League—come to pay their respects to Muhammad. Some then pledge their fealty upon meeting this great Prophet.

FORTY-ONE

ALL AWAIT
MUHAMMAD'S
ASSAULT ON MECCA

In the aftermath of the unexpected defeat of the League and the Meccans, there is a major power shift. Now the predominant military power, Yathrib is able to field an army of fifteen thousand warriors. When violated with a show of force, Muhammad does not hesitate to enforce certain agreements, thus exercising a kind of police power.

Under the guidance of the Prophet, Yathrib—unlike Mecca—opens its doors to all, confirming Yathrib as the new religious and commercial destination in Arabia. Many pledge to follow The Way, dropping tribal interests for the greater pursuit of emancipation. No longer simply serving its traditional role as a rest-and-replenish stop for caravans, Yathrib must grow. Its residents set to work creating an infrastructure designed to handle large numbers of migrants. The gardens established by Muhammad provide ample food, and Bedouin herders provide the meat. There is a carnival atmosphere to the city at certain times of the year, not unlike the glory days of the pilgrimages to Mecca. Yathrib has become a rallying point for hanifs, and the intellectual level of discourse, encouraged by Muhammad, is very high. Word of Yathrib's glory spreads well beyond Arabia, and spiritual figures come from far afield.

Muhammad, despite all this attention and the growing success of his movement, maintains his frugal and modest lifestyle. Some visiting delegations expect pomp and circumstance around such an exalted leader, only to find a man with worn sandals and homespun dress. Though after a few exchanges with the Prophet, they recognize him as a king without a crown.

At the beginning of the third year of this new reality in Arabia, Mother Nature takes center stage again. It begins to rain—the drought is broken. Meccans step outside looking skyward, reveling in the warm drops on their upturned faces. It will take some solid rainfall to restore the Zamzam spring and dried-up smaller aquifers. Certainly, it will be more than a year before they can even consider hosting another pilgrimage.

All of Arabia, especially Mecca, assumes Muhammad will make his move to conquer the city, settling scores while Mecca is still at it most vulnerable. But the Prophet makes no such move.

The fourth year comes, and Mecca announces they will host a pilgrimage during the traditional holy months.

�֍

After the morning prayers in the Yathrib mosque, Salman, the military strategist whose brilliance has both saved Yathrib and made it the strongest military force in Arabia, corrals Muhammad alone.

"My lord," Salman addresses the Prophet, "I am concerned that Mecca is gaining strength the longer we wait. It will mean as the attacking force, we will pay a higher price."

"The time has not yet come," responds Muhammad. "We will wait for the forbidden months. The long-standing Meccan lie, which empowered the strong against the weak, will be unmasked."

Salman, with his military optics, does not really understand this line of thinking, but those who know the Prophet well, like Bakr, realize the genius of this decision. Not only will Yathrib be stronger and better prepared, but most importantly, going during the period of nonviolence, the time of pilgrimage, tests Mecca to the core of their value system, a tradition that serves only the interest of the strong, not the weak.

For Sufyan and the other lords and their ancestors, confronting such a revolutionary force was unimaginable during the golden years of their little empire, when they were capable of striking an enemy as far as the Tigris and Euphrates. Now, they might not even be capable of defending their own gates. Before the forbidden months arrive, Sufyan, backed by the Notables, sends off emissaries to ask Muhammad to postpone his pilgrimage until the next year. This attempt to delay only brings back a firm no.

Mecca, unlike the unified nation under the Prophet, is divided in the face of this coming confrontation. Nowhere is this division playing out more sharply than in Sufyan's own home. Sufyan's son Muawiyah belongs to the rising new generation that witnessed Mecca's defeat at the trench and the shrinking of its power, which it won't accept.

The concerned Sufyan shares his fears with his son. "Muhammad rejected postponing his pilgrimage, vowing to give the Kaaba back to what he calls 'its true God.' He certainly intends to return to demolish our gods and displace us, the rightful leaders—"

"You're not going to let him in?" Muawiyah interrupts.

"Son, it is up to the council."

"You are the council! Better to die than let him in without an honorable fight!"

Hind interjects in her demanding voice, "Fight him! Fight him!"

"With what?" Sufyan asks. "A handful of scared men? My bare hands? Even Taif is choosing to hide behind their walls."

"If Mecca falls, Taif will follow!" Muawiyah insists.

"Taif is in denial, and Muhammad is returning with Arabia behind him—friends and foes! Children and women! Infants and elders. Look at us! We are incapable of fighting against one tribe, let alone against all of Arabia!"

"What about the blood debt? Do you think he will let that go?"

Sufyan doesn't answer as Hind comes up to him, putting one hand up to caress his neck. "I never even dreamed I would see the day when the 'great warrior Sufyan' would prostrate himself before the shepherd, offering his neck to have it cut off. You prefer to die on your knees rather than die on your feet with the sword in your hand."

Sufyan angrily sweeps her hand away and pushes her roughly aside. Hind falls backwards and knocks an idol off its stand. It breaks, cutting her hand.

"Damn you both!" Sufyan shouts. "I don't want to hear another word! You don't know what you're talking about!"

From the floor, Hind grabs his garment. "Fight him, my love! People only respect the strong. Better to die in honor than to live in shame."

Sufyan tears her hand away, sweeps another shelf clean with a clatter, and storms out.

Mother and son share a despairing look.

Later that evening, an agitated, sword-carrying crowd, privy to Muhammad's rejection of postponement, stands outside Nadwa House while the Meccan leaders meet inside. With the depletion in their ranks, several are new to the ruling group.

They must decide how to respond when Muhammad appears at the gate with an overwhelming force. There appear to be only two options.

"Surely we are not going to let him in," Amr says. "We cannot allow him to walk over our corpses!"

"We are defeated whether we let him in or not," Kasim reasons.

"Then what?" challenges Sufyan. "If we are defeated anyway, what is the point of shedding blood?"

"Dying in honor!" responds Amr. "Dammit! I prefer to die before I see Muhammad take the steps to the Kaaba."

"The Kaaba?" questions Sufyan. "You and your men can die an honorable death alone! I, Sufyan, will keep my vow—to not shed blood at the sacred shrine during the sacred months."

"Aren't you ashamed to use the sacred shrine to hide your cowardice? Are you suggesting that we surrender? You never knew what it took to be the leader of Mecca, leading us from defeat to defeat." Amr spits on the floor, expressing his disgust.

"Amr! Amr!" breaks in Habib. "Wait! Didn't we all take a firm stand against the Hashemites? We were hardheaded, just like you are being now. We were strong then, and Muhammad was weak. Now look at us!"

"If we couldn't defeat him then, how can we defeat him now?" Kasim wonders aloud. "I am with Sufyan—this is a losing fight."

Amr's face expresses his disagreement.

"We have no interest in continuing this endless fight against our own," continues Kasim. "It wasn't just Muhammad—we lost sight when we wronged our noble cousin Talib and punished him for protecting his nephew."

"Drought, hunger, pestilence, and a muddy Zamzam was our punishment," insists Habib. "And now this final blow awaits us. For how long will our pride blind us?"

"What Habib said is the truth—the bitter truth," says Kasim. "Listen, Amr, you and your handful of men can go confront Muhammad out of Mecca. I am with Sufyan. No bloodshed at the sacred shrine."

"We will keep our swords sheathed when Muhammad returns," vows Habib. "We will not violate the forbidden months."

✲

Thousands respond to the Prophet's call to gather in Yathrib. There is high excitement in the air of the oasis as men, women, and children continue to arrive, all with a sense that they are part of the founding of a new nation. With more than fifteen thousand assembled, the logistics required to sustain that number on the journey are awesome, but everyone pitches in, making sure their own families have sufficient provisions before helping others. The Prophet is pleased with the preparations, and word goes out that on the dawn of the next morrow, the great pilgrimage will begin.

The news of Muhammad's imminent return spreads around Mecca. Some who have waited years for this moment greet it joyfully. Others worry, seeing themselves as spectators to the coming clash between the Notables and Muhammad and his Meccan-born Companions. Are the Prophet's followers bent on revenge? Will the Notables stop them at the gate, leading to a war? Can anyone stop Muhammad?

Malik sits waiting with most of his guard colleagues in the shadow of the statue of Hubal. Accustomed to being on the offensive, the Meccans are now tasked with defending their home. Noisy birds perch on the statue's head until a large vulture descends, chasing all the little birds away.

"I have been a loyal guard to the holy city most of my life," Malik says, "but I was never accepted as a Meccan. Muhammad won't spare me at the hour of judgment."

"Muhammad is too clever to shed blood at the sacred shrine," one of the guards replies.

"He might spare his cousins, but not us. Family still weighs more heavily on the pardon side of the scales."

"He didn't kill prisoners when we surrendered at Badr," the guard says. "If we lay down our swords, he won't harm us."

"I say we have to run away before it is too late," Malik insists.

"I have no other place to go, and my wife and children are here."

Malik walks away from his fellow guards and approaches a beggar, who cowers at his approach. Malik orders the beggar to disrobe and hand his robe over. Shedding his outfit, which identifies him as a guard, Malik puts the beggar's filthy clothes on.

Muhammad is on his way, finally returning home after his long journey. But the question remains: Whose home is it, and whose home will it be?

FORTY-TWO

THE GREAT PILGRIMAGE

Tomorrow is the day of a great pilgrimage, toward the sacred home of our father Abraham!" the Prophet declares to his followers. "Those of you who have swords, keep them sheathed."

On 10 Ramadan January 630, the sun peeks over the eastern mountains, lighting up Muhammad on his camel, Qaswa. The Prophet is flanked by Bakr and Othman, as well as his family, including his three daughters, Ali, and Zayd. Muhammad waves his arm forward, signaling the beginning of the march as his camel takes the first steps. There are thousands upon thousands in the group, who have joined together from many tribes. Honoring his uncle's dream to return victorious, Muhammad is heading to Mecca with a nation, not a tribe.

As he leads the way south, the column behind him lengthens as each group takes their assigned place. Muhammad, looking back, sees Ka'ab, whom he welcomed to join in the journey. With a gesture, he signals him to come join his family and Companions. This is a pilgrimage, and all are welcome.

It would take until noon before all would clear the south entrance. With pennants and flags flying instead of totems and wooden gods, the spirit is one of joy and celebration. The last great march that came out of Mecca traveling this same trail north heard shouts of "Kill! Kill!"—which is the total opposite of what has motivated these thousands.

As Muhammad turns in his saddle to look behind him, the line appears never-ending, as though disappearing into infinity, moving at times in silence and keeping a steady, mesmerizing pace, at other times energized by women beating drums and playing flutes. They march as units, thousands of men with swords sheathed, with families following behind. Each tribe—some large, some small—is dressed in unthreaded white cotton. This most modest of attire reflects their letting go of the desire for the material, a rejection of flaunting their silk finery. By this, the Prophet tells them, they demonstrate surrender to the Creator—surrender of the self and its ambitions.

The magnificent nation continues its march south, day after day, as tribes along the way who didn't make the gathering in Yathrib join up with them. There is a general belief abroad in the land that this confrontation can only end in a fierce battle. Some of the tribes joining up no doubt envision capturing booty—the traditional reward for being part of the winning side.

On the seventh day, this endless caravan reaches Muhammad's first destination before approaching the gates of Mecca. That afternoon, Bakr and Muhammad, best friends who have gone through so much together, stand on a hill overlooking the mass gathering of followers who are busy with the daily chores of cooking, eating, and folding up tents. As the poets would later write, the number of campfires is more than the stars in the heavens.

Bakr gazes at the scene with evident pride. "We have come a long way. Your message has been heard. Should not you be pleased?"

"One day the path I have created will be emptied of its meaning," responds Muhammad. "Only the hard shell, not the fruit. Only the name."

Bakr is not sure he has heard right. Why such a dire prediction when his goal of ending paganism for oneness, for the one God, is at hand? But before he can say anything more, they are joined by Ali, Omar, and Othman, and the conversation turns to talk of how during the darkest years of atrocities, they would have never foreseen such a victorious return, nor foreseen this nation growing out of such a painful birth, an infant rising from a sand grave.

❋

The pilgrimage rests for three more nights, only a half day away from the walled city, preparing for the day when the forbidden city's idols fall as the one God of Muhammad rises. Most don't know the price the Prophet has paid to build this nation to which they now belong. Only a handful of Companions know what had to die in order for the movement to grow.

The Prophet's closest Companions are now planning how to orchestrate their entry into the holy city. As expected, Sufyan has sent word assuring Mecca's surrender, promising that the residents will stay closed up in their homes. The Companions, however, are skeptical of Sufyan's words after their previous experience with their mortal enemies, so the plan allows for the eventuality of a violent response. The Prophet is aware that his truth has prevailed and that his return to Mecca is mostly symbolic. However, from a practical standpoint, notably of governance, the future of Mecca is in his hands.

As all assemble, caught up in the excitement of the moment to cover the final distance to the gates of Mecca, the leaders of the various contingents surround Muhammad, waiting for their marching orders. All want to know who will enter Mecca first. Will it be the Prophet? The army? Or the pilgrims?

Muhammad soon answers their question. "The first-generation Companions, my disciples protected by the might of God's Army, will enter first. If Mecca drops its sword, the pilgrims can enter. Those who lift their swords shall be judged by the Lord of Death."

Departing on a moonlit night, a pilgrimage like no other arrives at the gates of the holy city with the rising of the sun. Thousands of drums and unified voices sound, greater than thunder, making the very walls of Mecca tremble.

Those with the honor to first enter their city through the main gate are the gray-haired veterans leading the main army. They have survived the persecution, the ban, the exile as refugees, and have experienced all the battles. Most are in tears. This is not the triumph of a military victory; it is a homecoming. And a vindication. Behind them come the younger warriors, all with their swords sheathed. At the same time, units of the army enter the other three gates, which have been left ajar and unguarded. A positive sign. However, could this be a trap?

Mecca is a ghost town. Many have fled; the rest have locked themselves behind their doors. Sufyan stands on the terrace, Hind positioned next to him, looking out at a scene she never believed she would witness. She wheels around to face her husband, her voice choked with bitterness. "You—the protector of Mecca! Look at you—a terrified sheep waiting to be slaughtered!"

"You must face the truth for once, Hind," Sufyan responds with resignation. "He has won. Are you blind? Who can win against such an overwhelming force?"

"The coward bows his head; the warrior fights to an honorable death."

"I do not fear death, but it is my vow not to shed blood in the sacred shrine. Let Muhammad violate the sacred place and the sacred months; I will not lift my sword to kill today. I prefer to be killed, and there is no more sacred place to die than this one."

Omar and Ali on horseback lead their force into the key Kaaba area, now empty, and begin the assigned task of rounding up their longtime opponents.

The traditionalists remember well how Believers were forced to kneel before Hubal and, when they refused, how they were tortured to death on Mount Nur. Would they have that same courage to refuse to bow before this God of their new overlords? Would their leaders set the example to refuse to bow before this God and defend Hubal and Manat? And yet it seems this one God was Al-lah, and they had, after all, always acknowledged Al-lah. Accepting Al-lah was not a problem; it might be difficult if they were required to denounce Hubal and the others.

No matter their diverse views, all wait to see what is going to happen. Where is Muhammad, and which Muhammad will it be who determines their fate?

Sufyan and the Notables watch from their terrace, where they have long enjoyed looking down at the populace from their lofty social and economic status. The Kaaba area fills with Muhammad's warriors, who fan out into the city on the hunt for their persecutors and any armed resistance while connecting up with the other army units that have entered Mecca through the other gates. Omar and Ali dismount from their horses and walk toward the terrace. Some of the Notables barely recognize them, as decades of war and exile have transformed their appearance. They look as tough and hardened as the million-year rock of Mount Nur.

Omar looks up at the mastermind who orchestrated and plotted decades of their pain and sorrow. The two men make eye contact, and Sufyan lowers his gaze. He knows it's over, that there is no hope and no escape this time. The Meccan chief drops to his knees, followed by his son Muawiyah and then all the others, Hind the last, who simply bends over, out of sight. Each Notable does not know whether they will live or die today. Each one of them is concerned only with their own skin. Sons ready to denounce fathers, husbands prepared to forget wives. The Day of Judgment is at hand.

Word has reached those waiting outside the walls that the city has been secured peacefully and is now safe for the pilgrims to enter. They rush in, celebrating. Women and children, those veterans who were exiled and those who defected from Mecca later, head for their familiar haunts and search for relatives in their city.

The pilgrims pour into the Kaaba area, where they witness Sufyan, Hind, and the Notables being led from the terrace in the same chains they used for slaves to sit in the center of the Kaaba area. There, they join others in chains, like Malik and Washi. Ammar faces his parents' killer, Malik, without showing any emotion. Omar and Ali pace back and forth, grasping their swords as they sort out the frightened prisoners. Knowing their death is imminent, some of the condemned can only whimper and lament. Others straighten up, affecting a brave face. Still others exchange recriminations and blame directed at the Notables, and some pray to Hubal for a miracle. Where is Muhammad? Some have never seen him and wonder if Omar is the man who styles himself as the Prophet.

A loud hammering draws their attention, and they look to where a group of Companions hammer at the clay feet of the statue of Hubal. The crowd watches as the feet give way. The statue totters, then collapses, shattering as the Companions scatter to get away from the flying shards of the monument. The head of Hubal breaks off and rolls away toward the prisoners. An alarming portent. The prisoners go back to staring at the ground.

Some Meccans who have barricaded themselves in their homes as a sign of submission hear the sounds of celebration, not combat, and venture outside, alongside secret Companions and Hashemites. Family members join the swirling crowds, embracing relatives they haven't seen for years.

Then the roar of excitement in this epic moment quiets, as though seized by anticipation. Sensing a yet-unseen presence, all eyes gravitate toward the main gate.

Muhammad on his camel, Qaswa, enters the sacred city— the forbidden city, his home. He is greeted not with cheers but with a kind of awe. A spiritual power in an individual not seen before has come out of the desert and conquered the jewel of Arabia. The fate of the city—and of thousands of Meccans—is in this man's hands.

Many are too young to have ever seen the Prophet, yet are caught up in the inspired moment as Muhammad regards all that once was so familiar. The densely crowded Kaaba area parts to form a pathway for him.

Muhammad reins up in the abundant space around the prisoners. Qaswa drops to her knees, and the Prophet dismounts. He walks toward the prisoners, surveys the situation of the some two hundred condemned. All have prostrated themselves on the ground. In the front row are his principal adversaries—Sufyan, Hind, Muawiyah, Khalid, Amr, Malik, and even Washi. A suspenseful hush settles over the crowd.

Muhammad raises his hand as though indicating everyone to wait. He walks to the temple that has served many gods, where 360 idols are stored. All eyes are on the Prophet. Will he make seven rounds around the Kaaba, the sacred ritual he has been deprived of for these many long, tempestuous years? No. He climbs up the steps to the locked door of the Kaaba and turns to face the vast crowd below, something he has never before been permitted to do. Muhammad has made his point with sheer numbers who have freely chosen to pledge loyalty to him and to the one God. The packed Kaaba area has rarely seen this many people.

The silence lengthens. For what seems like an eternity, Muhammad simply looks out at this vast assemblage. A few shouts come from the crowd, but the majority are held in the thrall of this most dramatic of moments, holding their collective breath.

The Prophet's strong voice projects out into the crowd. "In the name of the most compassionate and most merciful, today we return the Kaaba back to God." He pauses. "What say I to you? I say we are all born equals. All mankind are from Adam and Eve; no human is supreme to another. Arab or non-Arab, Black or white, Jew or Arab, man or woman. All are equal. O, my people, just as you regard this day, this city, as sacred, open to all"—he speaks as his eyes meet Kaab's—"regard all life as a gift from our Creator. Hurt no one so that no one may hurt you. Have love in your hearts for all, not hatred of the other. Be generous with those less fortunate than you. This is how we honor Al-lah, our Creator. Remember that one day, you will indeed meet your Lord, and you shall be judged by your actions in this life. So stray not from the path of righteousness."

A wave of hope passes over the prisoners.

Muhammad pauses and then steps down. There is an audible sound from the crowd as though they expected to hear more. Those who have not been exposed to any of his teachings are rather bewildered. His embrace of the tradition of the Kaaba gives some reassurance to those who feared this revolutionary would turn all continuity in their lives totally upside down.

Muhammad goes to the black cornerstone, places his right hand on it, closes his eyes, waits for a silent moment. He then walks briskly toward the waiting prisoners. Within the crowd, there are conflicting views, with many thirsty for revenge and hungry for a public beheading.

Muhammad stands in front of Sufyan and the others.

At this moment, the changed roles are clear, even to the stray dogs of Mecca. Will this master, this Prophet, be able to bring about a unifying vision of peace, a world of oneness of humanity, which he has just outlined from the steps of the Kaaba?

Muawiyah, lying prostrate between his two parents, looks up to make defiant eye contact with Ali. Muawiyah did not agree to surrender like this. Just an hour ago, he was a prince of Mecca, enjoying the limitless advantages his parents have given him. His arrogant gaze says it all. Ali, the leading fighter on the winning side, has not had such privilege and security. They are the two leading adversaries of the new generation. Each young man has been forged in their own truth. Both challenge the other, neither willing to be the first to drop their gaze.

Muawiyah's pride is greater than his fear. If it were only up to him, he would fight and die an honorable death, not take orders from slaves in this powerful city he used to rule. He suddenly rises to his feet, holding Ali's fixed gaze. This sends a shudder through the prisoners as they witness this act of rebellion that could cost them their lives.

Ali kicks him in the chest, knocking him back into the next row of prisoners. The Prophet watches this confrontation, but he says nothing. Ali knows what he is doing. Muawiyah and the others need to swallow their pride in order to live.

Ali raises his double-edged sword over the prone young Meccan. In a position of both might and authority, Ali kicks him again to keep him down, knocking the wind out of him. With his foot on his supine opponent, he raises his sword high to finish him off.

Ali looks toward the Prophet, his eyes asking whether to execute or not, but he cannot read a reaction. Ali hesitates.

In those seconds, Sufyan realizes his son is about to lose his head. He lunges forward on the ground begging, thrusting out his chained hands to touch the Prophet's feet. Omar and Sa'ad charge at Sufyan, brandishing their swords. Muhammad takes a step back and, with simply a gesture, stops his Companions.

"Have mercy on me—mercy now that I have seen the truth!" Sufyan cries. "The true God has granted Mecca to you. We were merciless, and now you are merciful. We surrender to you—and to your God!"

"Bow only to your Creator," the Prophet tells him. "My first and last command."

Sufyan and the others tentatively rise to a sitting position.

The Prophet waits for a moment, then speaks again. "The truth has prevailed. God is greater!"

"We are not worthy of your forgiveness," says Sufyan.

"Free your slaves and you shall go free," the Prophet instructs him. "Surrender to God and you shall be forgiven."

Having resigned themselves to their imminent execution, these terms are not hard to accept. How much sincerity there is behind the acceptance, though, remains to be seen.

Muhammad thus has found a way of freeing the largest number of slaves peacefully, and he will pursue the goal to the point where slavery will be completely rejected by the community. He also announces that killing infant girls will be treated for what it is—murder, punishable by death. This will be a new reality Mecca must adapt to immediately.

Muhammad indicates to Omar and the others to free the prisoners. So unexpected is this, there is a wave of doubt over those present.

The Prophet repeats his command. "Go. You are free."

The prisoners stand uncertainly. Muhammad then faces Sufyan and Hind. He cannot help but remember that day long ago, before he was called by Al-lah, when Sufyan offered to exchange his slave for Muhammad's horse. Now, the exchange is a slave for freedom, the greatest of all values. A bargain.

The Prophet faces Hind, perhaps the toughest challenge for forgiveness, as it is hard not to think of his beloved Hamza. Unlike the others who drop their gaze when facing Muhammad, she makes direct eye contact with him.

"Now that I have accepted your God, vengeance cannot be yours," states Hind. Though hardly a gentlelady, she has a point.

"You are free," the Prophet responds.

Hind is unable to suppress a slight smile.

"You are free," repeats the Prophet, "and equal to your former slaves."

Her smile vanishes.

The prisoners look at each other, then hurry away from the scene, afraid the Prophet might change his mind.

Bakr leads Muhammad through the crowd, still trying to absorb what they have heard and seen. A mother in tears, apparently crying in gratitude, hands her baby girl to the Prophet, who stops and gently holds the child. The child smiles as only a baby can and Muhammad breaks into one of his rare broad smiles. This produces *oohs* and *aahs* from those witnessing the moment.

Then Bakr and Muhammad mount the steps to the Nadwa House terrace, now empty of Notables. Omar, Ali, and Othman stay below, respecting the moment and holding back the crowd that wants to approach the Prophet. The two oldest of friends sit without speaking. There is only the hubbub of the crowd and the hammering noise of idols being smashed and dragged to a growing bonfire—dramatic proof of the change of regime, with Muhammad fulfilling his primary purpose of destroying idol worship in favor of the one true God.

Bakr feels a mix of awe and exhilaration. He looks at Muhammad. He has seen every expression on his closest friend's face, from anger to love, but now there is that familiar expression of calm, whether in victory or defeat. The true Prophet.

"Surely you are pleased at this moment," Bakr tells him.

Muhammad nods without changing expression. "I am pleased that all who followed us from Mecca and beyond are here living this moment." Unsaid are those closest to Muhammad who are not here.

"And surely you are pleased that you have brought a new order to Mecca, which you laid out many years ago in this very house."

"Well, a new order has been established," admits the Prophet, "yet this order, like the previous one, is finite—doomed to collapse when it is at its peak. Rulers think of it as eternal. Yet no earthly power is eternal."

Bakr searches for the positive. "Muhammad, the poets will celebrate you and this triumphant moment until the end of time."

Muhammad has to smile. "Poets will always tell their own versions. Who can ever know the truth of another man's life? Only Al-lah knows that." His gaze rises beyond the multitude below to Mount Nur, where his journey really began. "I am not important. If I am a Messenger, it is the message given to me by Al-lah that is important. I have said here at this moment what I needed to say—let them do with it what they may. I fear only the hard shell will survive, not the seed, the truth. I fear Al-lah will be turned into another idol to be worshipped by a confused crowd, only a shadow of the truth."

Bakr ponders the Prophet's words. "Yes, and even I at this moment of triumph worry about the future."

"My friend, no one knows the future except God. Just one truthful individual carrying the torch can provide light and warmth to many who surrender to darkness. A single flame can ignite an eternal fire. The architect of this universe will not allow the dark forces to take over, and when chaos begins, prophets are born to restore order."

Bakr looks over at Muhammad, whose mind seems elsewhere, his gaze looking toward Mount Nur. Aware of Bakr, the Prophet looks at him and smiles as he stands up, grasps his leather waterskin, and heads down the steps into the crowd. His Companions, unsure of his intentions, clear the way for the Prophet as he walks toward the Kaaba. The crowd follows him, but the Companions hold them back. Muhammad walks past the Kaaba and through the gate, heading toward the mountain.

Now alone, he begins the familiar climb, and soon this distant solitary figure in white is out of sight.

The Prophet died after a long illness on June 8, 632 CE.

Amidst the hysterical lamentations that erupted among those keeping vigil outside the sick room, Bakr speaks to calm those who could not believe their Prophet could actually ever die.

"Oh, people, I say to those who used to worship Muhammad—Muhammad is dead," Bakr begins. "But to those who worship God—God is alive and can never die. As Muhammad said, he was but a messenger, and messengers like him have in the past passed from this earthly plane. Does this mean you will now turn your backs on God, on all the magnificence the Prophet created? And have we not been blessed to live at this time in history and to have known the Prophet?"

POSTSCRIPT

After the Prophet's death, what happened to his close Companions, who had played such a key role in our story? And how did they influence the survival of this new Islamic nation and Abrahamic religion?

Bakr was chosen to lead the Muslim community in a consensus agreement. Ali was not present during the selection, and many—including Ali himself—felt that as the adopted son and closest relative, he was the logical successor. Though this breach was healed between the two men, it bore the seed of a split in Islam, all the way to today as the Sunni-Shia split. If Muhammad had had a surviving son, all of this might have been avoided, as the culture at the time was receptive to sons succeeding fathers. Hardly a rare event in today's world! Nor are schisms in major religions uncommon.

Bakr's reign was relatively short, but he played a significant role in establishing the foundation of the Islamic state. He is known for consolidating the Muslim community and spreading Islam beyond the Arabian Peninsula. During his reign, he faced several challenges, including the Ridda Wars, which were fought against tribes that rebelled against Muslim rule after the death of the Prophet. These conflicts resulted in tens of thousands of deaths. Bakr, already old by contemporary standards, died of natural causes in 634 CE.

Bakr was succeeded by Omar as the second caliph of Islam. He ruled for a decade and was known for his administrative reforms, expansion of the Islamic state, and social justice initiatives. Under his leadership, the Islamic empire expanded into Persia and Egypt. Omar was assassinated by a Persian slave in 644 CE.

Othman was the third caliph of Islam. His reign was marked by the rapid expansion of the Islamic empire, the standardization of the Quranic text, and the establishment of a naval fleet. However, his reign was also marred by controversies, including allegations of nepotism and corruption. These controversies led to a rebellion against his rule, and he was eventually assassinated by rebels in 656 CE.

After Othman's death, Ali was finally elected as the fourth caliph. Ali ibn Abi Talib is revered by the Shia sect as the rightful successor to the Prophet and the first Imam. However, his election was disputed by a faction that supported Muawiyah, the son of Sufyan and the governor of Syria. This dispute eventually led to the Battle of Siffin between the forces of Ali and those of Muawiyah. The battle was inconclusive. Ali was known for following Muhammad's principles of egalitarianism and justice. A Muslim ruler must not be tyrannical, as he is under God on par with his subjects and must be there to lighten the burden of the poor and the destitute. Ali was eventually assassinated by a member of the Kharijites sect in 661 CE.

Sufyan, a prominent figure during the early Islamic period, was the most prominent enemy of the Prophet. He converted to Islam after Muhammad peacefully captured Mecca, and he became a loyal supporter of the Prophet and Islam. After the death of the Prophet, Sufyan, a member of the Umayyad clan, played a role in the events that led to the Umayyad caliphate's establishment. He became the governor of Syria under the Umayyad dynasty and played a significant role in expanding the Islamic empire, which would spread from the Himalayas to the Pyrenees.

Though Muhammad had survived at least three assassination attempts, his message remained one of peace and tolerance. Yet his successors could not escape the human penchant for violence directed at those holding political power. Of the four close companions who succeeded the Prophet in establishing the Islamic state and its extraordinary rapid imperial expansion, three were assassinated.

The legacies of Bakr, Omar, Othman, Ali, and Sufyan continue to shape Islamic history and influence the contemporary Islamic world. Some look back on their reigns as the golden age of Islam. Today, there are 1.9 billion Muslims—25 percent of the world's population—and Islam is the fastest growing of the world's major religions.

GLOSSARY OF SIGNIFICANT CHARACTERS

Abbas: Talib's brother and defender of Muhammad

Abdullah: kills newborn daughter

Abdullah: Salul's oldest son

Ali: son of Talib; joined household of Muhammad and Khadija; great warrior and leader

Ammar: son of martyrs Yassir and Somaya

Arwa: Lahab's wife

Azora: leader of the Jewish Banu Qaynuqa'a

Bakr: Muhammad's best friend and constant companion

Bilaal: slave from Abyssinia and early follower of Muhammad

Eli: rabbi councilor to Ka'ab

Fatima: Muhammad's daughter, who marries Ali

Hamza: Mecca's number one warrior; Muhammad's uncle and close companion

Hind: Sufyan's adulterous wife, who loathes Muhammad

Jahl: "Father of Insolence"; leading Notable with a strong hatred for Muhammad

Ka'ab: head of the Banu Nadeer; has a fortress at the northern entrance to Yathrib

Khadija: wealthy merchant; Muhammad's wife and First Believer

Khalid: noted Meccan warrior; rival of Hamza and opponent of Muhammad

Lahab: keeper of the Kaaba; the high priest of Mecca's religion and a strong enemy of Muhammad; a Hashim who succeeded Talib

Malik: chief of the Meccan guards

Mas'ud: a young shepherd who is always where the action is

Mosaab: an early follower who has been disowned by his mother

Muawiyah: the son of Sufyan and Hind

Muhammad: also called "the Prophet"

Muttalieb: an early supporter of Muhammad who opposed the ban

Mu-Khairiq: a wealthy Jew in Yathrib; friend and supporter of Muhammad

Omar: a giant of a man who became one of Muhammad's closest companions

Otbah: Hind's father and a wealthy slave trader who is killed at Badr Wells

Othman: early loyal companion to Muhammad

Sa'ad: Yathrib leader of united tribes; longtime friend of Muhammad

Salman: Persian slave who has been freed; a military genius and key to Muhammad's military success

Salul: Khazraj chief who wants to be king and undermines Muhammad

Sufyan: Muhammad's main antagonist; the most powerful political figure in Mecca

Suhail: leader of Taif

Surakah: a renowned tracker who finds Muhammad

Talib: merchant, poet, and head of the Hashim clan; Muhammad's protector

Washi: Abyssinian slave who serves Hind

Zainab: wealthy mother of the disowned son Masaab

Zayd: Muhammad's adopted son who was rescued from slavery